IOU
New Writing on Money

EDITED BY

RON SLATE

CONCORD
FREE
PRESS

Copyright © 2010 by Concord Free Press
All rights reserved.

Published by Concord Free Press
152 Commonwealth Avenue
Concord, Massachusetts 01742
www.concordfreepress.com

ISBN 978-0-9817824-3-0

Designed by Chris DeFrancesco
www.alphabeticadesign.com

Cover Art
© 2009, Tabitha Vevers (see page 252)
www.tabithavevers.com

Printed in the United States by Recycled Paper Printing
www.recycledpaper.com

First edition limited to 3,000 numbered copies (see page 249)

A Norwegian man briefly became the richest person in the world after a mysterious bank error dumped 9,999,999,973,885.24 Norwegian crowns ($1.1 trillion) into his account. The Norwegian daily *Verdens Gang* said that Ole Andresen, 29, noticed the astronomical sum when checking his account via the Internet and reported it to his bank, Dennorske Bank. The bank, which said it had no explanation for the error, withdrew the fortune.

  — *Reuters*

Coins and Poems

AN INTRODUCTION

"Money is a kind of poetry," wrote Wallace Stevens, whose wife was a kind of money. After Stevens commissioned Adolph Weinman to produce a bust of his wife Elsie, she in turn became Weinman's model for the Liberty dime and half dollar. The silver coins and the little slips of paper on which he scribbled his ideas for poems mingled in Stevens' suit pockets. The prosperous burgher of Hartford could equably situate money and art in a single thought. Like a coin, he enjoyed "the pleasures of merely circulating."

Neither a coin nor a piece of imaginative writing is a commodity. Neither has anything but nominal immediate use in and of itself. The inscription on a coin usually does not reflect the language of the marketplace; its voice is quiet, specifying denomination but voicing generalities. About poetry, Stevens wrote, "We say ourselves in syllables that rise / From the floor, rising in speech we do not speak." Businessman by day, he accessed a different language by night. He was known to give away large sums to relatives and friends, but complained like a good Robert Taft Republican, "I am paying half my income for taxes."

Like everyone else, writers have complex relationships with and feelings about their finances. One of my novelist friends contends that if you can't write well about money, you probably can't write well about love either. The writers represented in *IOU: New Writing on Money* often confront the moral issues triggered by the consideration of money – but they also point, with subtlety or exuberance, towards the psychological complexities of their speakers' psyches or the thorny money-related issues of our communal situation. They are primarily makers of wonderfully expressive objects valued for the pleasure they offer.

Although we launched this project just nine months before its publication date, many writers have produced brand new work for us, including Michelle Huneven, Samantha Peale, Katie Ford, Geoffrey Becker, Catie Rosemurgy, Dan Pope, Jess Row, and others. Some who had not recently or even ever written about money took the assignment as a challenge. We also asked some writers to bring their published work on money to our attention; they include Mona Simpson, Robert Pinsky, Tony Hoagland, Michael Greenberg, Mark Doty, Elaine Sexton, Jonathan Ames, and Augusten Burroughs. Stona Fitch's interviews with two very different bank robbers resonate strangely alongside essays by Douglas Rushkoff and Dolly Freed, who both advocate for revolutionary models of exchange.

Some of our writers, like J. C. Hallman and Sonja Livingston, approach the topic through memory of childhood or employment, in their cases, the poverty of neighborhoods in Rochester, New York or the blackjack tables of Las Vegas. Others consider the topic through the lens of history, such as Jane Delury's narrative about "Plunder" in wartime France or Michael Hefferman's poem musing on Marcus Aurelius. Of course, all of our contributors and their publishers provided their work for no compensation. We're deeply grateful.

Although the "Free" in Concord Free Press is its calling card, the purpose of the Press is to stimulate the flow of dollars and empathy to those in need. With its disruptive business model and its titles gaining a broad and enthusiastic readership, CFP's role in the gift economy gives us the perfect stage for writers to address the topic of money head-on. This is where the idea for *IOU* came from. I hope you enjoy where this diverse group of engaged writers and thinkers takes us.

Ron Slate is the author of two books of poetry, *The Incentive of the Maggot* and *The Great Wave*, both published by Houghton Mifflin Harcourt. His work has been nominated for both the National Book Critics Circle and Lenore Marshall (Academy of American Poets) prizes for poetry. He spent 30 years earning his living as a business executive. Since 2007 he has reviewed books at his website "On the Seawall" and for other publications. He is on the Advisory Board of the Concord Free Press.

New Writing on Money

Contents

07	Interest MICHELLE HUNEVEN	79	Class ELAINE SEXTON
16	America TONY HOAGLAND	81	Having Discovered a Windfall by the Side of the Road, the Cautious Miser Is Visited by the Angel of Profligacy HAILEY LEITHAUSER
19	Tycoon MICHAEL GREENBERG		
22	Eros RANDALL MANN	82	Professor Lacy N. Igga Looks Up the Word *Parasomnia* RUTH ELLEN KOCHER
24	Money Standing Around TERESE SVOBODA		
27	On the Run KATHERINE ANN POWER	85	The Entrepreneurs TONY EPRILE
35	Dear Yale JESS ROW	99	Poetry and Blue Jeans JENNY BOULLY
47	Income DOLLY FREED	105	Broadway Taxes GEOFFREY BECKER
50	Skulls Are So Last Year MARK DOTY	109	When Bankers Steal DONNA LEE MUNSON
53	Stage DON BOGEN	117	Market KATIE FORD
54	Inman Square Incantation ROBERT PINSKY	119	Living on Someone Else's Money TOM HEALY
57	Free Meals JONATHAN AMES	121	Local Money DOUGLAS RUSHKOFF
63	From *Ghostbread* SONJA LIVINGSTON	127	An Inheritance DAN POPE
67	Coins MONA SIMPSON		

| 141 | Barter
CATIE ROSEMURGY

| 142 | Change
DORA MALECH

| 145 | Immorally Bankrupt
AUGUSTEN BURROUGHS

| 149 | The Back of the House
J. C. HALLMAN

| 167 | Old Money
MICHAEL HEFFERNAN

| 169 | Limited Time Offer
RONALD WALLACE

| 170 | $5 American Poem
L. B. THOMPSON

| 173 | Nannies, Maids,
and Money
KATE CLANCHY

| 179 | The Price of Waterfalls
MICHAEL GUISTA

| 184 | Loaded
DENISE DUHAMEL

| 187 | Fair Is Fair:
A Dialogue Between
Husband and Wife
KELLY CHERRY

| 189 | Money as Water
KURT BROWN

| 191 | Sixty per Bird
SAMANTHA PEALE

| 200 | The Economist's Daughter
dawn lonsinger

| 203 | A Consistent Property
REGINA DERIEVA
TRANSLATED FROM RUSSIAN
BY J. KATES

| 204 | Old Soup
DREW DEGENNARO

| 207 | Old Money
TERESE SVOBODA

| 211 | The Price of a View
CASTLE FREEMAN, JR.

| 215 | Plunder
JANE DELURY

| 228 | Back of the Envelope
GREG MCBRIDE

| 231 | Money
TOM SLEIGH

| 232 | Money
C. J. SAGE

| 235 | Where the Money Went
KEVIN CANTY

Interest

MICHELLE HUNEVEN

Ned's daughter Coral needs $30,000. She wants to buy a house.

He has hung up the phone from their conversation and now stands in the kitchen of his duplex in Carpenteria. He smears his own homemade fig jam on a Saltine, eats it, and thinks.

He has the money, of course. That is not an issue. He has his home, fully paid for, plus $978,600.00 and change according to his most recent statements – and they're a week old. Not bad for a retired schoolteacher. His money is in treasury bills and Franklin funds and a few bonds. A few thousand in CDs. And he's carrying three mortgages, is looking for more. He does not believe in the stock market – who needs it? He makes a sweet side income from those mortgages. Interest payments, month after month. Balloons at the end. If they can't come up with the cash, he ends up with the properties. Guaranteed.

Another cracker. The sweet jam and the salt and the grit of the fig seeds make him eat another, and another. He will bring some fig jam to Coral, and a square tube of Saltines. Some pleasures come cheap.

It is not surprising that Coral has turned to him when she wants to buy a house; he is something of a mortgage broker, after all. Only she doesn't want a mortgage. She wants a down payment. No financial gain in that. She has found a house, or rather, her friends are trying to foist one on her. These friends have singled Coral out as their ideal buyer, or so they say. They claim to have put their heart and soul into remodeling the place and now that they've outgrown it (a toddler followed by twins), they want a friend to live there: Coral. More likely they have heard that Coral is an heiress and are eager to take advantage of her. They claim to be offering her the house at 10% under asking price, but what they are asking is a fortune, even in this housing bubble.

Coral, his youngest, has always been credulous, extremely easy to talk into things, and impossible to talk out of them. He heard it in her voice when she talked about the house – drought resistant garden! orchard! clerestories! – that she's deep in their thrall.

He would like to help her out. Her life is lonely.

A house in the suburbs may not be the solution.

He takes a jar of fig jam from the cupboard and puts it on the table, where he will see it tomorrow morning, and remember to take it to her.

Funny, he thinks, driving north on Olive Avenue in Monrovia, that Coral would want to live so near the old home place. Even he has moved away. And his older daughter, the daughter he'd been closest to, Diana, has always lived far away: Paris, Oslo, now Montclair, New Jersey. He would've thought that Coral, with whom he has always struggled, would be the one to go far afield and that Diana would be nearby.

The old neighborhood is looking trim and bright, the small yards mown and blooming. No mystery there: interest rates are low, people are borrowing, fixing up their places, as they always do during a bubble. Later, they will have to pay, of course, with interest. Upwardly adjusted interest.

His daughters, while intelligent and even talented – Diana is a musician and Coral a museum curator of "installations" – have both chosen difficult lives. Neither is well off. Nor have they managed their meager finances well. He likes to say that one (Diana) spends too little, and the other (Coral) spends too much. When they were young, he claimed that having daughters was like a stream of pure affection running through his life. Now that they're out in the world, living their own lives, those affections are thinner, duller, directed elsewhere. He's been hoping for grandchildren, but neither of Diana's marriages produced any, and Coral, at 33, remains single.

He brakes to turn onto Orange Blossom Street. Diana too had once wanted a down payment from him, for an apartment in a co-op in New York City. He had flown there and was shocked by her choice: a dim one-bedroom unit on an airshaft for a quarter million dollars that Diana insisted was a bargain. He had to point out to her that the initial outlay in these situations was just the beginning. This building was old, the monthly fees, already astronomical (somebody was pocketing a tidy sum), would only increase – and there would be assessments for new electrical wiring, new plumbing, new furnace, new elevator, new carpeting for the corridors; the list was endless. He was forced to refuse Diana's request for her own good. Since then, she has moved to Montclair. He wants to visit her there, but so far, they can't seem to arrange a time. The orchestra keeps her busy, so much so she rarely even phones.

He checks the paper with the address. 2980 Orange Blossom Street. The number has a familiar ring, and of course, he knows the street, which is looking tidy and smart, each house freshly painted, with flowers blooming. Orange Blossom has always been one of the better streets in this neighborhood, its wooden bungalows built in orange groves during the teens as winter cottages for well-off Midwestern asthmatics and tuberculars. After WWII, the cottages became popular starter homes for young professionals. He and Eleanor had looked at a home on this street, but had bought further down the hill, in Duarte, for considerably less. For what two schoolteachers could afford.

Coral stands in the driveway of a green bungalow. Behind her is a big black Jaguar. Somebody has money. The house itself strikes a chord; he sees past the new paint job to recognize the home of a boyhood friend. Except that the driveway should be on the west side, and this driveway is on the east.

Coral, spotting him, waves and rushes down to meet him. In her brown skirt and straight long hair, she looks like a religious Jew, except that her arms are bare, and she wears strappy sandals. She wears the same outfit in solid black at her museum openings downtown. He has stopped attending; the drive from Carpenteria is too long, the so-called installations do not interest him.

Hi Dad, says Coral. Thanks for driving down. You're looking dapper.

His heart lifts. Up close, she smells good, and her skin is tanned and clear. She kisses his cheek and taking his arm, pivots him around to face a front yard full of cacti, long grasses, and gray bushes. Rocks. A small patch of scrubby desert. She leads him through the thick of it on a path of compacted decomposed granite.

Coral is only five three, shorter that her own mother. Neither of his girls, he has to admit, are lookers. Diana has grown into the spitting image of his own grandmother, complete with Grandma Ulla's tics and laugh – eerie to hear that laugh after a silence of thirty years. And Coral has the air of an orphan, or a religious penitent. She dresses only in solid colors and her hair is eternally straggled and droopy. Eleanor had fought long wars with that hair, taking Coral to countless salons, sending her money for cuts and permanent waves only to have it appear again and again long and lank and naturally separating into strings. At her museum openings, noisy, swank affairs, there is her hair, a waif's limp locks.

Neither daughter has had success with men. Diana had tried a Korean husband for nine years, but he proved alcoholic. Then, she had married a Syrian psychiatrist she met in Damascus; he divorced her minutes after his green card came through. Coral has never married, and has had a long string of boyfriends, every one of them what Eleanor called, a wounded bird. And really, if she buys this house, any normal man who sees her front yard would be warned off: far too eccentric. What's the matter with lawn?

Coral, her hand grasping his arm, pulls him up the stoop, onto the porch and into the living room, where the name arrives. Yes. This is Jeff Granger's old house. Jeffrey Granger! How many times had he dashed up those front steps behind Jeff, letting the screen door slam behind them. And Peggy Granger's voice ringing out, The door, boys, please!

Sorry Mom!

Sorry Mrs. Granger!

How tiny the living room looks now, and how different: the walls are painted the color of cinnamon and a terrible gold-orange that makes the space dark and unappealing.

Jarrod did research and found all the original Craftsman colors, Coral is saying. And refinished all the wood, himself. Feel it, Dad. Smooth as skin.

He runs his hand over wainscoting. Eh.

Two bedrooms flank a narrow bathroom. The smaller bedroom, at the back of the house, Jeff's old room, has a single bed with an old fashioned white bedspread, the kind with wicking that looks like a frosted cake. An oak desk and tall boy, nothing more. A simple room, old fashioned, pleasing.

This is your room, Dad, Coral says, whenever you come for a visit.

In the kitchen, the Realtor waits for them at the kitchen table. The owner, clever Jarrod, is wisely nowhere in sight. His agent, a woman in her fifties, has short bottled blonde hair, red nails, and a crisp directness. Strands of gold and pearls loop over her breasts. If these people intended to sell to Coral, why did they bring in an agent? He could've handled all the details for no fee. Or a very modest one.

He lets the agent give her pitch. She does, in fact, address his concerns. Copper repiping. Updated electrical. Furnace new three years ago. Also the roof. She goes to fetch some documents; apparently, it's her Jag in the driveway. He musters respect, then, for a fellow professional. Returning, she hands him a list of comps for the neighborhood, no doubt doctored or at least selectively edited. If he can get her alone, he means to ask, since he is essentially representing Coral in this transaction, if she will split the commission with him. That way, he can earn a little back – approximately $6000 by his calculations – and offset the full loss of the down payment. He asks for her card.

She prattles on about inspections and sewer lines. It has been sixty years since he sat in this kitchen and he combs it for details to match his memories. He would swear that the Granger's kitchen was on the opposite side of the house, but his mind is slowing reorienting itself, the remembered kitchen swinging around to align with reality. The Grangers, he recalls, ate on thin, flowered china; there was always a tablecloth, and their sink was white porcelain, not the dark gray, chipped stone at his house.

The agent and Coral stand. He stands too and follows them into the backyard where the famous Jarrod has also revived and augmented the orchard. Peach, plum, and apple trees, loaded with green fruit, are evenly spaced in rows. At the back of the property are three aged orange trees. He looks over the rear fence; in all the backyards up and down the block, he can trace the vestigial rows of the original orange grove, which once stretched for acres beyond the fence. As a teenager during the depression, he and Jeff Granger had stolen buckets of oranges from that grove and sold them door to door further down the hill, making enough for a ticket to the movies and a bag of day old pastries from Laidlaws. Once, on an endless Sunday afternoon in June, when the Valencias were ripe, he and Jeff and Jeff's brothers had juiced dozens and dozens of oranges, 90 dozen oranges. They had scrubbed and rinsed the Granger's bathtub, then filled it to the brim with orange juice. All the neighbors had come with pitchers and helped themselves. At a time when nobody had any money, he and Jeff had cheered everyone up with such excess.

He stands between two old trees with their smooth gray trunks, and takes a deep breath. How many nights had he and Jeff Granger slept out in the green canvas pup tent! This very scent of pulverized orange rind and dirt and blossoms, the smell of the orange grove floor, brings wave upon wave of sensation, evoking Peggy Granger's warm dry hand on his arm, her lovely black curly hair, the smell and starchiness of the clean clothes she gave him to wear when he and Jeff muddied themselves in the canyon. She'd given him a whole bag of clothes, in fact, which he took home proudly, pants and shirts Jeff had outgrown, all of them ironed and folded and good for many more wearings.

What do you think, Dad? Coral's dark green eyes are focused on him with an eagerness that disturbs him. He wishes for a knob or a dial to tone down her intensity. Her face looks pointy, desperate. In her bloom, there had been a touch of beauty, a trace of Slavic cheekbones and almond eyes from her mother but that has faded. She'll age, he sees, as a sprightly, difficult woman, eager yet on edge. Her mother was similarly high strung. Quick to turn on you, to lash out. He has to watch his step.

I'd like to have a word alone with the Realtor, he says.

They walk to the driveway and stand in front of her car. He clasps the chrome jaguar hood ornament, warmed by the sun. Since I am acting as my daughter's agent, he says, I would be curious to know what percentage of the commission you would be willing to offer.

Her red-tipped fingers twist in gold chain and pearls. Oh, but Mr. Tilgman, she says, there's a misunderstanding. I am your daughter's agent.

I see, he says. Well then.

I must think this through, he tells Coral on the stoop. I will let you know what I decide.

He is already on the freeway when he sees the jar of fig jam, undelivered. The square column of Saltines. Securing the Mason jar between his thighs, he pries off the lid, dips in the crackers, eats and dips again, all the way home.

That night, he writes Coral a letter.

June 12, 2001, he begins, and the words pour out of him. To set the stage for his decision, he begins with his years as a teenager during the Depression, when he worked at two dairies in Monrovia, juggling two and three jobs at a time, wiping udders, hauling bottles, loading trucks, starting at 3 a.m. with the first milking. He dropped out of high school for a whole year, he writes, so that his parents would not lose their little wooden house down on Oaklawn which, although not nearly as nice as a house on Orange Blossom, was still a home worth saving.

It may also interest you, he writes, *that I am not unfamiliar with the property you showed me today.*

He describes Jeff Granger as older, taller, stronger but not so bright. He tells about the buckets of purloined fruit, the bathtub of juice, and the clothes Peggy Granger gave to him, so clean and neatly folded.

Long forgotten details stream through his fingers, and who best to receive them but his own daughter. A legacy, of sorts.

He tells her that he and her mother had once looked at a house on Orange Blossom, a house beyond their means. They did not buy it, and lived to tell the tale.

As she will. This house she likes so much, he regrets to say, is far from ideal, financially or personally. She can't see it now, she has been too well versed in its alleged virtues. She is infatuated. A cooler head – his – knows that it is too expensive for what it is. The resale value is low; the property has no curb appeal thanks to the eccentric desert yard, and a dark, gloomy interior is never an easy sell. As an aside – this occurs to him as he writes – those same qualities (gloominess, eccentricity) could discourage suitors who, naturally, would be interested to see what kind of home she makes.

Even if you and I differ in these matters of taste, he writes, *even if the house were indeed perfection itself, keep in mind that we are in a housing bubble that will shortly pop. Buy now and, in a matter of months, you could easily owe far more than what the house is worth.*

When your mother was dying, he writes, *she told me to take good care of you and your sister. Although you may not see it now, that is exactly what I am doing.*

On impulse, he adds a caveat, a generous one which he may well have to make good on: *The house will no doubt languish on the market for some time to come,* he writes. *The price will come down considerably. I wouldn't be surprised if it comes down as much as 30%. If and when it does, I'd be happy to revisit the issue.*

And still, he keeps writing.

I should add that single women are notoriously poor risks, and even if I provided you with a down payment, it is unlikely you could qualify for a loan. And really, paying interest, any interest, is never a good idea.

In due time, you will be able to afford to buy a home flat out. You are an heiress, don't forget.

He tries to reread the letter, but he has written for so long, his eyes are tired. He folds it and sticks it in an envelope and walks it to the mailbox and raises the little red flag. The next day, when he goes to get the mail, the flag is down, the letter is gone, and the box is full of letters and statements addressed to him.

Walking back to the duplex, it comes to him that he has made a mistake. A mistake and also an omission: Jeff Granger lived on Mountain View, not Orange Blossom Street. And those clothes, those folded shirts and creased pants? He brought them home and his mother stuffed the whole sackfull into the incinerator.

In the days, weeks, months to come, he cannot find Coral anywhere. Her phone is disconnected, all correspondence – letter after letter expanding upon and re-explaining his position – is returned to him unopened, stamped *Moved, No Forwarding Address*. No matter when he phones the museum, Coral is in a meeting. Diana refuses to discuss it. He has called the blonde Realtor twice; she claims no knowledge of Coral's whereabouts. She does tell him that nine bids were made on the Orange Blossom house. It sold for twenty-five thousand dollars over asking price.

He finds some comfort there. When the housing bubble pops, his daughter will not be the one underwater with a crazy loan.

She will get her house, and it will be interest free.

At odd moments, in his chair, or washing up after a meal, at night as he drifts toward sleep, he does recall with some pain the single bed with its candlewick spread, the simple, old-fashioned room he might have occupied in his daughter's house.

America

TONY HOAGLAND

Then one of the students with blue hair and a tongue stud
Says that America is for him a maximum-security prison

Whose walls are made of RadioShacks and Burger Kings, and MTV episodes
Where you can't tell the show from the commercials,

And as I consider how to express how full of shit I think he is,
He says that even when he's driving to the mall in his Isuzu

Trooper with a gang of his friends, letting rap music pour over them
Like a boiling Jacuzzi full of ballpeen hammers, even then he feels

Buried alive, captured and suffocated in the folds
Of the thick satin quilt of America

And I wonder if this is a legitimate category of pain,
or whether he is just spin doctoring a better grade,

And then I remember that when I stabbed my father in the dream last night,
It was not blood but money

That gushed out of him, bright green hundred-dollar bills
Spilling from his wounds, and – this is the weird part –,

He gasped "Thank god – those Ben Franklins were
Clogging up my heart –

And so I perish happily,
Freed from that which kept me from my liberty" –

Which was when I knew it was a dream, since my dad
Would never speak in rhymed couplets,

And I look at the student with his acne and cell phone and phony
    ghetto clothes
And I think, "I am asleep in America too,

And I don't know how to wake myself either,"
And I remember what Marx said near the end of his life:

"I was listening to the cries of the past,
When I should have been listening to the cries of the future."

But how could he have imagined 100 channels of 24-hour cable
Or what kind of nightmare it might be

When each day you watch rivers of bright merchandise run past you
And you are floating in your pleasure boat upon this river

Even while others are drowning underneath you
And you see their faces twisting in the surface of the waters

And yet it seems to be your own hand
Which turns the volume higher?

Tycoon

MICHAEL GREENBERG

The other day I came across something I had scribbled in an old notebook: "Reverend Ike, wearing gold, tells his broke congregants that money is an article of faith. Like God."

It was 1978. I was making my living moving furniture in a used van with a hired helper. Between jobs I looked after my two-year-old son and worked on my novel. On the subway, I had been handed a flyer advertising one of Reverend Ike's inspirational talks about prosperity. The only obstacle to wealth, preached the reverend, is "your poor person's state of mind." I studied Ike's neon smile, crumpled the flyer into a ball and threw it in the garbage.

I had just lost five thousand dollars in the stock market. I had made the investment, my first, with the hope that from its return I would be able to buy more time for my novel, on which I had already spent four years. Where money is concerned, however, hope is counterproductive. Skepticism would have been a more useful attitude. "Consider it an educational loss," said the broker who had sold me the security. "You can't know beans about the market until you've been burned."

Two years later, I sold the novel, only to have its publication canceled when the publishing company changed corporate hands and my editor was fired. This confirmed my growing belief that my literary efforts were a mockery of the basic relationship between money and labor – I was working for virtually nothing.

The stock market, of course, distorts that relationship in the opposite way. Buying shares in a company turns you into an economic parasite. You are the silent partner, hidden, inert. Your money is the productive one, not you. I was in the absurd position of working hard for no pay, while trying to make money by not working. My so-called publisher's new corporate parent, I noticed, was listed on the New

York Stock Exchange.

I immediately began raising a stake for another foray into the market – "discretionary capital," the financial advisers call it. I felt like Saul Bellow's character Wilky, in *Seize the Day*, who had persisted in his quest to be an actor just long enough to make himself unfit for the more lucrative professions. Wilky falls under the spell of a fast talker called Tamkin. Like Reverend Ike, Tamkin sees prosperity in strictly psychological terms: it's all a question of self-confidence and nerve. He claims to have cracked the "guilt-aggression cycle" that is behind the market's ups and downs. Investing, he says, "is filled with hostile feeling and lust. People come to the market to kill. They say, 'I'm going to make a killing.' Only they haven't got the genuine courage to kill, and they erect a symbol to it. The money."

Tamkin takes Wilky to a brokerage office where gnomic old men seem to be weaving gold from thin air. Following Tamkin's advice, Wilky bets his entire savings on lard, and loses.

Playing the market may be the respectable cousin of gambling, but for me there are no thrills in the game. After getting burned the first time out, I have become like the plodding card counter you sometimes see at the casino blackjack table, methodically trying to tilt the odds in his favor. I have discovered that I have an improbable facility for assessing gross profit margins, debt-to-asset ratios, and lurking areas of growth in a company's revenue stream. This activity, I tell myself, brings out a level-headedness that is in short supply in other areas of my life. However, for years I have kept it a secret, fearing that it somehow discredits me as a writer. In some circles it would be regarded as a point of social and political shame. I occasionally wonder if I missed my true calling, as a stock analyst poring over corporate reports in the back office of some Wall Street firm.

Unfortunately, when my analysis is accurate, my timing usually isn't. After the collapse of the Mexican peso in 1994, I threw everything I had into Telmex, the Mexican telephone monopoly, betting that the U.S. Treasury would come to the rescue. The peso would stabilize, I figured, and shares of Telmex would rise.

It was a bold move, but I didn't have the stomach for it; I lacked Tamkin's aggressive impulse toward risk. After scouring the financial papers each morning for information that might shed light on my investment, I would finally sit down to work. I would write a few sentences, go over to the local bar, and drink bourbon while gazing at the stock ticker that ran along the bottom of a silent television screen. After a couple of months, I sold Telmex in order to be able to think straight again.

During the entire next year, I watched the shares I no longer owned dramatically increase in value.

Finding myself in Lower Manhattan, I wander over to the Stock Exchange, a Greek Revival mass whose Corinthian columns are wreathed in frosted light for Hanukkah and Christmas. A giant menorah hangs over the entrance where shivering traders gather to smoke. Six brightly painted nutcracker soldiers stand guard on the balconies, while below, in front of the barricades, are the real guards, gray-faced and bored.

I am studying the colossal sculpture in the pediment – Integrity with wings in her skull protecting the commercial endeavors of Man – when one of the guards approaches, wanting to know what I am writing in my notebook. Dissatisfied with my answer, he demands to see identification, then returns to his post with a warning stare.

The incident reminds me of the day, in 1968, when our high school history teacher canceled class to lead us down to an anti-Vietnam War demonstration at the Exchange. "You're looking at the vault in which the industrial-military complex throbs," announced our teacher. But it's also like a department store, I thought, where the country's entire productive capacity is for sale. As I marched miserably in the cold, a policeman whacked me in the hams with his billy club. "You're too close to the building!" he barked. Hard not to loathe such a place. But the instant I sank my money into the market, the revolutionary inside me retreated.

A survey in 2003 found that nearly 20 percent of Americans believe they are among the wealthiest 1 percent. Another 30 percent are convinced they will get there before long. I credit myself with not having yet descended to this level of delusion, but I know really it's just my poor person's state of mind.

Eros

RANDALL MANN

Giving the man behind the counter my money,
I take from him a fresh white towel
and walk into the sex club – the safe
one – called, mythically, Eros.
I go there, as one does, to kill an hour
or two in the hopeful dark.

Out of my clothes, I step into the dark
of the back rooms, where not money
but flesh is the currency of the hour.
I wrap my torso in the towel
and grab a condom: at Eros,
the only sex allowed is safe,

management insisting that we "Play safe
or be thrown out" into the outer dark.
Life's much simpler inside Eros,
where for a little money
I find what I need, in my towel,
cruising the sticky floors for an hour.

But it's been nearly an hour,
and nothing – I am not going to be safe
with just anyone! Then a man without a towel –
beautiful, in the dark –
puts a hand on my chest. He smells like money.
This is why I go to Eros.

(It's hardly my first Eros
experience: there comes an hour
when, in spite of the money,
no matter how unsafe,
I find what I need only in the dark.)
The man without a towel

removes my towel:
I fall into the arms of Eros;
that world, an underworld, dark
no matter the hour.
And it is good. And we are safe.
It is good to have more sex than money.

Money Standing Around

TERESE SVOBODA

Capillaries and leucocytes tingle
as the great banks of blood
busy themselves, sloughing
and harrowing our insides.
I'm not writing *like money*.

Statistics show the great fiscal decisions
are most often made by whim,
not by women. The world nods.
The great bear and bull act –
animal rights aside –

insist on the curtain, *We agree
honey/money/honey*.
I'm not explaining all I know.
Wads kept in the freezer
groan for acronym,

CD/IRA/SEP/KEOGH,
instruments that play well
at a certain tempo, as long as
no fireman checks for ice cream
and cash, the smoking cables

snaking through the walls,
fire all the time about power.
I'm not holding my breath,
I'm not even shaking my head
if barter's revived.

Consider the Predator droning
overhead, surgically, as it were,
striking – there's money.
You lay down your number,
your code, your expiration date.

Money ebbs in a meadow:
the bear unshot for dinner,
the witnessing trees exchanging air,
the air not acid out of agreement.
Evil so often remains unchallengeable,

the box unchecked but the cookie set,
the crowds cajoling the man to jump,
an abstract hand at his back.
The chief orders his men to shoot.
Everyone's wet.

On the Run

AN INTERVIEW WITH KATHERINE ANN POWER

Katherine Ann Power gained notoriety in the spring of 1970, when she and other Brandeis anti-war activists robbed a bank in Brighton, Massachusetts. During the robbery, one of Power's associates shot and killed Boston Police Officer Walter Schroeder. Power fled and spent more than twenty years underground, most of them on the FBI Ten Most Wanted Fugitives list. She lived under an assumed name – Alice Louise Metzinger – in Oregon, where she became a successful cook and food writer. In 1993, she turned herself in, ending 23 years on the run, and pleaded guilty to two counts of armed robbery and manslaughter in Boston. She served six years in federal prison.

Power was released in 1999 and now works for a non-profit organization near Boston. Her controversial sentencing agreement precludes her from making any money from her story during her 20-year probation period. Concord Free Press Founder Stona Fitch interviewed Power in March, 2010. This is one of her first public interviews. Like all *IOU* contributors, she will receive no payment for her work.

KP: The Concord Free Press really is a subversive business model.
SF: Thank you.
KP: Subversive is one of my highest values.

SF: In thinking about your life story, I find it very resonant and complicated. Looking at it in the context of money, I was intrigued by the notion that it wasn't necessarily your ideals or your politics that landed you in trouble. Ultimately, it was the quest for funds to pursue your radical goals. And the way that you chose to get those funds, which was robbing a bank.

KP: That is an interesting take on it. Because to me, I think I would have landed in trouble anyway. It was the summer of 1970. Kent State had just happened. Half of the campuses in the country didn't have final exams that year. It was a really big crisis. Henry Kissinger later described it as the country being on the edge of civil war. All I wanted to do was make thermite devices that would weld train wheels to the track so they couldn't move the weapons and the troops. That's what I wanted to do. That was my idea, and I was looking for a Vietnam vet who knew about things like that.

SF: So that was the ultimate goal for the money from the robbery?
KP: No. That was way before there was ever any money. This was my first idea for direct action. I wanted to make the war stop.

SF: That's a very scientific way to go about it.
KP: Yes. It's very literal-minded. And I knew I had to find someone else to help. So eventually, Stanley Bond,[1] who was on campus said *I heard that you want to do something more.* And I said *yeah.* And he said *I'm trying to put together a revolutionary action group, do you want to be part of it?* And here is the kind of shocking and culpable naiveté – I really had not a clue what that meant in practice. We were all talking revolution. It was on the horizon. Our professors were talking about it. We all had this kind of rarified view that was hopelessly naïve about the violence that accompanies deep power struggles.

SF: So you were making a subtle step-by-step shift from abstract to applied radicalism.
KP: Exactly. A lot of little decisions.

SF: And what was your ultimate intent for the money that you were going to get from these robberies?
KP: To tell you the truth, Stona, I don't really know that we knew. We just knew that if you're going to make a revolution, you're going to have to finance it. So we did the Newburyport Armory break-in.[2] And we actually got guns and detonators and all that kind of stuff. And I don't think we even knew what we were going to do with those

things, except that if you're going to have a revolution, you're going to have guns and you're going to have money. And I don't think that we had any comprehension what the next step was.

SF: You were sort of like a start-up organization just getting all of its venture capital together. But in this case, it was money and guns.
KP: Yeah. And at that point there was a bombing somewhere in America every day. Revolution was in the air. But the Weather people had already gone down one of their dead ends, which ended up in the town house that exploded in New York City.[3] And that was a really ugly anti-personnel thing that they were headed toward in that act.

SF: But you weren't officially or even non-officially part of the Weather Underground?
KP: No, we weren't.

SF: So you were on your own. You had this group that needed money and guns, but after the event you ended up with $26,000, is that right?
KP: That was the proceeds of the robbery, but Stanley Bond was apprehended with more than half of it.

SF: So you and one of your cohorts ended up escaping with a certain amount of cash from that robbery and setting out for parts unknown. How did it feel to be on the run, fueled by this money that must have felt tainted to you?
KP: I think that there's a more visceral level that everything operates on when you're on the run. It's really all about survival. So if you need cash, there it is. The shock and the shame were so huge that they were literally compartmentalized in what I think of as a really inaccessible place in myself. My consciousness was utterly focused on survival.

SF: How long did the proceeds from the robbery last? Was it a couple of years? When did you realize that you needed to get a job?

KP: Pretty soon, I got a job at a department store. It wasn't just about money. It was about life.

SF: You were doing this at a time when the methods that track people were very different. There weren't ATMs. There wasn't the Internet. But were you concerned that when you took that job, the need for money would expose you?

KP: No. I figured that they reported to the IRS at the end of the year. So at the end of the year, I would have to leave that job and that made-up identity. That was just a walk in and say your name kind of identity. At that time, if you were a white woman with some education and you wanted way less than a middle class job, you got the job. I was always at the top of the pile.

SF: But you had to quit every year?

KP: Until I had a continuous I.D. I did. When I took up the identity of Alice,[4] I actually applied for a Social Security number and got one. I got a bank loan, even.

SF: Did you pay taxes?

KP: Oh yeah.

SF: When you were Alice, you did all the things a normal, financially responsible person did, correct?

KP: After I surrendered and went to prison, more than eighty solicitations still came in the mail to my home. Did I want to get a Mastercard or VISA?

SF: You've gone through so much. Being a student radical, involved with a notorious robbery, on the run for years, then trying to make a new life. You spent years in prison. And now you're released, and still not so far from Brandeis, where it all started. How do these experiences change the way you feel about money?

KP: First of all, I was always ambitiously aspiring to the middle class. I started as a scholarship girl. So the first drive that I had was to earn the kind of money that would let you be secure. I came from a home of financial insecurity. Real fragility. My aspiration was to be secure. And my path to that was going to be to go to Brandeis and get a scholarship. I was working on this from the time I was a kid. I got a scholarship to a private high school and I knew that I would get a scholarship to college. That was the work I was doing to secure my future earning capacity. When I got into Brandeis, I had never thought beyond that stuff. And then I got there and nothing made sense anymore. No next step made sense in 1970. I think that's part of why I literally stepped out of that life.

SF: So you were self-sufficient at an early age. In high school, even. Then it continued and you became self-funding as a fugitive. You were like an entrepreneur. A radical entrepreneur.
KP: Well, I am an entrepreneur. That's the personality that I have. At one point, in one of the sociology classes the professor was saying something about how we were all going to be part of bureaucracies some day, and I thought what do you mean we're going to be part of a bureaucracy? I couldn't comprehend that idea.

SF: How many years were you in prison?
KP: Six.

SF: Even though you were living under an alias when you were on the run, you were still free. How did you adjust to prison?
KP: When I first got to prison I thought: This feels really familiar. This feels like a story that I know about. I started to remember a story that my friend told me about a visit to East Germany and how there are cameras on every pole. And I'd been reading a lot about the Soviet Union before the end of communism. And there was a sense of this really grim life where you had enough but it really wasn't very attractive and there wasn't any freedom. And I looked around and thought: *Oh my God. I'm living in communism.* It was the most punishing thing you could do to people in America then – make them live in communism.

SF: What else did you realize in prison?
KP: Market economies work really, really well for the strongest and the smartest and the most ambitious and frankly, the most selfish. You don't have to be all of those things, but you have to be one of those things. They don't work very well for people whose competitive position is much weaker. And I was in prison with women who would leave and go out to the streets and find that they didn't fit there and come back to prison. Because it was the only way to survive. It wasn't their limits, it was the limit of the market economy. These women didn't lack imagination or talent. This was at the same time that some Russians who weren't doing so well under the market economy were voting to bring back communism. These two things seemed really similar to me.

SF: How has your complicated experience changed the way you feel about money and the desire for it?
KP: Well, you know, it's one thing to be kind of reckless about your society's values or economic system when you're young. It's extremely hard to come out of prison and be a fifty-year-old ex-con on probation, prohibited from the only natural opportunity that I might have for making a living[5], which would be to engage, for a living, in conversation about some of the most important ideas of our time. The rules said that I had to either work full time or go to school full time. I found an $8 an hour job at a Montessori school and applied for it. But because I was on probation and had a criminal conviction, they couldn't just give me the job, they had to advocate for me to get the job, and the process involved a series of investigations involving the FBI. I don't know if you can imagine what it feels like to have no assets, at fifty, and be denied an $8 an hour job.

SF: Well, that's the result of all you've been through, isn't it? You have no real way to provide for yourself.
KP: Yeah, but ultimately I got my Master's degree and now I work for a non-profit. So I found my way, which is what I've always done. I've been off the tracks a lot of times. But then I just go to work, and get myself back on the track, at least to a level of being comfortable.

No one in America has any kind of economic security. One thing I learned early on during my life as a fugitive was that I kept getting offered jobs in management. But it didn't make any sense to me to try to earn more money. The only thing I aspired to, but didn't have, was economic security. But no one in our country really has economic security. So all through my fugitive years, I valued autonomy and artistic satisfaction over having more money. I valued that over money and prestige.

SF: So by being a fugitive, it enforced a purity in your life, freeing it from a lot of the expectations that come with our culture.
KP: Yes. This is a tremendously aspirational culture. If you're not smart, it will just sweep you up. I broke that conditioning. I walked away from it. I just kept choosing what I valued, and what was important to me. The promise of more money didn't mean more happiness. It didn't mean anything.

SF: So now it seems like your life has circled around, and you're living on your own terms again.
KP: I have what seems most important at this stage of life. My son, who is working class, is living really well, raising his kids with his wife. It's everything I could want. I have incredible beauty and joy and richness around me.

NOTES

[1] Stanley Bond was a former convict enrolled at Brandeis as part of a government-sponsored program for ex-convicts on parole. He was captured following the robbery of the Brighton bank and died in prison awaiting trial when a bomb he built to use in an escape attempt detonated.

[2] On September 20, 1970, Power, Bond, and others burglarized and torched the Massachusetts National Guard armory, stealing a significant cache of guns and ammunition.

[3] On March 6, 1970, a nail bomb being assembled by members of the Weathermen exploded in the basement of a Greenwich Village townhouse, killing three and reducing the townhouse to rubble.

[4] Her alias, Alice Louise Metzinger, came from the birth certificate of an infant who died.

[5] Power is precluded from selling her story or profiting from it in any way.

Dear Yale

JESS ROW

It's been much too long.

But enough about that. Don't think of me angry. Think of me as I am, standing at the mailbox on a sunny September mid-morning, a light breeze kicking up a swirl of dust and aster leaves around my legs. Cane hooked over my arm, I steady myself against the post, and run my finger under the flap, heedless of paper cuts, like a little boy with a birthday card. There are still those of us who love the smell of fresh ink and newly pulped wood, the sweet gum of the envelope flap; who when we see, in amongst the telephone bills and the Humane Society pity letters, a simple blue silhouette of Nathan Hale, experience a perineal clench, an involuntary rectal bunching-up of joy.

Today, in celebration, I put on Black Watch tartan pants, with a navy v-neck sweater, a white button-down, and a kelly-green tie dotted with canvasback ducks. My granddaughter Mackenzie, the colorblind one, gave it to me last Christmas. Why grow old if you can't dress the way you like? I always say, though Tilda sees things differently. She says I dress like a country club Republican. I remind her that we *are* country club Republicans, and she says, oh no we're not, not anymore, not since Monkeyface invited his drooling henchmen to squat in the Lincoln Bedroom and do their dirt on the floor.

Tilda's father knew Preston Bush rather well, even wrote the family's automobile policies at one point, and she took the whole Texas move rather hard.

I make up errands for myself nearly every day; today it's Wofford's Hardware, where I buy a set of solar-powered walkway lights on sale, reduced to $99 from $299, because the sun never shines in Connecticut long enough to charge the damn things. Michael will put them in anyway. We have few visitors, day or night, and I don't mind if they stumble. And then, yes, though it's out of the way, and there's split pea soup with ham at home, I drive up the long curving driveway to the Club, past the tennis courts, the young women in the short boxy skirts that flap so invitingly around their bottoms, and park in the Senior Members lot, next to the wheelchair ramp. A young man comes out to greet me, and I don't mind saying he's black, no more than I mind that I still think of him as a Negro, and still believe that Negroes make the best help, the most deferential and kind, because, after all, they are still human, which is more than I can say of myself on some days, and Tilda hardly ever. And it is only then, seated at my customary window table overlooking the lawn where all three of my daughters were married in a five year period during the Reagan administration, that I take your letter out of my inner jacket pocket, right side, and lay it on the white tablecloth where it belongs, where a letter from Yale deserves to be read.

But not quite yet. There are other rituals to be observed. There is the removal of the toothpicks, the salting and peppering of the egg salad. There is the first glassy taste of iced tea, my first and only caffeine of the day, unless I sneak the dregs of Tilda's instant coffee at breakfast. There is the spreading of the *Journal* and the scanning of the headlines. I keep my head down, intent, industrious. No one interrupts a man of my age while he's reading. We fear heart attacks, sudden jolts, little arrythmias. I could stay here all afternoon, three shifts' worth of waiters silently refilling my glass. I have nothing but time. But at least I have that.

Dear Yale Family,

There was a young woman from the Office of Alumni Giving – a name I have always loved, because it never hints, grammatically, at who is doing the giving and who the receiving – who came to see me once, some years ago. We had lunch at this very table. It was May. The old beeches on the lawn still had that look of wetness, that intense, astringent green of spring. Her name was Melissa Hardwick; she had pale blond hair tucked behind her ears and sat up very straight, as if she'd only recently become accustomed to sitting in chairs at all. Her hometown, incredibly, was Hailey, Idaho, Ezra Pound's birthplace. She had been captain of the ski team. Her major was Ethics, Politics, and Economics. We discussed Machiavelli. I don't blame her at all for what happened afterwards. I gave her the plans in a sealed envelope, and told her, with best wishes, to pass them onward, upward, to you. Imagine, she had no idea who Jonathan Edwards was!

I bear no ill will toward the Melissa Hardwicks of the world. But to you, I still say, there was no need to inform the authorities.

It's the time of year when I come to you hat in hand for contributions to the Alumni Annual Fund. There are, of course, many ways that you already support Yale – donations to your class fund, to Capital Campaigns, to individual institutions, through legacy giving – but only the Alumni Annual Fund provides us with the unrestricted resources we need to meet the ever-changing needs of Yale's students and faculty. Our most pressing concern this year is a 14% increase in applications for financial aid.

I nibble the crust of my wheat toast. I take up a soupspoon and prod among the swollen noodles for a shard of dark meat. Last year the club did away with its old recipe and introduced institutional canned soup, with perfect white discs of chicken, precise cubes of carrot and celery: a bizarre food-lab experiment, courtesy of some land grant college in the Midwest, Porcine State. I admit that I overdid it at the member's meeting. Mark Philpot, the president, is a perfectly nice man; I told him so afterward in his office, over a glass of sherry. But there are ways and ways to economize.

I want you to sit here and watch me as I think about the nature of the phrase *financial aid*. I want this to be part of our time together. The last child I interviewed before the unpleasantness began, before the AYA removed me from its list of Faculty Interviewers, was a young lady named Zhihua Liang, whose parents literally owned a laundry. In Hartford, on Butler Street; I drove by afterward myself to make sure. Zhihua Liang, as you surely know, had perfect SAT scores, and had already received the highest possible grade on five Advanced Placement tests in her junior year. She had invented a software program that had to do with testing the screens on something called a *Tablet PC*. She had filed a patent application. She played one of Bach's partitas on the violin and then discoursed for nearly an hour on Bach's relationship with the choirmasters of his father's generation, quoting extensively from German sources. From her mother she had learned a form of reflexology that she demonstrated on the balls of my aching feet. She took my pulse and gave me a kind of scalp massage. She was wearing a rather low-cut knit sweater with a demure silver heart pendant above her small but well-defined breasts. We made love for an hour on the couch in my study, and then I wrote her a check for five hundred thousand dollars, to cover the cost of tuition and books. That, according to my lights, was nothing more than financial aid. I did not need it demonstrated to me in a court of law – my check, in a plastic envelope, marked "exhibit 439c"! I knew what I was doing. I said so at the time.

Recently I had a conversation with Izameyake Ogundigasagare, a sophomore (SY '12) who lost both her parents in the Rwandan genocide when she was only two years old. Izameyake, who still smiles when her friends address her by her new American nickname, "Izzy," came to Yale with the assistance of the Alumni Fund's Aid to International Students program. Raised in an orphanage in Kenya, she was invited to apply after a chance meeting with Bill Clinton at the African AIDS and Tuberculosis Summit in the spring of 2006.

I am an enthusiast; that is the worst of my faults. A late interloper in realms where I have no authority, unlike, say, the realm of reinsurance for highly capitalized multilateral corporations, where I quite literally wrote the book. I waited too long to pursue my graduate degree. Melissa Hardwick, in whom green optimism sprang eternal, suggested that I would benefit from Yale's enormous range of, as she put it, non-credit, Adult Education programs. In declining I had to explain to her that basic precept of American philosophy, that there is no such thing as knowledge for its own sake. I was hungry, I told her. I *am* hungry, hungrier than any twenty-five-year-old. I wanted, I want, to get in the game. There are other schools, she said, and I laughed, again. In every age there is only one school. And I have applied, in my late life, to nearly every one of its branches and tentacles: law school, engineering school, philosophy, classics, English, economics, Poly Sci. The chair of one department, I forget which, wrote me a personal letter, in which he commended my enthusiasm but suggested that my ideas belong to *a discipline which may have once existed but has now vanished for lack of empirical evidence.* This, to me, seemed a most ringing endorsement. Indeed, almost an invitation.

Why do I say this to you, you who must be embarrassed, and a little bored, by a recitation of such unpleasant, tender, warty facts, as if I had stood up in the steam room, shucked my towel, and displayed my shriveled member with its silver shock of hair, an ivy-choked window of the old ancestral manse? Finally I have grown too old for pretense. Dr. Harriman has assured me that barring the no-salt, no-fat diet he's harped on for years, the Gilbey's poured down the sink, the day closed with a bowl of lentil soup, a bucket of wheatgrass, a whole-oat cracker, I'll be gone in three to five, that is, my eightieth birthday or thereabound. A handsome and fitting event horizon. And thus it is time to discuss my Major Gift. There, I'm warming to my subject. I've finagled the last globule of fat from my soup bowl, and drained the last of my third glass of tea. The afternoon awaits in all its buzzing glory.

> At Yale we're used to meeting extraordinary people and hearing incredible life stories, but Izzy's to me was in a class of its own, and I felt I had to share it with you. It speaks to our greatest aspirations as leaders in global higher education for the 21st century. The only way we can meet these goals is to grow our financial resources at an unprecedented rate. You're all well aware of the excellence represented by our endowment managers and the success they've had over the last decade, but you may not know that income from the endowment covers only the university's general operating expenses and scheduled financial aid. When we have those special scenarios – students who require not only tuition, books and board but plane tickets, visa fees, living and clothing stipends – we turn to our alumni as our most longstanding, generous, and passionate supporters.

I recall, now – following Pomander Street down to Greenwich Parkway, my window open, elbow jutting into a stiff breeze – how

Father and I once argued over Spengler's definition of the word *blood.* Blood, I said, means exactly what we think it means, family belonging, and only by extension racial belonging, only insofar as we can associate people of the same race with our own origins, our own rituals and feeling of most intimate belonging, or *heimlich,* as the Germans say, *homely.*

Nonsense, Father said. His mouth convulsed; he spat a ribbon of phlegm into his handkerchief. Spengler couldn't have cared less about *family.* Do I have a proprietary concern for my family? Certainly. Do I have a *spiritual* concern for my family? Not at all. *The blood is the symbol of the living,* he recited, eyes closed, *the blood of the ancestors flows through the chain of generations and binds them in a great linkage of destiny, beat, and time.* All you're saying is that he wasn't superstitious. Does *anyone* believe anymore in that octoroon nonsense, all that stuff about Aryan skulls and Semitic noses? Why even bother, when the obvious is right in front of our noses? There's *them,* and *them,* and *them,* and *us.* It doesn't take a scholar or a scientist to figure out the difference between me and Herschel Rosensweig. Why debate definitions of an iceberg when you're on the Titanic's tilting deck?

This was, to him, the alpha and omega of my education, *Der Untergang des Abendlandes, The Decline of the West,* for which I was required to spend my junior year of high school at the Kopf Gymnasium in Tübingen, learning to curse in Bavarian. It lay on my bedside table beginning in sixth grade; we read it at night, alongside Adam Smith, *The Prince*, Martin Luther, Karl Barth, *The Protestant Ethic and the Spirit of Capitalism.* Like all closet intellectuals, Father had a book of his own, too, a yellowing cinderblock-sized manuscript held together with cracking rubber bands. Occasionally he took it from its locked drawer and read me a chapter. There was a Thomist critique of Nietzsche, an inventory of fallacies in Freud, a section titled "Andrew Carnegie, Presbyterian *Übermensch.*" He had once dreamed of reconciling the Industrial Revolution with Biblical prophecy, predestination and the Will to Power. But then – around the time he was turned down for President at Chubb, I learned, years later – he read Spengler, and his passion for synthesis, for the final proof, simply melted away, like ice in gin. Our world is collapsing, he was so fond of repeating, and all we can preserve is our dignity and honor. And a sense of *proportion*. That's the first thing that goes, isn't it? Why make a loan at six percent if you can convert it to a credit card at twenty-five? We've gone from the logic of men to the logic of leeches.

All of us have bad habits, our little bugbears, our red-nosed playground hatreds, and what else is education, viewed from a certain angle, than a process of smoothing, streamlining, subsuming, if not extinguishing, them? That was what always impressed me about Father. He could have been a John Bircher. He could have been a Lindbergh. But he funneled his rage into books, seeking, as it were, a justification for himself. A way of living without apology. When I mentioned Spengler to my professors at the Gymnasium they pretended never to have heard of him. Oh yes, one said, finally, he was one of those Weimar cult figures, an eccentric mystic. His work was translated into English? Really? I came home with Jung instead, and Hermann Hesse, and a first edition of *The Tin Drum*. I went for long walks in the snow behind our house. I watched coverage of the Emmett Till trial on the eleven o'clock news, tears rolling down my cheeks. Across the dinner table my father gazed at me sorrowfully, an El Greco Christ. *May you never have a son,* his eyes said. I would have liked to find a way of saying I still respected him.

It wasn't until his mind started to fail – this was in the late Fifties, the atrophying ease of the Eisenhower years – that Father began speaking in company about The Jews, and what had lain submerged all those years released itself in a torrent. There were a few unpleasant Thanksgivings and Christmases until I managed to have Dr. Cromwell declare him delusional and pack him away to the Thetford Rest Home, where he had no rest at all and gave none to the staff. He would talk to anyone who was listening, or not listening, about the great genius of an ethnic group devoted only to enriching and pleasing itself, a club maintained by one absolute rule, tradition, and a rulebook as old as writing itself. He, too, wrote letters. In another era – when there was only the Alumni Office, and I was the corresponding secretary of the Greenwich Yale Club – the office manager in New Haven showed me the file of Father's letters to President Griswold, with photostats of the checks attached. The later ones were no more than rants, scrawled across his old Chubb stationery, and the checks were for fantastic amounts: one for twenty million dollars, back when that was still a lot of money. In the end, after the policies had been revised, he began addressing the letters to *President Rothschild.*

What I don't understand, he often said aloud, regardless of who was listening, is, why do they want *our* schools? Don't they have their own, better, schools? Brandeis, Brown, Columbia? Why should they waste their money, their energy, where it's not wanted? It's nonsense, this business of assimilation. Can't they see where it got them, the last time they tried it? At one point he even tried to set up a scholarship fund at the Hebrew University of Jerusalem, solely for American Jews who promised not to apply to Yale. The Israeli embassy contacted the FBI, and two agents actually visited him and Mother up in Booth Bay. *Mossad tracked me down,* he wrote me in a telegram. *Phones tapped. No further contact til Labor Day.*

In his last week of life – early October of 1962 – I maneuvered him in his wheelchair to the south-facing porch of the Home, looking out over Mt. Tom. Someone had handed him a *LIFE* magazine, and he flapped the pages back and forth, staring at pictures of Kennedy and Khruschev. What I can't stand, he said finally, isn't *this,* though this is bad enough. It's knowing that in your lifetime we'll have one of *them* in the White House. The Catholics, well, they don't have Kennedy in the pocket. They don't have a *plan.*

At least you won't be around to see it.

Some legacy I've left you, he said. Never let it be said I didn't do what I could to stop them.

I couldn't resist; I bent over his snowy head, and whispered, *God preordained, for his own glory and the display of His attributes of mercy and justice, a part of the human race, without any merit of their own, to eternal salvation, and another part, in just punishment of their sin, to eternal damnation.*

What's that? he said. Speak up!

Oh, nothing, I said. A bit of Calvin. Something you believed in once.

You've never heard of Franciscus Gormarus, then. He took care of that business at the Synod of Dordecht in 1618. Those who reject the offer of conversion are excluded by default. But theologically speaking I've always held to Luther's view. *Von den Jüden und iren Lügen.*

Father, I said, you wouldn't presume to divine interference.

It isn't interference to try and preserve what's yours.

But it isn't ours. That's my point.

Call Hymes Thayer, he said. I'm changing the will. I always knew you were a closet socialist. No wonder I wouldn't let them tap you for Bones.

The money isn't *ours*, I persisted. It – it – flows through us, doesn't it? For the next generation. The question is, who gets to choose? *We* don't. The universe chooses. Or God, if that makes you happier. For his own reasons. Isn't that the whole point? I mean, for heaven's sake, *we're* not particularly special.

I'd rather see it go up in smoke. Ha! Like certain people I could mention. Certain people who missed their calling the last time around.

His face had become a gargoyle's: the witch's peak, the pointed chin, the scythe-shaped nose. I stood up and walked away. It was all I could do. At the front desk I asked the nurse to take charge of Mr. Proctor while I placed a call from the pay phone; then I found my car and drove home. Needless to say, it was a closed-casket funeral.

Not long ago, I spoke over the phone with one of our most senior alumni, Sam Winslow, SY '28. Sam, the only living member of his class, remembers visits to campus by Calvin Coolidge, George Bernard Shaw, and Edith Wharton. He regretted not being able to attend last year's reunion due to ill health, but he was delighted to receive a visit by Tiffany Jackson, president of the class of 2009. Sam, who calls himself "a lifelong believer in progress and development," says of Yale in the twenty-first century that "it's different from the Yale I attended in every conceivable way, except the ways that matter most." He credits his own longevity to one word: "adaptability."

I shouldn't have to mention this here, but I was, very briefly, brought in as a consultant on reinsurance matters to the meetings of the Yale Corporation, from April to August of 1983. Professionally it should go without saying that those were the happiest months of my career. I worked myself literally to a froth. I had night sweats. I slept on the couch in my office. I took on, and abandoned, a smoking habit. When it was all over I went to a party at the home of a younger colleague, Class of 1967, on East 77th Street and Park, and snorted cocaine for the first and only time in my life. And it was in that ecstatic state – on a rooftop patio, at some ungodly hour of the morning, after the exquisite Thai prostitutes had left – that I had the first of my visions.

Portfolio managers, I'm told, visualize their largest accounts in bar graphs and flow charts. The true visionaries see numbers as swans, their feathers ruffled by the winds of market turbulence, or as sand dunes in the Sahara, their tops delicately shaved away minute by minute as the manager's fees accumulate. I have never had this talent. In insurance we don't *see* risk. But on that rooftop I did: I saw the number, our number, as a tower, an obelisk, three-sided, shining, and absolutely black. Light seemed to fall into it.

The Gnostics, as you know, say that at the moment of true knowledge our earthly trappings simply evaporate; we no longer feel our bodies or see our surroundings, except briefly, fleetingly, as the mirage dissipates, and we are suffused with glowing joy at being united with the light. And I ask you, as I have asked myself my entire life, where *is* Yale, exactly? Can we locate it in its symbols, in beloved old Harkness, in *Veritas et Lux?* Of course not. We are our money. How much more baldly can I put things? Our money which is not ours, which belongs to the future, our life-giving fountain, may it ever accumulate, may it gather power unto itself!

Occasionally I'm asked why it is I feel such commitment to a position raising money for an institution that already has a great deal of money. My answer is always very simple: with our great resources comes great responsibility. Staying the same size – staying the same in any way – is not an option in a complex and expanding world. It's because you appreciate this fact that I know you'll make this another successful year for the Alumni Fund.

My proposal, then? My Institute. The Proctor Institute. I see it in one of the stone mansions on Hillhouse, but I leave the real estate concerns up to you. It could be in a basement. It could be a rural retreat. What matters is that it exists, and that every undergraduate, on the day they arrive, receive a letter in his or her box in Yale Station, giving them a day and time for an Appointment.

They arrive, I see it now, one at a time, in their scrubby clothes, their hooded sweatshirts and fashionably ripped jeans, and find a dimly lit, plush-carpeted, sweet-smelling room. Beautiful olive-skinned women invite them to change into robes and escort them to a bubbling hot bath. There is champagne, and a lovely light meal. There are massages offered in private rooms. There are other experiences available, only for the asking. After an interval of two hours, the students arrive, flushed and sleek, in a conference room, with a circle of couches around an advanced holographic computer. More women arrive, bearing pots of exquisite tea, slow-brewed Ethiopian coffee. A Yale representative greets them and dims the lights. And there, in front of them, a glowing orb, a monument, a number in dancing laser beams, as the market fluctuates that day.

What should he say to them? What do we all wish we could say to them, our precious offspring, these striplings, these fawns? Look around. Take note of one another. What meaning do you have, separately, individually? A thousand people wanted to take your place. Why are *you* here? The truth is, it doesn't really matter, does it? This is America; we don't have titles, we don't have pedigrees, we have money. And what is the meaning of money? Like water, it flows everywhere, but always returns to its source. What do *you* want in life? We can give it to you. As long as you return the favor.

Look around. I have tears in my eyes, soppy old soul that I am, and have to pull over onto the narrow grassy strip. *Look around,* I want to say to them. Touch each other. Love each other. Conjugate, for God's sakes, you Changs and Al-Abiyas, you Wheatcrofts and Gopals! Pool your lucky genes!

Spengler was, in the end, a prisoner of his own Alpine romance, a rapture of Goethe and Heine, edelweiss and *kuchen* made by hand. What would he say now, if he found himself in any airport's first-class lounge, in a club chair, with a rum and Coke, a pocketful of Viagra, and a beautiful blonde Silliman College graduate, watching the jets take off and land in a grave, continuous motion? What would Father say? All the liquids we bear around, all our semen, all our blood, the luscious rinse of our membranes, why shouldn't it flow into the one place where liquidity actually matters? Why *shouldn't* we live a life without apology?

Yours,

Our house is set back nearly a quarter of a mile from the road, on a slight rise; the whole front of the property is a long, sloping lawn, that comes down to a fringe of old oaks around Warbling Brook, and to the left of the driveway, behind post fences, are the horse pastures, the barn just visible next to the woods on the opposite side. When the girls were still at home we owned four and five horses at a time, Morgans, and had family rides on Sundays. Now the pastures are overgrown with ragweed and thistle, impossible to mow, and pitted with hidden sinkholes, thanks to poor drainage. Ride a horse there now and you'd break his leg. I park at the mailbox, leaving the keys inside for Michael, and walk up the driveway: my daily constitutional, such as it is. This way, if I pitch over, at the very least I'll be on my own property, not a burden to the taxpayers.

Tilda, who has been watercoloring, and haranguing one child or another over the phone, comes out onto the front porch to watch me, hands on her hips. I make slow but steady progress. In one hand I bear a letter from Yale; it flaps lightly, teasingly, with every jolting step. You who are looking at me now, who have been with me for this journey, you who see me, frankly, now, as an integer, see me now turned back into material, if only for a minute, before I go up to my study and call my accountant. See me for this once as the human being I might have been, and then I will dissolve myself, joyfully, finally, but with a tiny residue of sadness for the world I have excreted and left behind.

Income

DOLLY FREED

It's really ridiculously easy to pick up the little bit of money we spend each year. I do babysitting for a working mother, and housework for an elderly couple sometimes. These people are neighbors, so it's no hassle. A friend of ours has a craft shop and I make up packaged items for her on a piece-rate basis every now and then. I pick up the materials, then do the work here at home.

We pick up a buck or two selling bunnies and herb plants. We just put up a sign on the front lawn when we have extra to sell.

Daddy does yardwork and handyman jobs for the neighbors occasionally, and even goes so far as to take on a regular job for a week or two at a time when the spirit moves him.

When we lived near Philadelphia and the candle business was slow, as it is in the summer, Daddy used to work for Manpower, the temporary help people. They pay coolie wages, of course, but you go to different jobs all the time and meet people, so it's very interesting. You don't stay on any one job long enough to become bored with it, and if you happen to dislike a particular job, you can turn it down without their holding it against you.

Much as I hate to admit it, you can really earn good money by making candles in your kitchen and selling them. Daddy and I would rather mug old ladies in the park for money than sell candles, but that's only because of our overdose experience. There's no reason *you* couldn't do it. If you're interested, go to any craft or specialty store and tell them what you want to do. Since they'll want to sell you the equipment and supplies, they'll be most helpful and cooperative. If you do try it, I hope you have enough sense to regard it as a business venture and don't get hung up on it as a hobby. Unfortunately, if you don't happen to have a sales personality you won't do well with candles or any other craft item. Trite, but true, though, quality candles practically sell themselves, and it's not really hard to make a candle of higher quality than the ordinary factory-made item.

Consignment placing in gift shops doesn't pay. The shopkeeper wants too big a bite, and also isn't going to push your item when he has a store full of things he has money tied up in. Flea markets are also bummers. You pay for your spot, then nickel-and-dime it all day. Partnership arrangements whereby one party produces and his or her friend sells *never* work unless both partners eat at the same table. Otherwise there are bound to be difficulties, and you're more likely to lose a friend than to make money. Most craft items such as ceramics or leather goods don't sell as well as candles or tasteful, well-made jewelry. I don't know why, but that's the way it seems, and we have a lot of experience in this field. However, if you have an unusual craft and can get some publicity on it, a fad might develop with you sitting right on top of the situation. Mom got her start by simply calling up the women's page editor of the local newspaper and saying she had a feature article for them. She got a half-page interview complete with photos out of it, free. It would have cost a good $200 to buy that advertisement.

Here are two good ways to sell craft items:

If someone who eats at your table goes to school or works in an office or factory, they periodically take in samples and show them around. Orders taken must be promptly filled with quality merchandise or there won't be repeat business.

Find a gregarious type to act as hostess and hold a "party" or "demonstration." She invites 12 to 25 friends over for a display and demonstration of your craft. (It had better be good.) Then you take orders. Afterward there's coffee or drinks and snacks or a buffet. The hostess gets $15 plus 10% of the gross (in merchandise) for her troubles, and $5 for every party booked at her party. (These things breed like rabbits.)

The question of sales tax might come up. Don't collect it if you aren't going to pay it! You might just be quiet about it. If some busybody brings it up, say you have applied for a tax number but haven't received it yet and can't collect tax till you do. If pressed on the matter, play dumb. (We were always good at that.) Or you can get a number and collect the tax, but that increases the price to your customers and complicates your life. Some unscrupulous folks rake off 30% or 40% from the state's share for their trouble.

Don't suppose that because people live in nice neighborhoods and act graciously, they won't dead-beat on you, because they sometimes will. Explain to the hostess, *before* the party, that she is to collect the money and that it must be paid in full before the merchandise is delivered. Be polite but firm.

It shouldn't cost you more than about $20 to get started. Then you want to shop around for your supplies – there's a wide disparity in prices in this market.

Pricing your merchandise shouldn't be difficult. Keep track of your expenses and your time for making and selling the stuff, and you should be able to calculate it okay. You know what your time is worth to you. You might also note prices of comparable items for sale in local stores. Being handmade, your item might be of higher quality than the store item, and if it is, you shouldn't be shy about charging a bit more.

There are so many ways to pick up money without actually (shudder) 9-to-5ing, that whole books have been written on just that subject. Check your library. There are also periodicals devoted to the subject, but these are mostly vehicles for people hawking various franchise deals, some of pretty dubious worth. Use your common sense and instincts to evaluate them.

But enough. Rather than make a lot of money, which sets you up as a John for the various taxing agencies and other predators, learn instead to do without much money. Make your own way, without buying what you need. Do it for yourself, instead. You become free that way.

Skulls Are So Last Year

MARK DOTY
(Including Half a Line by Thomas McGrath)

Unattended money may be searched or destroyed

Woman in the doorway of Dunkin' Donuts
reciting *will you help me get
something to eat will you help me
get something to eat will you
help me get something*
painful revision of WCW's
modernist syntax of insistence

Please hold on money is leaving the station

In New York at five past money
many small vacancies open

Debt clock broke down whirling exhilarating
proliferation of zeroes we just don't have
that many light bulbs

Do not accept money from persons unknown to you

In New York at a quarter past money
I'd put my queer shoulder to the wheel if I could find it

Be careful when opening money as contents may have shifted

Put my shoulder to the wheel but I'd go tumbling
through the absence of value to the lack of a floor
flat on my face in this fiction of a symbol

That can itself be sold
or you can sell the absence of the symbol
bundle the absences and divide them among a multiplicity
build a whole towering extravagance

Something like the way in Tallinn this month
the Estonian Philharmonic is holding a Festival of Perfect Silence
so we are planning to celebrate the completed

Vanished tower of abstract money

A little reminiscent of that fading fashion for vertical foods in
    restaurants
an edible structure that would allow your meal to rise from your plate
toward you mirror of an entire economic architecture shimmying
    upward

Into the thinning atmosphere the most tenuous needles of money

And maybe why today the barrista who's charging me
do you want cash back with that
wears around her neck a cameo
no antique but sly parodic black oval
upon which a coral-red skull and crossbones are looming

That's why skulls were everywhere last year
on jeans pockets backpacks wallets china your wristwatch

Sign of piracy

Would you like another transaction

Stage

DON BOGEN

As he walks on stage
The president of fruit spreads his name in legacy
His business school, his family amphitheater
A museum he paid for, with a hall of heroes
His name gleams on the monitor among others: Gandhi, Cesar Chávez
Brilliant in pixels, it will always be remembered
The fruit company never existed now
History is a billboard to be painted over
The paint is money, the money blood

Inman Square Incantation

ROBERT PINSKY

Forgive us, we don't exactly believe or disbelieve
What the President tells us regarding the great issues
Of peace, justice and war – skeptical, but distracted

By the swarm of things. The young Romanian poet in LA:
She said, "In Romania, bums are just bums, but here
In America the bum pushes a cart loaded with his *things*."

With a mean elfin look one of the homeless carters
In Alfred Vellucci Park sometimes begs using
A stuffed dog, bear or bunny as a prop: the paper cup

Panhandled toward us passing marks puppetwise –
Can you spare a little for Teddy? Or *The Doggie's hungry* –
Crooning maternal parody, a wheedling mock-innocence.

The noseringed leather kids who haunt the T station seem
The reverse – feigned menace. But one bashed some black girls
On the train, using the kind of metal rod called an "asp."

Some money to feed the bunny? His little poetry reading.
And the plush animal a street sign among signs, his ad
For something more personal and abounding than just need.

His smirk knows a thing sharper than pity to block my way by
The brazen ten-foot tenor saxophone that marks *Ryles,*
To *Top Cleaners,* the bank machine and *Patel Quick Food Mart.*

The dictionary says that a *thing* is first of all an assembly.
Forgive the word "bums." Forgive "homeless," our sheepish
Euphemism. "Derelict" is better for these forsaken.

Across the street from *Cerveija e Vinhos* and *Boston Improv,*
The Romanesque firehouse's arches frame bas-reliefs
Of horse-drawn ladder & hose. Amid these signs of civic

Rescue and cleansing, diversion and provender, let's
Remember, you rat-faced beggar: I dislike you. Forgive me.
And if as I pass again from where I've been I choose to take

A dead president from my breast pocket where I stowed the thing
To put it in your cup, it isn't Charity, but superstition – a provisional
Wishful conspiring with the artist in you, son of a bitch, bastard.

Free Meals

JONATHAN AMES

I was eating dinner at Café Gitane. I had ravenously gone through most of my Greek salad and then I forked what appeared to be the torn-off end of a used condom. "WHAT'S THIS?" I shouted.

My lovely waitress came over to me. She was Audrey Hepburn-like, which seems to be the way to describe all women who have the beauty of a fragile dark bird. I held up my fork with the shredded rubber and I exclaimed: "I FOUND THIS IN MY FOOD! A TORN CONDOM! I COULD GET PREGNANT! I COULD GET AIDS!" All the Europeans in the café looked at me.

"It's the sanitary glove the cook wears. The finger end," she explained, trying to make sense of it all.

"Did the cook cut off a finger? Maybe I ate the finger. I might have mistaken a fingertip for an olive."

"I'm so sorry," she said.

"I wanted a salad, not finger food. Well, I won't pay for this."

"Of course not. Let me show the manager what happened."

She took my fork and plate and went behind the counter, where a pretty, dark woman was preparing food. She was the cook *and* the manager. She looked at the piece of rubber and then looked at me. She smiled a smile of profound apology. I walked over to the counter.

"You didn't lose a finger, did you?"

"Oh, no," she said. "I'm really embarrassed."

"You don't have TB or hepatitis, do you?"

She laughed. She thought I was joking.

"The salad is on us," she said. "And order anything else you like."

"My appetite is destroyed . . . Well, I'll have a café au lait and a piece of pie."

I went home. I was feeling pretty good. It's always nice to get a free meal. And emboldened by my good luck at Gitane, I called my parents: I needed an emergency infusion of cash. I was down to thirty-five dollars. They were both on the phone with me and I tried to be brave and ask for the money, but I chickened out. It was too humiliating. But after I hung up I knew that I had no recourse – all my friends had already been tapped.

So I called back and said, "I have to tell you something – "

But before I could continue, my father said gruffly, "How much?"

I went on with dignity. "I was just wondering if you could pay my health insurance for a few months. A few deals, as you know, haven't come through."

My parents knew that I had been expecting a royalty check from my publisher in Turkey. My first novel is a best-seller over there. It's considered pornographic and indecent, and so it's a great success. I'm the D. H. Lawrence of Istanbul, but I'm broke in New York. My publisher had to seal the book in plastic so that the Turkish children wouldn't read it accidentally, and he claims that legal fees and the cost of the plastic sealing are eating up my royalties.

So my parents kindly agreed to help me, and late the next afternoon, I headed home to get the check. I didn't have time to wait for them to mail it. Just for leaving your apartment in New York, you're charged fifteen dollars.

I took the PATH train to Hoboken. I had twenty minutes before my rail connection to northern New Jersey and decided to explore the little port town, which I'd never done before. I was hoping to see lots of hobos and find tough bars, but Hoboken has been destroyed: The streets are clean and there is a Barnes and Noble and a Starbucks. And I didn't spot it, but I was sure that a Gap was lurking somewhere nearby. I usually don't care about things like this – the destruction of America – but when I'm traveling, it's nice to find a town with personality.

I was starving, so I went into a deli to buy a sandwich, but even the sandwiches were gentrified. I picked a smoked turkey with sundried tomatoes and olive paste. A young counterman with a big nose prepared my sandwich and made a phone call at the same time. With the receiver tucked against his shoulder, he grabbed slices of pale, translucent turkey. And because of the incident at Café Gitane, I realized he wasn't wearing rubber gloves.

He nonchalantly touched the phone with his hand and then took the same hand and spread the turkey on my whole wheat. Who had touched the phone before him? It was a daisy chain of germs. And where had his hands been before the phone? Food preparers should wear gloves, as if they are taking blood. The whole thing was grotesque. Eating the turkey would be like kissing his fingers. Then he stopped making the sandwich just to talk on the phone.

I thought of skipping out of there. I could run to the station. Then a fat manager-type emerged from the back before I could escape and asked me, "Are you being helped?"

"Yes," I said. "But I do have a train to catch."

I was hoping that this authority figure would then excuse me from having to eat the sandwich, but he scolded his counterman: "Get off the phone." The kid got off and finished my sandwich. But he forgot the olive paste. I wanted olive paste with the germs.

"Isn't there supposed to be olive paste?"

The manager overheard my question and snarled at the kid, "This sandwich is on me." A free sandwich! My second free meal in two days, but both meals were tainted.

I thought of throwing the sandwich away, but I couldn't – it was free. I got on my train and ate the thing. I tried to be brave, to be like everyone else – people who can eat other people's germs and not care. I finished the sandwich and I stared out the window at the polluted meadowlands.

I felt myself falling asleep; my eyes were closing, and then I thought, Maybe I should just kill myself. Suicidal thoughts always sneak up on me like that. But I don't mind them. They're like aspirin. They calm me down.

My father was waiting for me at the station. We drove home. I felt the old distance, the old repulsion. I fought this. Appreciate him, love him, I told myself.

Whenever I'm with my father, I think of Thorton Wilder's *Our Town* and the scene where the young woman, Emily, who has died in childbirth, gets to leave her grave and go back in time to the day of her twelfth birthday. But it's too painful for her to relive it, and she cries, "I can't. I can't go on. It goes so fast. We don't have time to look at one another."

I played her husband, George, in my high-school production, and I love *Our Town*. I don't care if its brush strokes are broad and sentimental. Its message is good. So I tried to be in the moment with my dad in the car, to *look at him, to be with him.* "How are you?" I asked gently.

"I have a sty in my right eye, and I have numbness in my left foot, but other than that I'm all right."

We were silent for the rest of the car ride. We went home and picked up my mom and headed out for sushi. Before the miso soup arrived, my dad wrote me a check for a couple hundred dollars.

"I should be getting a check from Turkey any day now," I said. "And the new book is coming out in August, in six months. I'll get some more money then."

"We know you're going to make it," said my dad. He has his good moments.

We ate our sushi. It was my third free meal in two days. I thought of telling this to my parents, buy my mother also abhors germs, and both the Café Gitane and Hoboken stories would have upset her.

They took me to the train station. My mother sat in the back. We waited in the car.

"We support you," my mother said.

"Thank you," I said. "And thank you for the check, and for dinner."

Then the train came. My mother leaned over the front seat and kissed me and said she loved me. I shook my dad's hand and sort of rubbed his shoulder. He smiled at me.

I got out of the car and I leaned in just a little and I said to both of them, "I love you." And then I closed the door.

I took the train back to Hoboken, and then the PATH to Ninth Street. From there I walked home and I had an odd pain in my big toe. Something was in my shoe. Whenever this happens, I always remember that in health class in the third grade they showed us a film about a boy who was limping. But then he stopped trying to walk and took off his shoe. Out came a pebble. We were told to always do this if something in our shoe was hurting us – that taking care of one's feet was very important. But I've always been too lazy to empty out the pebbles in my shoes, and this particular night, having gone begging to my parents, I thought I deserved a little suffering.

When I got to my apartment, I took off my shoe and nothing came out. Then I took off my sock and out fell a hard, brown lentil. I hadn't cooked lentils in years. Where had this lentil come from? It was all very strange. Then I thought of all the charity I had received in the last twenty-four hours, so I opened my window and threw the lentil outside. It wasn't much, but I hoped some poor pigeon might be able to eat it.

From *Ghostbread*

SONJA LIVINGSTON

Something big happened.

I found five dollars and discovered what it felt like to swallow the sky. The money was folded on the sidewalk in front of our apartment. I saw its color first, a tight rectangle of green lying flat against the gray walk. It was sitting there like a gift, so I picked it up and handed it over to my mother who thanked me, hugged me, adored me.

"Honestly," she said, "I didn't know how we would eat tonight."

To be taken by the hand to the corner store and allowed to choose a special candy – that's something. To be talked of with gratitude and pleasure, my name coming out of her mouth like a song. To be lifted over the shoulder, made to feel like the sun and the moon – it was almost too much to bear.

But there was a twist. There's always a twist.

Because when things are found, it is also true that they are lost, and the five dollars that made me family hero and benefactress of a macaroni and cheese dinner was the very same bill dropped by someone else. So when my mother lifted me up to the counter, I smiled and let my fingers skim the ruffled faces of penny candy, but remembered the Brownie troop that had passed our place just minutes before my find.

I selected my candy reward and thought of the double-file line of brown-uniformed girls, giggling in their cocoa-colored berets, one of them not knowing she'd lost her money, one of them looking, digging perhaps, into her tiny brown pouch the exact moment the atomic fireball settled into my mouth.

The dead end of the street was a fenced-in park that sealed off the street like a cork. The weedy lot was used by kids for baseball and running, by men for drinking and fighting, and as access to Goodman

Plaza – a square of rundown shops, including a large grocery, a Laundromat, and a furniture store that sold pressed wood dinette sets to neighborhood women on layaway plans. The pavement in the plaza was smooth, providing a good place to ride bikes and a cut-through to the old Italian bakeries where we bought sweets and pizzas when money was available.

Though I preferred to bury myself under a pile of blankets and read Nancy Drew and Greek mythology all day, Steph was always there, standing over me, pulling me from Persephone on a regular basis. Once she had me in her hold, she'd convince me to ride bikes to Tyron Park or East High School, or to find old sticks and a puck and start up a game of street hockey. Groups of kids headed to the park for sweaty games of baseball and football. We'd spend cool nights playing porch games – *Mother May I?* and *What Time Is It Mr. Fox?* – and street games of Spud, Kick the Can, and Hide & Seek.

Girls spent hours twirling bits of rope stolen from mothers' clotheslines. We drew chalk lines and played endless varieties of hopscotch. An older neighbor would inevitably call the police when games went too late and the laughter failed to die and a blue and white patrol car would skim down the street and ask us to quiet down, which we always did, at least until the police car was out of sight.

We learned to look out for utility vans and police cars. Most people on the street didn't drive, so any real traffic came from those who turned onto Lamont Place on accident. We waited as the slow coasting cars made their approach. Strangers looked out from windows as if they were seeing ghosts and wondering where the hell they were. We hated having to suspend our play, and stood near the curb, balls set to rest in the dips of our waists, faces wet with sweat, staring into the cars as they finally realized their mistake, screwed up their faces, and turned back around in someone's driveway.

There was nothing worse than a utility van coming down the street. They weren't coming to repair lines and wires. They were coming to cut someone's power off.

Very likely ours.

When my mother couldn't pay a bill, she'd simply toss it aside, unopened, like a paper boat set upon a stream. As her ability to pay lessened, heaps of unopened mail accumulated on bookshelves and tables. Instead of throwing them away, she'd add each bill to the piles until they grew through the house like a mountain chain.

Utility vans rolled slow and steady toward our house. We'd see them coming, peek out from windows, and pray they wouldn't stop at our house. When they did, and a uniformed man approached our door, we'd scatter like roaches.

"Shhhh," someone always said, "If we don't open the door, they can't cut off our power."

This bit of urban lore was true for only a few days. Eventually they'd access the wires from outside the house and we'd suffer the pity of neighbors who donated battery-powered camping lamps and snaked extension cords through their windows and into ours.

We learned to jump at knocks to the door, cringe when the telephone rang. When bill collectors called, I learned to say what they wanted to hear.

"I think she mailed that check out this week," or "I'll be sure and tell her to call."

I became an expert at pretending to write down return numbers. What's the point, I thought, since my mother won't be calling them back?

I was caught once. Lying. By a sharp-tongued bill collector whose voice reached through the pumpkin-colored phone mounted to the kitchen wall and grabbed hold of my ear.

"Are you *sure* you wrote that number down, young lady?"

When I said "yeah," she asked me to read it back. I stuttered and stalled; my face went red. I considered hanging up, but lacked the courage. When she asked for my name, I dumbly gave it, and she began to use it. Often, and with authority.

"Let's be honest now, Sonja, we never wrote that number down, did we?"

My humiliation was thorough. Convinced she could see me through the phone, I felt real nausea as I admitted that I'd never written the number down. Even as I wandered off in search of a pen, I hated her for her tone, her use of the word "we," the thoroughness of her power over me.

The phone's ring was not a delight for me, as it was for other pre-teen girls. Instead it sounded like a police whistle, making me stand at attention, pointing at me like a finger.

I never knew who was calling. It could have been Rochester Gas & Electric, Rochester Telephone, or the man who sold appliances out of the back of his van – though he usually came in person to collect payment.

My mother bought a TV from him. Steph had done the math and told her it was a bad deal. She told her she'd be paying much more than it was worth, and was being cheated. My mother knew Steph was right, but was annoyed at her interference. She couldn't have a child telling her what to do. So she bought the damn TV, and added one more person wanting money we did not have, one more van to look out for, one more reason to hide from knocks to the door.

Coins

MONA SIMPSON

I always say, We are the second oldest profession. That is because we serve the needs of women. And what we do is harder. Because we are giving more than only our bodies. Our bodies too – I carry him, he is already now forty pounds.

We may be selling our time – we are here in America for the money, that is our purpose – but still we give our love.

Dee told me, when I first came here, I don't need to teach you children. You have been a mother to give, she said, you know. Children, they are not hard.

But most you need to think about the mother. Here, the mothers are the ones who throw the tantrums.

You may have had nannies, but you have not before been a nanny.

Dee has always been my teacher, of America. I was never the only one learning. No, in the house of Dee there is always a crowd. After only one month, I was no longer even the newest. But I understood that I was the teacher's favorite pupil. I had never before been the favorite of any teacher; I used to be the favorite of the class. When the teacher turned around to the blackboard, I stood up and made the face that caused everyone to laugh. Dee believed I had the talent for baby-sitting, because of the schools my children attend in Manila. Even in the provinces, people know the names of our best colleges. I was the only one Dee ever asked for a job from her employer. "The others, they are not for Beverly Hills," she said, quiet because that is Dee's way of talking.

I hold my hands open in front of me to take away whatever my employer is beginning. If she starts to sew a button, I finish. If she runs water to rinse a lettuce, I say, I will be the one. When the husband spills something and pounds a wet napkin at the spot, I reach out my hands and say, Give it to me. I will make it clean.

All the while with a smile. It is not hard. Not when you have a purpose. And I have five purposes, the youngest seventeen, entering medicine.

But I have a good job. The parents of Ricardo get him in the morning, while they eat their breakfast. I fix their bed, take the glass of water from the side table, pick up Kleenexes.

Always the parents first, Dee said. A kid cannot fire you. Even here. They can love you but they cannot pay you. And anyway, they will forgive.

When I started with Richard, Dee said, I'm not going to tell you how to love, because either that will happen or it won't. And in six jobs, twenty-five years, she said, only once it did not happen to her. And then you need to quit. Because you cannot do the job if you do not love the baby.

But children, they are easy to love. Especially if you have them from a baby. Ricardo, they put him in my hands the first day at the hospital. They gave him to me.

Call me Lola, I whispered. That will be my name for you. (I was two years in America, I had been only a housekeeper. He is my first baby here.)

For me it is the parents who are more hard to love.

No, Dee said, at the beginning, I will not tell you how to love. I wouldn't if I could, because what would I tell you if I knew would be how not to so much. Because you will love him the same as your own and he never will. They love you, but it is not the same.

"I know, I *know*," I told her then. "I am a mother too."

But now I think, if you can keep them until they are five, then they will not forget you. I ask Ricardo, "Will you remember your Lola?"

"Why? You are not going away," he says.

"Someday," I tell him, "I will return to my place."

"And what will you do there?"

I will just sit in my house. Look at my kids' diplomas.

"Comeon comeon comeon comeon comeon. CometoLola. I have something for you," I say. Because he is very angry.

Usually it is the dad. But today it was the mother he was hitting. She has her hand on her eye and I dab ice, the way I do with his boo-boos. My employer when she is hurt sounds like an animal.

So I take him in my arms, away. We turn on ground now in the yard and he is strong, three years old, I cannot so easily hold him. And Lola told a lie. I do not have anything for him. So I make promises.

"Someday," I whisper, "I am going to take you home with me. And there we will make the ice candy."

He lies still in my arms, not any longer fighting. His bones they feel different now, not pushing to get out. They fall in a pattern, like the veins of a leaf.

"I will put you in my pocket and I will feed you one candy every day. And you will be happy. Because the ocean at our place it is very blue. The sky, higher than here. And the fruits that grow on trees, very sweet. Durians, mangos, atis."

His head hangs down between his knees, but he is listening.

"In my pocket I will give you one lichee. You can bounce it for a ball."

"If you were a kangaroo you would have a pouch," he grumbles. He is better now, slower his heart.

Through the window I see my employer on the telephone. She holds the ice to her eye and thumps around the kitchen talking to her friend, long distance, a woman who reads many books about the raising of children. When my employer becomes upset she calls this friend, the full-time mother.

My employer works and she has the American problem of being guilty. But you should not be guilty about your children. It is for them that you are working. I am here for my own, to pay for their professional education.

He is better now. Only his mouth smears outside the edges. He will come with me. I lift him into the stroller and promise candy, not the ice candy, just candy we can buy here. "But-ah, do not tell your mother." I call, "Excuse but, we are going now."

"Is that okay? Thanks, Lola." This is how my employer believes she cannot live without me. She is telling her friend who reads the books that he is better with me than with her.

And her friend will say to her that it is perfectly normal.

"Play date," she says into the phone cross-country. "I can't even stand the word."

"Smell," I say. "Do you have a poo-poo?" I pull his diaper back. I am paid to smell that. By the time I change him and we are ready to leave, the mother is going too.

Claire walks out into the world, away from us, holding keys in front of her, ready to start her car.

With a child small small it is a little like a ball and chain. You are never free. Not even sleeping. So with her it is a prance almost, an escape. She can walk under the old pines of the university, talking about an even older book.

But what she said to her friend on the phone is true. With me, he is no problem. When she takes him with her, it is not the same for me. Some weight is lifted off my lap. I have no purpose. For me alone here, I am too light.

My employer she says, When the baby comes home from the hospital, a Filipina should arrive with him. That, for her, would make a perfect world.

I take Ricardo to the store to show him our place on the map.

I say, Where is Lola from, and he points.

Very good.

I told my employers already. When they go to Europe to celebrate their tenth anniversary, I will take Ricardo to the Philippines. We are already saving for the tickets. I have one hundred twenty-five put away. I cannot save much because every month I have many tuitions. I even wrote in a letter to my husband that I will bring Ricardo home. Only my kids, they do not yet know. They are a little jealous, especially BongBong, my son, who has two children. And it is true. I am closer to Richard than I am to my own grandchildren. Because I see him every day. He is my albino grandson.

We are just alone. This neighborhood is ours, during the daytime. You do not see the white mothers walking. Only sliding in and out of cars, carrying shopping bags. In my place, I was at one time one of these ladies. Now that I see from afar, it looks like a lot of work.

I push him in the stroller and he sits. That is the good of fighting: it makes them very tired. The sun is solid, like many small weights on our arms. We pass the park, and in the distance we see the baby-sitters and children, so I roll him under the tall trees.

All the while, I keep talking to him. Dee told me, You have always to talk to him. Even a baby, it is very important that they hear words. And I always talked to him, more than to my kids, because my kids I had one after the other, five in ten years. But with Richard, I talk and talk, I tell him everything, and see, now, he is very *madaldal*. He understands more than one hundred words Tagalog.

In the class of 2020, at Harvard University, which is where the parents of Ricardo would like him to go, there will be six Santa Monica boys saying to the cooks in the cafeteria, Excuse, where is my adobo?

Lola by then will be swaying in a hammock, back in the Philippines.

"What for?" he says to me.

He is young. He does not yet understand the importance of rest.

"They change when they move to the big house," Rita says, kneeling in the sandbox, holding a sieve, "they really change."

For your salary, I am thinking, let them change! Rita gets one hundred dollars a day. Six months ago, her employers transferred to a fourteen-room mansion they had custom-built for themselves. My employer's house is the smallest. We compare jobs, the same as women will compare their husbands. Usually you would trade a part of what you have, but not all. If you are wanting to trade all, then there is trouble.

"But-ah, your employers, they are good," I say. I am always the one telling baby-sitters to stay in their jobs. Because too much change, it is bad for the children. I look at the two little girls in the sandbox. Of all of our kids, those two of Rita are the best behaved. Maybe because they are Asian (Chinese, adopted).

"They don't think I will leave but I can leave," Rita says. "Lot of people they are looking for Filipinos."

"The richest people all want Filipinos," Kitkat says.

"Like a BMW," I say. "We are status symbols." With only women, I can make them laugh.

"No, you know why? You know what Prudence told me? Rita whispers. "It is because we are quiet. Prudence told me in the hospital they have a joke: What does *yes* mean in Tagalog. *Yes* means fuck you."

"That is right. Fuck you," Kitkat says out loud.

"Shhh," I say. Ricardo is a mynah bird, and sure enough the head springs up.

"What?" he says. Always. What? He is very intelligent.

I have never said out loud but I have thought before, I am not the same as other baby-sitters. A part of me, I want to be known for what I can do. I want to be seen alone. At a few certain things, maybe I am the best.

The baby-sitters stand and brush sand off their laps, ready to go. "Tomorrow at the house of Rita," Kitkat calls, hitting me in the stomach.

"I want to go there now," Ricardo says. "To Ritahouse."

In their voices, that is the only time it is our house.

Back home, I have ready a project. We put into cardboard all the coins we can find. His mother told us we could have the pennies for the choo-choo bank, our place to save for tickets to the Philippines.

We also find nickels, dimes, and quarters, and I have brown tubes from the bank for those too. There is always money in this house, little puddles, where people empty their pockets. "It is a hunt," I tell Ricardo, and we discover nests in the carpets, piles on counters, little dishes filled. If someone came to the door with a pizza and I needed ten dollars, I could always collect, in coat pockets and cups, next to little slips of paper with writing. My house in the Philipines is like this too. I leave money places I forget. That way if I become very low I can dig.

That is what Lola calls her secret garden. People who too much like order, they do not have this security, the many seeds.

Richard is a very good worker. We pile the tubes of coins. We build with them an American log cabin, using Richard's Play-Doh for the mortar. If we can also keep the quarters and dimes and nickels, we will have a lot. The pennies they are ours already. But the rest I will have to call and ask.

Claire answers her office phone, "Hey."

"We are wanting," I explain. "Can we have the money also for the silver coins we find?"

"Sure, Lola," she says. Usually she will say to me, "Sure, Lola." There are certain people in life, you know, they will always say to you yes.

At the bank, we wait in line a long time. Then we go to the front, the lady acts all business, making a total of the rolled dimes. I say to her, "This little man rolled the nickels by himself."

While she finishes the silver coins, I lift a bag of pennies from his wagon. It is very heavy. We have many pennies. We took apart the fort and the log cabin. We counted forty dollars from nickels, twenty-seven dollars from dimes, and one hundred and three dollars from pennies. I lift Ricardo up so he can see.

But the lady pushes our tubes out of the cage. "We cannot take pennies," she says.

Richard picks one roll in his hand, to give it back to her. I remember this moment, again and again. It is like the giving of a flower. He does not yet understand.

"We don't take these," she says.

For a second then his face changes, what his mother calls berry-with-a-frown. Cartoon looks, they are really true on children. The upside-down smile, an open mouth, then he is bawling. And he throws the roll of pennies at the lady's face.

Her hand goes to a place above her eye. "I cannot help you," she says, setting the teeth. She has already given us the paper money for the other coins. She looks at me with hate. I have seen real hate only a few times in my life. The shape of diamonds, it is shocking. But she is hurt above the eye and I am not white.

"Come, Ricardo." I fight him down into the wagon. I will have to pull all the rolls of pennies and him. "We will make our getaway."

But he runs dragging pennies to a garbage can and begins dumping the tubes in the open top. Still crying but he is mad now. Also mad. I have to stop him. This is not right. All our effort. With him what I do is almost tackle. Lola is not a big person. But I get on the floor and hold him until the fight is out. Then I tell him a story, keeping him in my lap.

"Once upon a time," I say," I work in Beverly Hills. In a house that is very fancy. Three layers. Floors like a checkerboard. All marble.

"When I was first here, new, the lady she open the door and saw me and right away she said, You are hired. She told me, she knew like that – and when she said that she snap her fingers – you will never guess from why. She said, because of the way I tie my sneakers."

"How did you, Lola?"

"She thought Lola was a tidy person. But Lola is not so very tidy, not really. I can be. If I have to. And for her I was neat. I clean everything. But that is not the way I live my life. It is too much time, always straightening. I would rather see people, taste some part of life.

"The lady's husband, he had an office, and she wanted that to be neat too. She hired me extra to go on the Saturday and straighten. He was there working while I clean. And he had one jar like this, up to my waist, full with pennies. I asked him did he want me to get tubes from the bank. And he said, 'You can take the pennies.' But I could not lift.

"And so I came back Sunday, my day off, and I sat on the floor out of is way and put all the pennies into tubes. He stepped around me when he went down the hall to use the restroom or the machines. He'd ask me how much money it was as he went by, and I'd tell him the total so far.

" 'Thirty-six dollars,' I said.

" 'Good job, Lola.'

"The next time it was ninety-two.

"By the last time he passed, I was at two hundred and six. That time his face looked strange, like two lines cross over it. He went down the hall and I heard xeroxing.

"On his way back, he stopped over my legs and said, 'Maybe you better leave the pennies.'

" 'Whatever you say. It is up to you.'

"When he was back in his office, on the phone, I stood and left it all there, the rolled pennies, the pile on the floor, the jar turned over. I took the bus to the place of Dee, and I never went back to that house. That was the end of my career for a Beverly Hills nanny."

"Is that when you came to me?"

"That is before," I say. "You were not yet born. Still I had to wait one year more. But-ah, when the husband took the pennies I rolled to the bank, you know what they are telling him? They are telling him too what they are telling us. 'We cannot help you.' And you know what he will do then?"

"He shouldn't have taken your pennies, Lola. He is a bad man."

"A little bad. Listen, you know what he will do? He will throw the pennies in the garbage and walk away in a hurry, he is always in a hurry. He is too busy, see?"

Now I fish with my arm in the garbage, feeling among wet things for our tubes, the ones Ricardo threw.

"But we will do something else. Come. You watch Lola." I pull him in the wagon out of the bank into the bright air. We go to the five-and-dime. And then the candy shop. And then the Discovery Store, where we study the globe. Each place, I count out the money in pennies. I put in piles of ten on the counter, so it is easy for the register clerk.

My father always told me, Spend your small money first. He remembered in our place when money became light, the smaller denominations would not buy anymore. And still at that time, he told me, there was so much wealth.

In the wagon, Ricardo is eating long orange and green candy worms.

"See, in the bank it is nothing, but out here in the world it is money. Not for the Philippines, but we can still buy. Every day a little. It is our own private fund. Our trust fund. I trust you and you trust me. You have your candy. Now, we will use some pennies to buy Lola her cup of coffee."

That is what my kids and Ricardo, they will remember. That Lola loved her coffee.

When we return home, the hallways round to caves, warm, dark already. I hear the mother of Richard making dinner in the kitchen.

I take the tomatoes from my employer. "I will be the one," I say. That is our way. My employer did not grow up living with helpers. She cannot easily ask. Also, my employer is a very good cook. I am happy to chop chop, while Ricardo plays on the floor with his action figures.

Tonight, Claire's eye, where he hit, shines black and blue, there is yellow also. Over it she has applied makeup.

"Now he's fine," she sighs when I bend to look closer. "I don't know what I'm doing wrong."

"It is the age too," I say. But my children, they were not like this, not even my boy. Here in America, they are different. They are also taller.

My employer whispers, "May I should find a psychologist for him. Do you think this is all still normal?"

Really, I do not know. The hitting too, I worry. I cannot tell her the woman at the bank. "You are talking to the wrong person," I say. "Because-ah, I like naughty boys."

She sighs, but she is better. We are like magicians. With us too there is what the employer sees and there is sleight of hand.

I feed him his dinner because that is easier for the baby-sitter.

Then, when Ricardo has eaten enough, I get out of the way and let the family sit together. My employer gives me my plate, covered with a napkin, and I carry it back to my own place.

At first they used to ask me to eat with them, but I always said no.

Dee advised me, Don't, even if they ask. Americans do not know what they want. They will invite you, and then later on they will pine for their privacy. Americans need very much privacy. Because it is a big land.

And the parents of Richard work all day, it is their only time together. Also, if I was eating with them, when Ricardo needed more milk or the salt was not on the table, I would be the one getting up and down. I like to put my feet up, watch the TV. It is important to have hours in the day when you are comfortable.

Later on, he can come back to my place, but then it is not my job anymore, he is a visitor, my buddy-buddy. And he is very good in my house. He never breaks anything. He looks at my pictures, he knows the names of my children, and we study the map.

We will save for the globe, on a layaway plan. Each day we will give the man fifty pennies. It will help teach Ricardo counting.

The parents do not come out here. My work is done. They leave the dishes, I do them in the morning. My money is earned. I can sit. That is my day.

So, some people across the Pacific, they had better be studying.

Class

ELAINE SEXTON

I lasted three days minding a child
at the beach club on a thin strand
of sand, where my family lived
but did not belong. I took over the job

my sisters had before me,
my sisters, who sat every summer,
gladly, reading books, getting tans,
earning money for college.

On the second day I knelt by the pool,
the north Atlantic in sight,
the Isles of Shoals clearly raised
in the distance. I watched a girl

not much younger than I swimming
laps. The sun bleached the water
in the pool, licking its sides
the way my soft drink

licked my glass. Idle, like the idle rich
parents at the bar, I watched this girl
as if reading would be stealing
the attention they paid for. This was

my lesson. Back and forth she swam,
back and forth I weighed belonging
and not belonging, the salt water,
always free, the steps to it already mine.

Having Discovered a Windfall by the Side of the Road, the Cautious Miser Is Visited by the Angel of Profligacy

HAILEY LEITHAUSER

Our most perfect machine.
    See it wink in the dirt. See it flirt.

How it warms in the hand.
    See it rubbed in the glove. See it shine.

See it deepen and gleam. *How it bursts.*
    No coin is an island;

no tender unclean.
    How it sweetens the feast of the beast of the heart.

How the heart is a box with a contraband
    slot. *Let us splurge. Let us supper like swine*

in our troughs. Let it burn, let us thirst.
    Let us fill if you will. Let us spend.

Let it tend like a fire-coal dark in the pocket,
    like a radiant coffer. *Unlock it, unlock it.*

Professor Lacy N. Igga Looks Up the Word *Parasomnia*

RUTH ELLEN KOCHER

the evening is first waves and shackles
smells of rotting wood and skin, shit, sea
stink and then 1-800 numbers . . . miracle juicers

flowers in long boxes
a lifestyle slave collar that can pass
for vanilla jewelery

somehow bought, boxed, shipped
and delivered to Lacy's door.

how a dream about captivity
results in sleep-shopping is anybody's
guess. on campus she will seem

removed. on campus her
white students will see the groggy grey
sheen on her eyes and think

how very affirmative action
how very unprofessional

Lacy speaks louder than usual
during her lecture. She tosses words
out to anchor the room.

blub blub blub what she talkin a-bout
blub blub blub exclusivity?

Her students blink absently at each splash
as the ship that cruises her sleep slowly
trolls above their blank open faces.

She watches them. Pink Cashmier™ sweater 49.99
ski jacket 389.99. designer satchel 550.00
and thinks freedom. She watches

with a deep compulsion to close her eyes
over the grey sheen, to sit down in front of them
and talk about marketing, she sees the

patent leather ballet shoes right
from the runway and struggles
against the static white noise of sleep.

The Entrepreneurs

TONY EPRILE

They pulled off the highway in a spurt of dust and gravel. "That's the road up there." The driver of the Zola pointed to the opposite side of the motorway. "You just walk, walk, walk until you get to where the peach tree used to be, then you follow your left hand past some koppies and tin huts. You'll find your man there, I promise you."

The Toyota minivan darted back onto the highway again, causing a speeding Mercedes to swerve sharply and hoot in anger. The van beep-beeped cheerily in reply, or perhaps simply as encouragement to Naboth, who watched it recede into the distance. On the van's back panel was a slogan lovingly hand-painted in gold lettering: "Rode To Riches."

"You can talk," Naboth spoke out loud, thinking bitterly of the three five-rand notes he had handed the jovial driver. These minivan taxis – which were known by the ironic name of Zola Budds because they moved fast, stopped suddenly, and had a habit of knocking people over – provided a good livelihood. The trouble was, you didn't try to break in uninvited . . . not if you had the ordinary kind of human skin that could be penetrated with sharp objects.

Gauging an interval in the stream of fast-moving traffic, Naboth ran across the highway, his Natal Leather Company suitcase banging against the side of his leg. He started up the gravel road cheerfully enough, pausing only to remove the sharp-edged stones that kept slipping into his city shoes. He would have liked to take the shoes off to save their finish, but years in town had sloughed away the habit of walking barefoot. After about a mile of painful hiking, he passed a group of women going the other way. They waved and smiled at him and he envied the ease with which they balanced their burdens on their heads and benefited from the resulting shade. A hundred yards or so farther on, there was the ping of flying brass studs as the suitcase handle came unmoored. The heavy bag wrenched out of his grasp, spraining the muscle of his upper arm. Naboth rubbed the injured spot ruefully, looked back to make sure none of the women was watching, and then seized the suitcase in both hands and headed into the veld. He slipped it under a thicket of thornbush, adding several more branches to better conceal it. As he stepped back, there was a tearing sound: the sleeve of his polyester jacket had snagged on a thorn. A light line of displaced threads ran through the darker blue.

He walked on, cursing the heat, the dust that parched his throat, the plants that pricked and cut and jabbed his tender flesh. A world without shelter or shade, that was rural life! He heard a car grinding its way up the road in the direction he was taking, and he stuck his thumb out hopefully, only to be given an angry glare by the pale-fleshed woman who was driving. He cursed her and the car, too, but carefully, when it was not likely that anyone glancing into the rearview mirror could see him doing so. This was the countryside, after all, where things are different in that they haven't changed.

Naboth paused at the top of a hill, his eyes stinging as sweat dripped into them, the land around shimmering in the heat. You could die here easily, of sunstroke or thirst, and all that would be left would be a dried-out shell like the broken white cases of dead millipedes. No one would know; only the State, after a few years, would note the inactivity of your bank account and swallow up the contents. Naboth wandered down a barely discernible footpath to relieve himself, amazed that his body still contained any superfluous liquid. As he zipped up, he realized that the stump overgrown with sawgrass must be the former peach tree the driver had told him about. That idiot! How was anyone who'd never been there in the first place supposed to know to turn off where something isn't there anymore? How was this country ever going to prosper if people couldn't even give you decent directions? Perhaps it was a good omen, though. The ancestors had tickled his bladder at just the right moment and saved him from wandering uselessly down this hellish road.

He continued on slowly, squinting his eyes to avoid the glare. Yes, there were the koppies, standing tall like welcoming sentinels to either side of him. The road meandered past a brownish, evil-looking stream, its narrow trickle of water foaming unnaturally with runoff fertilizer from the surrounding farmland. At last, there were some tin-roofed huts and, lying on his side in the sparse shade of a thinly leaved tree, was a man wearing what clearly were once city clothes: a dusty pair of charcoal-gray trousers, a faded blue Oxford shirt.

"Hey, my friend," Naboth called, his voice unnaturally loud in the stillness of the afternoon. "Can you provide me with something to drink? I think my head is going to burst and fly off in a thousand pieces."

The man listlessly pointed toward a jerry can resting against the side of the hut. Naboth took the tin mug from the top of the jerry can, poured some acrid-smelling water into it, and drank gratefully. He refilled the cup and poured some of the liquid over his left wrist to cool himself, only to be interrupted by an angry shout from the man under the tree. "Hey, stranger. Drink, but don't waste! You think you just turn on a tap around here?"

"Excuse me, I wasn't thinking" – And you needn't have talked so sharply, either. You live in the country, but you know nothing of the laws of hospitality – "Are you by any chance Teacher Makize?"

The man laughed bitterly. "You can call me that, but I haven't been in a school for a year now. And I won't be in front of a classroom again if the DET has anything to say about it." A suspicious look appeared on his face. "How do you know who I am? What do you want from me?"

"It's all right, baba. I was sent by your cousin Sipho."

The man sank wearily back into his former posture. "What's that troublemaker done now?"

"He told me you could help me get rich like him. I want a secret like the spell you gave Sipho."

"Sipho? He's not rich. Not unless he's been stealing." The man's voice rose a pitch in irritation.

"Hai, baba! I've seen his Mercedes. It was bright and clean and shone like a mirror. He was on his way to pick up his girlfriend to take her to a *restauran*t and to a drive-in cinema!"

"Oh, god. Sipho's lying to you. Even when he was this small, he was a big, big liar."

"No, you have it wrong. I saw the car with my own eyes. Sipho said he got the secret to get rich from you. I want you to help me, so I can get money, too." Naboth took another cup of water and squatted down on his heels to show his patience. He knew the man wouldn't turn over his secret just for the asking, but he wasn't leaving until he got the answer he wanted.

"So Sipho told you I gave him some medicine, some *muti*, and that's how he acquired all his wealth?"

"That's right. Now I'm here." If you persist, they always come around. Just persist, persist. "I'll give you my wristwatch – Timex – for this medicine. It cost me a hundred rand."

The teacher's eyes flickered, his guess that Naboth was a Zulu confirmed by his pronunciation of the English words: *a hundled iLandi*. The headmaster of Makize's school had been a Zulu, and stubborn just like this one. "What am I going to do with a wristwatch out here? Tell me how much time I have to hang out doing nothing in the middle of nowhere?" The former teacher spat into the red dust at his side. "Keep your bloody watch, man. I'll tell you the secret. But then you must promise to leave right away and never bother me again. "

"Thank you, my friend. I am too happy!"

"Okay, but it's not easy. You have to work to get rich, you know that? You have to accomplish a task, or the *muti* won't work. Come over here!" The teacher spoke with a new firm tone of command. Pleased, Naboth went and sat down before him. The other man dipped a finger into the tin cup, rubbed the wet finger into the red dust, and drew two parallel lines on Naboth's forehead. "First of all, you have to lose your name . . ."

"My name?"

"Yes. From now until four Sundays from now, you cannot have a name. Throw away your identity card. And if anyone asks your name, you can't just make up a new one, you have to tell them you don't have any name."

"That's hard . . ." Naboth murmured. He didn't like the idea of getting rid of his identity card.

"Well, you don't have to do any of this," the teacher said impatiently. "You can go home, go about your business, forget this nonsense about getting rich."

"No, no, I will do it. Is that everything?"

"There's one more thing; after the fourth Sunday, you must go home to KwaZulu and stay there. Any business you put your hand to will prosper after that. Provided you fulfill the conditions exactly as I told you. Now, go!"

Naboth carefully placed his wristwatch on the other man's lap – you always paid for medicine, otherwise it wouldn't work – then he stood, nodded respectfully, and began walking back down the path with jaunty steps.

"Why did you tell him those lies, you useless?" a woman said, coming out of the hut.

"It's Sipho's fault. You know how he always plays practical jokes. I'll bet you he told this idiot that his employer's Mercedes was his own. How else was I supposed to get rid of him? Besides, the crazy stranger drank up all the water." The man strapped Naboth's watch around his own wrist. It was a perfect fit.

"Nevertheless, you shouldn't have told him to throw away his identity card," the woman grumbled.

The teacher waved her words away as if he were shooing flies, then lay back in the shade to rest.

The man walked down the gravel road, each step taking him farther from his identity card. He had overturned a large rock about a hundred yards back, brushed away the earwigs and woodlice that were lurking underneath, and dug a small hole. As soon as he took the ID card out of his wallet, it began objecting. "What do you think you're doing?" it said. "If you lose me, you'll be in deep trouble!" Amazingly, it spoke in exactly the clipped English tones of the sergeant of police who had stopped the man's father on the way back from a church service many years before. As he wrapped the little plastic square in a paper handkerchief, he remembered watching his father's growing terror as he searched first the right inside pocket of his jacket, then the left, while the policeman berated him in this same voice. Carefully, he placed the rock over the small declivity that now contained his identity.

"Come back at once or you'll be sorry," he heard the voice in his ears, fainter now. It was not too late to turn back. He had made some scratches on the stone with his nail trimmers, and he would still be able to identify it among all the other rocks. Half a mile farther on, he knew that that was it; he was not going back. He felt a peculiar lifting of his spirits, a sense of freedom that he had never felt before. All his adult life he had carried some form of official document, first the hated passbook, the *dompas,* with its rubber stamps and employer endorsement, then the identity card, less hateful but still coded for race and ethnic origin. Now he had nothing. He strode easily, his shoulders squared back, his step firm. The sun was not quite so high now, and the heat was less bothersome than before. Even his suitcase, when he retrieved it, felt lighter than it had earlier, and he was able to rig up an improvised carrying strap with the canvas belt to his other pair of trousers. He felt ready to start a new life.

He turned left when he reached the motorway, heading out toward Natal but with no clear destination in mind. After he had been walking for a while, he paused for a moment to rest. It was just as well that he did, because a string of fast-moving bicyclists came pouring out from behind a hedge that hid another side road. With their white helmets, plastic goggles, Lycra bodysuits, their awkward postures hunched over the expensive racing bikes, and the strident whirring of their tires, they resembled some sort of large, swift insects . . . locusts, perhaps. Watching them pass, Naboth admired the precision of their limbs, the rapidity of their progress. He hoisted up his suitcase and stepped forth again on his own way, but as he passed the side road, he was halted by a shout and a rush of wind past his face. The straggler, who had narrowly missed running into him, skidded where the road surface changed from Tarmac to gravel. The rider almost regained his balance, but the angle was too steep and, as if in slow motion, he fell to one side while the bicycle shot into the roadway under the wheels of a passing goods lorry.

Naboth stared at the unconscious cyclist who lay prostrate almost at his very feet. Behind him, he could hear the belated screech of brakes and the cries and yells of African workers who had been waiting for a bus on the other side of the road. He felt as if he saw the injured man from very far off – an absurd figure lying in the dirt like a shotgunned guinea fowl. There were more shouts, the sound of running feet, further shrieking brakepads as cars slowed to avoid hitting the erstwhile bus passengers who ran without heed across the busy road. Naboth caught the eye of the terrified lorry driver, who had now reversed and had stuck his head out of the window to see what he'd hit. "Aiii, you killed him!" a man shouted, reaching the prone body. "You hit him and you killed him." Naboth could see decision take shape on the driver's face; there was a grinding of gears and the lorry hurtled out onto the motorway and sped away.

Naboth leaned down and unbuckled the strap to the cyclist's helmet. He gently extricated the man's head and removed the helmet with its yellow foam padding, soft and secure as the inside of a weaverbird's nest. The cyclist's eyelids fluttered and he gave a faint sigh. The crowd pressing around Naboth murmured in satisfaction at these signs of life. "Shame," a woman's voice said, "that bloody driver didn't even stop."

The cyclist sat up and looked around in surprise at the crowd of African faces peering down at him. "What's going on?" he asked conversationally, causing a subdued titter.

"What's going on is that you are coming off your bicycle," Naboth replied, causing a few members of the crowd to laugh outright. He hadn't meant to make a joke, but already the crowd behind him was repeating the exchange for the benefit of newcomers. At this moment, a police car passing on the other side of the road performed a U-turn across two lanes and skidded to a halt near them. A young white officer and an African constable got out and approached the crowd. A minivan with the words "Raleigh Racing Tour" made the same U-turn and pulled up behind the police car.

"What's the disturbance?" the white policeman demanded, unconsciously tugging at his Sam Browne belt.

"This man was run over by a lorry and now he has come back to life," a man in the crowd responded. "It is a miracle of God,"

"I fell off my effing bike," the cyclist said, standing up painfully. "And this idiot thinks it's funny!" He pointed at Naboth, who looked around for some support against this injustice. No one else seemed ready to come to his aid – the crowd was watching him with interest in anticipation of new signs of wit; the policemen were staring at him with officious distrust; the only people not looking at him were two men in white overalls who had gotten out of the minivan and who were carefully straightening out the bent front rim of the bicycle.

"I saw you fall down . . . I was worried about you," he tried to explain. The two men in white overalls came up to the cyclist and began feeling his legs and arms with the same assiduous care they had shown toward his bicycle.

By now, the policeman had taken out a notebook and a stubby pencil. "You were a witness to the accident?"

"Yes. I was standing here. He came down the hill very fast . . ."

"He was run over by a big truck," interrupted the same man who had spoken up earlier. "It is God's will that he's not dead."

"First he fell off, then a lorry ran over the bike," Naboth hurriedly interjected.

"And then you started making jokes," the cyclist said, advancing angrily toward Naboth. "I hit my head; I wreck a four thousand-rand bike, and you think it's a big bloody joke. Ha! Ha!"

One of the overalled men, who had an Australian accent and a distinct black handprint in chain grease on his bleached pants, succeeded in calming the errant rider and convincing him that they could replace the tire "quicker than a wombat's fart" and get him back on the tour. The policeman, meanwhile, was getting increasingly frustrated at the divergent descriptions of the hit-and-run vehicle: a gray minivan, a lorry fetching lumber from the Houtkop mill up the road, a dusty white Ford pickup.

"You can't leave," he told the cyclist. "I has to file a report."

"Sorry, mate," the Australian said. "No time for that. Just forget about it."

"I has to make a report," the officer complained, but the other white men insistently ignored him as they climbed into the Raleigh minivan. In frustration, the policeman ordered the crowd to disperse, telling them they were creating an illegal assembly.

"Not you," he said, grabbing Naboth's arm. "I needs your name for the report."

"I can't tell you my name, sir," Naboth replied.

"Stop your nonsense, my boy. You is my witness. Give me your name and address and then you can bugger off."

"I can't tell you that," Naboth said sorrowfully. The officer had gotten quite red in the face by now and was clearly on the verge of losing his temper.

"Right," he said, pushing Naboth toward the police car. "Obstructing justice, resisting arrest, and I'll think of something else, too. You're going to laugh on the other side of your face, you skellum."

Naboth found himself in the back seat of the police car, behind the wire grille. The African policeman plunked himself beside him, folded his arms so that his hands accentuated the bulge of biceps beneath his short-sleeved shirt, and eyed Naboth ironically from just an inch or two away. "What have I done wrong?" Naboth asked plaintively, but the African policeman just continued to peer at him in this intimidating way and the driver, too, said nothing, his pimpled neck flaming red with exasperation.

When they finally arrived at the police station, the black policeman stuck a mallet-sized fist beneath Naboth's nose and murmured, "Now you're going to shit."

Naboth's hands were roughly forced behind his back and cuffed at the wrists, then he was left alone in a small anteroom. In the next room over, he could hear a senior officer telling off the policeman who had arrested him. "Three murders in the township last week, a patrol car shot at, and what do you do? You bring in a nameless witness to an accident that never happened!" The man's voice rose in a high insistent whine, tireless as a lone mosquito in a darkened room. After enjoying his excoriation of the young cop for some time, the senior officer came in and looked at Naboth.

"Okay, Nkabi," he said to the African constable, "take him to the fingerprint room and get his prints. We'll put them in the computer and find out soon enough if our friend here is a terrorist. And, Nkabi, maybe if you ask him nicely he'll tell you his name."

Steely fingers gripped his sprained arm by the elbow and Naboth fell over his own feet as he was thrust down the stairs leading to the fingerprint room. The handcuffs were removed and his hands crammed first against an inkpad, then against a white sheet of paper – the four fingers crunched down and rotated separately from the thumb – to leave a clear and unsmudged impress, tribute to the policeman's practiced art. He was handed a rag smelling evilly of turpentine, and then the black constable stood before him, very close, a newly sharpened pencil still smelling of wood shavings in one hand, a clipboard in the other.

"Your name?"

"I'm sorry – " Naboth's words were lost in the sudden expulsion of his breath as the blunt end of the pencil was rammed, stiletto-like, into his solar plexus. He doubled over, his face meeting a rapidly rising knee in a meld of brilliant light, deep blackness, and scalding flesh.

"You think you're hard, but you're soft, soft, soft. I can break you like that!" Nkabi said, snapping the pencil neatly in two. Naboth lay quietly, his face pulsing with waves of heat, salt liquid burning its way down his throat. When he was able to focus again, the first objects that came into sight were the constable's muscular calves and shiny, reinforced leather boots. He was going to have to do something before those boots trampled over him.

"Listen, there's a reason I can't tell you my name. It has to do with a Sangoma."

"Don't talk lies. When you open your mouth, worms fall out."

"Seriously. This is the truth, not worms." The booted feet shuffled impatiently, and Naboth sped up the course of his tale despite the pain from his swelling lips. "I hired a Sangoma to help me dream a lucky number for the Fah-Fee, but I only paid her half. *As sure as my name is my name*, I said, *I'll give you the remainder when I get my Friday paypacket.*

"Well, I didn't win. And I thought to myself: this one's medicine is not good, why should I pay her the rest of the money? A few days later I went out to buy some beer, but it was very hot and I got confused. I wandered all over the township without finding the shop, and then when I opened a door that I thought was it, there was the Sangoma waiting for me. *You swear too lightly on your name*, she told me. *The next time you open your mouth to say your name, you will die. And the person who asked you your name, they will die too."*

"This is more rubbish. Am I wearing a blanket that you think I'm some stupid country bumpkin?" The voice drifting down to Naboth was angry, but the feet did not kick him.

A few moments later, the young white cop came in. He stopped abruptly when he saw the broken pencil. "Ag, Nkabi, what did you do that for? You think pencils is grown on trees?"

"It can still be used," the other replied morosely.

"Nooo, man. And what am I supposed to tell Captain Van Rooyen when he wants to know why we use up more supplies than anyone else? And what about this joker; did you find out his name?"

"He has forgotten his name. Truly." The black constable tapped his head with his finger significantly.

"'Strue? I saw a film like that. This guy goes outside one day and somebody hits him on the head and he gets ammonia. He doesn't know who he is anymore. Then this nice rich lady takes care of him and they fall in love. Just when they're going to get married, a flowerpot falls out of a window and hits him on the head, and he remembers everything – his name, his bloody nagging wife, and screaming, bratty children – and he has to tell the nice lady he can't marry her even though he loves her. Ag, I cried when that happened. I couldn't help it. You know, maybe if we hit this guy on the head again, he'll remember who he is." He peered down at Naboth and asked in an unnaturally loud voice: "Who are you? What is your name?"

"Please, boss, I don't know."

The following morning, Naboth was arraigned on charges of vagrancy, resisting arrest, and loitering with the intent of creating a public nuisance. The examining magistrate, the Honorable Brits Van Stossel, pondered the prisoner in the dock while he calculated how much work was still needed on his terraced garden. Despite his city clothes, this miscreant had broad shoulders and strong hands and, like most Africans, was probably quite used to physical labor.

"Four weeks. To be spent on work detail, not idling around at government expense!" The magistrate was not through yet, though, for presently he addressed the young white policeman. "Perhaps, Officer

Botha, if it's not too much trouble, you might consider devoting a little of your precious time to chasing a real criminal now and then?"

This remark made Constable Nkabi chuckle under his breath, and his hold on Naboth's upper arm while leading him out of the courtroom was not quite so fierce. "You're lucky," Nkabi said to him. "Now you'll get to answer to a number and you won't have to worry about your name until we let you out again."

The Honorable Brits Van Stossel's substantial white brick house sat atop a small rise. The native flora of scrubby underbrush had been plucked and shaved into near invisibility, replaced with carefully tended green lawn and baked flower beds, smelling richly of black, peat-enriched humus. The shape of the hill itself had been changed by tasteful brick terracing that kept the cherished flower beds from washing away in the area's violent downpours. Naboth found his place in a crew of three (supervised by a bored warder armed with a high-powered rifle), who were reinforcing the lowest tier of the garden at the edge of the property. Naboth's job was to pass bricks from a wheelbarrow to Stokvels, a wiry South Sotho with a peppering of silver in his hair and a fixed, anxious smile. Stokvels then handed the brick to Spaza, a brawny younger man from the local township, who carefully set it in place before using a trowel to scrape off any excess cement. Naboth could see that Spaza was using too much mortar – it would contract as it dried and begin to crack from the contrasting heat and chill of passing days and nights – but he did not bother to say anything. The other two were already annoyed with him because he refused to tell them his name, and he did not want to reiterate the Sangoma story: these things have a habit of coming true with the saying of them. He did not mind that they relegated him to the worst job: wheeling the heavy barrow back and forth from the prison pickup when fresh bricks were needed. It took the edge off their suspiciousness of him.

"Hell, I could use a Castle lager right now," Stokvels said, wiping sweat from his forehead with the side of his arm. He had made this remark about once every half hour. "A nice barrowful of ice-cold cans instead of this load of focking bricks."

Spaza took the brick handed to him and mimed flipping the top of it open, then pretended to pour the cool liquid down his throat. "To your health," he declared, holding up the rough, red brick. He had a deep, gravelly voice, like that of the "the lion," Mahlathini.

"Don't even joke like that," Stokvels grumbled. "A couple weeks ago, I could walk over to my refrigerator any time I wanted and pull out a nice cold one. That's what got that bastard local policeman, Thomas Kakala, to jealous me. He told me that he had also bought a fridge on the hire purchase. He told me exactly how much he had to pay each month. 'That's nice,' I said to him. 'Enjoy it.' I knew he wanted me to give him money, but the hell! I let him come free to my house; I let him drink all the beer he wanted."

"Where did you get so rich?" Naboth asked.

"NoName speaks! When NoName speaks, Nobody listens." Stokvels laughed a surprisingly shrill laugh. "I wasn't rich yet, but I was on the path; my feet were on the path. It's easy what I did: I bought a television from a friend in town. I put up chairs, served cold beer, brewed my own liquor. M-Net! Sports! Orlando Pirates versus the Umtata Bucks! Then that Kakala turned me in. No license for the television, no license for the liquor, no license for the chairs, no license for being without a license. I'm drinking bricks now, and I'm going to be drinking bricks for a long time."

"It's your own fault," Spaza asserted. "Kakala has to eat. You've got to bribe. It's as simple as that. I'm a businessman. I *know*."

"You're a businessman? Busy with a trowel." Stokvels sneered. Spaza looked as if he were ready to take the little man's head and slap it on the mortar in place of the next brick.

"Hey, we're all here, all in the same shit," Naboth interjected, seeking to make peace. "Tell me how you were a businessman."

"Everybody has to eat, that's my motto. I was selling food boxes to the people who had to commute to work. Early, early I was out there when the taxis were waiting with their engines running. People knew, those commuters knew they could sleep a few minutes longer and not have to be hungry all day. When they came back from work, they could buy dinner and not have to go home and start the charcoal or fire up the gas. I had seven women working for me. I had boerewors. I had chicken. I had putu, Ting, you name it. Everybody's got to eat."

"Then some Kakala turned you in, right?" Stokvels said glumly.

"Nobody turned me in. I gave the drivers free, the best food. I gave the police free. Everybody's got to eat. You bribe, you stay in business. No, man, it's because I have a temper. This one guy, he didn't want to pay up. A couple of weeks I let him go; he said he hadn't been paid. No problem. Lots of people, they didn't have money this week, they gave me the end of next week. You don't want to be too tight. Then I told him: *My friend, it's time.*

The food was bad, he said. He had to throw the chicken out the window. Why should he pay for chicken with maggots in it? He said all this with my other customers standing where they could hear. I cut him, man. I cut him fast. He didn't even see it coming, just blood, and then him squealing like a pig."

"Au, that's hard," Stokvels, said, regret at his earlier rash remark explicit on his face.

"No, I'm fair. If someone's hungry, pay me tomorrow. Everybody's got to eat. If it wasn't for that thief, I'd still be in business."

"When I get free from here, I'm going to start up again. I'll get a license for everything, and Kakala can go to hell," Stokvels mused. "Maybe I'll even serve food."

"Food is the best. Soon as I'm free, I'm back to business. Everybody's got to eat. But I got thirty months for cutting that guy. It's hard."

"I got one year, and I lost all my money. But I'll start again. You can't lose with television, 'specially sports." He looked over at Naboth, who pretended disinterest but had been drinking in every word. "What about you, NoName? What are you going to do when they let you go?"

Naboth smiled mysteriously. "I have my plans," he said softly.

"Sure," his companions jeered in unison. "NoName has plans!"

Poetry and Blue Jeans

JENNY BOULLY

I want to know how many of us who buy blue jeans have also bought poetry. I mean, if you buy blue jeans, I want to know how much money you have spent on both blue jeans and poetry.

This past year was not a particularly good year for me in terms of blue jeans. Although I would have liked to have had more blue jeans, I only bought one new pair from a discount store, and although they fit well, I did not particularly like the fitting in the crotch but had to live with them anyway as my tolerance for trying on clothes and returning them is low. My other pair had slowly worn away in the butt area, as so many of my jeans do, my butt ultimately being too much butt for the cut of the jeans. Right below each butt cheek, a slow wearing away that will eventually thin enough to reveal skin.

In terms of poetry, however, this year was a particularly good year. I am a tenure-track professor of literature and creative writing. This means that I can buy many books related to research or teaching and have my purchases reimbursed by my department. It also means that I can assign poetry books that I would like to read in my classes and request free instructor's copies, and I do. In terms of poetry, I have spent much money this year.

I'm wondering about blue jeans and poetry and money because Levi's, the company that in the 1980s had famously, through a particular commercial, let us know that a pair of their blue jeans was worth more than an automobile in developing countries, is telling me to Go Forth; however, they aren't really telling *me* to Go Forth. They are telling that part of me that would like to be young and beautiful and unencumbered and adventurous and lanky and sexually uninhibited to Go Forth. And they are using Walt Whitman to do it.

Whitman, an American poet who wrote to the poor, the encumbered, the old and the not so beautiful.

Levi's would like for us to believe that their blue jeans are quintessentially American. One of the two commercials in their recent ad campaign is in black and white. The soundtrack incorporates the wax recording of Whitman reading "America" and shows a lit billboard with the word "America" slightly submerged in dark water. The images, of children and young adults of mixed socio-economic backgrounds, are intended to make us feel united through our differences in wealth and resources and employment. Essentially, however, everyone is quite young and fit and seems carefree.

In third grade, the Levi's factory donated Stay in School Kits to the school district where I went to school. I went to school in the South San Antonio Independent School District. I did not know it then, but the high school I went to was the second poorest high school in the city. The Levi's factory donated the Stay in School Kits because their factory was very close to our schools and our neighborhoods, and so many of the mothers of the children who were schooled in this district sewed blue jeans for Levi's, which were the jeans that everyone had to wear at the time.

If you have never lived in San Antonio, then I am not sure if you can understand what I mean when I say that the South San Antonio Independent School District served the poorest area of San Antonio, but I can tell you this: when it is cloudy, I don't feel very smart; whenever I have worked indoors in an office, I feel a certain and sure sense that my clarity is becoming dull; if I don't see the sun for few days, I grow extremely depressed. There were no windows in any of the classrooms in my schools. Some rooms had a small pane of glass, about three by twelve inches, and the teachers were told to cover them with construction paper. The tables sat six children to a desk, and the desks had "dividers" on them, wooden walls that separated the children from each other.

One teacher, Mrs. Eng, wouldn't allow you to show more than your eyes above the dividers. If she saw your nose or mouth rise from the top of the divider, you had to stand in a corner. It happened to me once: I peered up more than I should have because I couldn't see the board, and I cried the whole time I was in the corner.

Perhaps this doesn't tell you anything at all. Maybe I should tell you about the barbed wire that was on top all of the fences that surrounded the schools. And then maybe I should tell you about the little boy in third grade who got all cut up in that wire rather than face the other little boy who was also cutting him up in the school yard. Or maybe I should tell you about how we lived and walked in graffiti and random gunshots or how children went to the park and went missing so no children ever really went to the park.

Maybe I should tell you that in San Antonio, the schools receive money from business taxes, taken from businesses within the district. There were hardly any businesses in our district: a failing flower shop, a meat market, a gas station, a self-service car wash. On the north side, where the other children who had windows and sunlight lived, there were banks and corporations. Through the years, there was sometimes legislation introduced to pool all the money together and distribute it evenly among the school districts, but of course, such legislation never stood a chance, never went through.

The Stay in School Kit was, to a third grader, absolutely amazing. It was a shrink-wrapped Levi's folder full of school supplies. The folder had a photograph of a chalkboard on it, and on the chalkboard were stay in school messages. I remember in particular "you can't teach an old dog new tricks" was written on that chalkboard. There were pencils and a ruler, among other items that would help us to stay in school.

My high school no longer exists. After a flood in 2007, the school was closed. The district didn't have the money to fix it.

The last statistics I could find on the zip code where I grew up: students eligible for free or reduced lunch: 81% (Texas average: 38%); students who identify as white: 7% (Texas average 46%); graduation rate: 77% (Texas average: 97%); median household income: $27,566 (Texas average: $42,049).

Towards the middle of the school year, when I was in fourth grade, our teacher, Mrs. Morgan, who sometimes gave us grapefruit from her trees or shared her peanut brittle with us if we had memorized our multiplication tables, produced – they must have been leftovers from the previous year – a new Levi's Stay in School Kit for everyone in my class, and it was like Christmas again.

At the beginning of each school year, we wrapped our books with book covers that were furnished by San Antonio businesses, and everyone wanted the Levi's one: it featured a drawing of the back of their jeans, a rear pocket on each side of your book. You could write your name, subject, teacher, and homeroom number on one of those pockets.

Levi's would like for us to think of their jeans, especially during these "war" times, as American, but I know differently. I know for certain that in 1990, they took their factory and they themselves went forth. They and their American jobs went forth to Costa Rica. I know this for certain because many of my Mexican-American classmates in grade school had mothers who sewed those blue jeans in the Levi's factory that could be traded for automobiles overseas. When Levi's went forth into the third world and the cheap labor that such a venturing entails, they left American families, particularly Mexican-American families, particularly the families in my school district, with no way to further their own livelihoods. My neighborhood became less and less lively as a result of Levi's going forth. Whitman's "Pioneers! O Pioneers!" begins with giving an order and then asking a question: "Come, my tan-faced children, / Follow well in order, get your weapons ready; / Have you your pistols? Have you your sharp edged axes? Pioneers! O Pioneers!"

A house on my street was abandoned for years and then set fire to over and over again. My classmate Eugene, who had just been let out of juvenile, was found dead on the train tracks in front of my old elementary school. It was the summer of 1990, and we would have been starting freshman year. He had been shot in the head. In 1991, my friend John was shot by another kid in school in his own backyard, just around the corner from me. In 1993, another classmate of mine was found dead, shot and left to die under a drainage ditch, the bridge of which was always covered in graffiti despite the community's best efforts. I crossed that bridge each day as I walked to school and home again. Margarita, a girl who I had in homeroom several times in elementary school, was the murderer's sister. She was also in juvenile and then dropped out. These are just a handful of things that happened in my zip code after Levi's went forth.

The other commercial for Levi's Go Forth ad campaign plays "Pioneers! O Pioneers" along with a soundtrack that also features panic-inducing noises such as thunder and gunshots and fireworks while showcasing young and beautiful Americans who seem to be fleeing from danger or else on their way to someplace important. There is an air of the perilous. There are scenes suggesting that either animal slaughter or sex has just taken place or else the "youthful sinewy races" are unabashedly accustomed to changing into and out of their blue jeans in front of others. There are young men necking young men, or else there is much androgynous necking. As viewers, we catch the young and carefree in the middle of their seemingly rebellious, naughty, and private acts and are led to believe by their stern and strict faces that these acts are seriously and gravely important. The place where the young and beautiful are going forth, at commercial's end, is revealed as some outdoor, nighttime gathering of serious looks and more fleeing accomplished with water drops on one's body.

I have been told that Levi's *is*, by taking their jobs away from Americans, American: that capitalism and exploitation of people's livelihoods is *American*. Whitman was, at first, for abolition, and then, he was against abolition because it might harm democracy.

In 1855, Whitman included a portrait of himself in *Leaves of Grass*. In the picture, he's wearing a dark hat, a light button-up collared shirt, and his pants, I always thought, were blue jeans, but now, I'm not so sure.

I, too, feel as if I have somewhere important to go and that perhaps I should embark on this perilous journey, but I do not believe that Levi's or its commodification of Whitman has anything to do with my getting there.

Broadway Taxes

GEOFFREY BECKER

Come on in. I'm so glad you could make it. There's coffee in the kitchen. Shall I get you coffee? No? All right, then, I'll just show you around and let you know about everything.

This is Mary. She's going home now. Goodnight, sweetheart. Are you sure you don't want coffee?

Now that she's gone, I can tell you her salary. Three hundred and fifty dollars a week. You should keep her. She's the soul of the operation, and a bargain. Seriously, I'd keep her. But of course, that's up to you.

Here is the waiting area. You'll see I keep a selection of different magazines out, appropriate to various tastes. Yes, that is *Playboy*. People seem to enjoy it. I have *Playgirl*, too. And *The New York Times*, of course.

In here is my office. That's my big chair, there. It's Italian leather. So are my shoes. Your shoes, I notice, are rather less fashionable. That's fine. But our clients are mostly in show business, and they appreciate a little flash.

Over here is the bathroom. There's another in the back bedroom, where the computer is. I know, I know, this doesn't feel like an office, exactly, and that's because it's not – it's an apartment. Paul and I have two apartments. This one is mine, and the one on West End is his. But we both live there – along with Imogene, our Sheltie – and I use this one purely for business. It's rent-controlled, which makes things a bit dodgy. But that's not your problem. You have a regular office, don't you? With standard-issue furniture and ugly steel filing cabinets and all that? It will be a shock for some of my clients. They don't think of this as just a business. They come to me because I'm one of them. I was an actor for many years. I did soaps, commercials, a bit of modeling. That's all right, I know you don't recognize me. And the fact is, I've looked better. I've been staying home quite a bit lately. The tax preparation business, well, I've done it a long time now. If I wait until I'm old to retire, what fun will I be able to have? And they keep changing the laws. Reagan. Oh, my, you're not a big fan are you? Accelerated depreciation. Five-year property, ten-year property. Who can keep up?

Here, in the back, this is where we do our data processing. That's our computer, there. It's called a Vector 5000. I have no idea how it works. Interestingly, five thousand is exactly what it cost me. And of course, there's the service contract, that's additional. I have a young man, Max, who comes in and puts all the information on it, then prints out the returns. He uses that printer over there. He watches television all day, on that old black and white, which is mine from years ago. He doesn't know I know, but I know. His favorite show is *The Waltons* – he's been known to tear up watching it. I pay him $300 a week, January through August, at which point I fire him and he goes on unemployment. He still comes in, of course, and I pay him, just off the books. Come tax season, I rehire him. My accountant can explain this to you when you meet with him. It's probably not legal at all, but it's what we do. Max lives in Queens and is writing a musical about Trotsky.

Yes, of course you can smoke.

This is my assistant LaLanne's office. She's from Haiti. I have no idea where she got that name. I thought Haitians had French names. She may have made it up. But she's very good. I pay her $700 a week. She's stealing clients. She and Mary have a plan to open their own business. I know all about it, although they don't know I know. That framed advertisement for cough medicine up on the wall? That's me in the photograph. Just look at that hair.

I should tell you about the audits. We do a lot of them. That's because our clients are in the entertainment business, and they have unusual expenses. We let them deduct haircuts, gym memberships, travel – well, just about anything. You can't get a part in a film without a decent haircut! And tickets, of course. Tickets to movies, tickets to the theater, tickets to concerts, the symphony, the opera. Mary has a whole drawer full of them out front – clients bring them in when they come each year. Research Expense – an old Schedule A standby. When a client gets audited, we just dig in the drawer and put together as many ticket stubs as we need to prove the expense. Five hundred dollars, a thousand dollars – it doesn't matter. After the audit, back in the drawer! You'd think the IRS would get wise, but they don't. I bet we've used the same set of tickets for *Cats* upwards of thirty times by now.

That's Zero Mostel's signature on that framed *Playbill*. He was never a client.

I want to tell you something about our clients. They aren't all actors, or singers, or musicians, or whatever. When one is in the arts, one must of necessity also do other things. At least at first. That often means waiting tables. A lot of our people wait tables. This can lead to some peculiar-looking tax returns. You make ten thousand dollars as a waiter in 1983, but your expenses – acting classes, hair, clothes, travel to auditions – add up to eleven thousand. Adjusted gross income? Negative one thousand dollars. Yes, it's a bit of a red flag.

Let's go back to the kitchen. I'll have some of that coffee, even if you won't. You will take care of them, won't you? My clients? Because, here's the thing. We're a bit unusual, we artists. Take that young man I was telling you about. All year long, he struggles, hoping for his big break. Perhaps he's done industrials, had a bit part in a film, understudied at a summer stock company. Each January comes the reckoning. That W-2 arrives, and what does it say to him? It says, "You are a waiter." Or a secretary. Or a shop clerk. Or whatever. This is a painful moment, and one I encountered more than once myself. A body blow. What I do is tell him it's not true. And it's not! It's not true! I've had clients go from waiter to movie star overnight. Do you know Rex Callahan? You don't watch soaps? Well, he made over $100,000 last year on *Santa Barbara*. The year before? Six thousand, serving puff pastries at parties. We got to fill out a Schedule G, Income Averaging, for Rex.

I hope you'll make an offer, I really do. I'm pretty sure I can get Max to go with you. You'll get the Vector 5000. I already told you about Mary and LaLanne, but you might still see if you could hire Mary. I think a raise would help. I'm afraid that's all I've got time for, and to tell you the truth, I need to sit down. My accountant will provide you with all you need to see in terms of how much we book each year, what our profit margin is, that sort of thing. I really don't know the numbers – I've never been much of a numbers person. Funny, isn't it? I get five, six, seven hundred dollars per tax return, and I'm not an accountant. Not even close. I couldn't tell you a credit from a debit. I know people. That's my forte. That's where I'm worth everything. I really *am* this business, you know. I built it from scratch, starting out doing returns for Irv Scheinbaum, Accountant to the Stars, back when he had a second floor office on 43rd Street. Just to pick up a little extra income. And then after a few years I went out on my own, taking some of his folks with me, which is why I know what's going on with LaLanne. That's just business, right? You understand, I can tell looking at you. The marketplace has no heart. But we artists, we're all about heart. And that's what I've provided. An ear, a shoulder to cry on, my heart. Some of my clients, we'll cry together. I know their families, I know their lovers, I know their heartbreaks, I know their successes. I'm family. And while most of them are just fine, there are others – those waiters – for whom their visit to me each April validates them. It gives them self-respect, it gives them courage to keep going.

You don't mind showing yourself out, do you? I'm just going to sit here a while. Later, I might turn on that little TV on top of the fridge. I like to watch the news, although I don't trust a thing on it, except maybe the weather. Do you know how Trotsky died? He invited someone to tea who then brained him with a pickaxe. I don't know how you set something like that to music. They're saying it may snow tonight. I haven't done any of my holiday shopping yet. Then before you know it, it'll be W-2 time, all over again. One last time into the breach! Isn't it amazing the things that end up measuring our lives, things we never expected?

But I don't need to tell you. It's like that for you, too.

When Bankers Steal

AN INTERVIEW WITH DONNA LEE MUNSON

High-flying swindlers may grab the headlines. But most financial fraud happens in the mundane branch offices and back rooms of banks. In February, 2009, Donna Lee Munson pled guilty to embezzling almost $200,000 from the community bank in Georgia, where she worked as assistant vice president. The Concord Free Press interviewed Munson in June, 2009, just weeks before she began a three-year sentence in a federal facility.

Employee fraud remains one of banking's unsolved problems and best-kept secrets. This is one of the few known interviews with a bank executive turned felon.

CFP: Did you like working at the bank?
DLM: I loved it.

CFP: What did you like about it?
DLM: It was very family-oriented. I was in the public. Got to see people all day. I met tons of people on a daily basis that became very close friends of ours. I loved my staff. I had a great staff. We'd do things together on the weekends. My kids would babysit their younger kids. We were one big family. I wasn't just a bunch of employees.

CFP: Did you feel like you were well-treated by the bank?
DLM: Perfect. You couldn't ask for anything better.

CFP: So why did you steal money from your bank? From customers you knew, even?
DLM: It's complicated. It was easy the first time, but it got out of hand. And we had some serious bills. We were living way beyond our

means. The money was just paper to me . . . a piece of paper. I never took any cash. Cash seemed wrong to me. Cash seemed like a tool of my job. But the paper part of it just seemed different. It didn't faze me at all in the beginning.

CFP: So to you, the money you were stealing was kind of abstract, just a piece of paper or numbers on a screen?
DLM: Yes. But I always intended to repay it. It started in little amounts and it seemed like I could repay it and it's not going to be a big deal. But then it was more, and it got to the point where I couldn't repay it in a timely way that no one would have noticed.

CFP: The first time, how much was it?
DLM: It was like $300 the first time.

CFP: And what did it work its way up to?
DLM: Never more than $1,000. Well, I take that back, maybe $1,500. But they were small amounts.

CFP: But you were probably taking them out more frequently, too.
DLM: Yes.

CFP: You said that it got out of hand. Was it just that the stealing was so easy, or that the money didn't seem real?
DLM: Both of those. Not getting caught was another. It just seemed that, well, nobody's picking up on it so it just seemed easier to do.

CFP: You mentioned that you knew that stealing money would catch up with you.
DLM: Yes. I was robbing Peter to pay Paul and you know there's only so many Peters you can rob from to pay so many Pauls. I always knew it would get caught. It was very stressful. I worked every day of the week because I was afraid to take a day off because I was afraid somehow I would get caught. When we took vacations I always figured I would come back and not have my job. I always checked to see if there were different cars in the parking lot. Every single morning,

to see if there was anybody out of the ordinary there waiting for me.

CFP: So you were waiting for the axe to fall.
DLM: Yep.

CFP: And you were waiting for a couple of years?
DLM: Yep.

CFP: Every day you would look in the parking lot and think: *there's an investigator or policeman or someone waiting for me?*
DLM: Yes.

CFP: Did that have a physical effect on you?
DLM: It was very . . . you know, we laugh about being psychotic over it. [*breaking down, crying*]. At the same time, my mom passed away. That kind of did me in.

CFP: And on top of this, you were in serious financial trouble too, yes?
DLM: Yes. They made it sound worse than it actually was. It was about $250,000 total. The majority of that was a mortgage. It wasn't like we had $250,000 worth of credit card debt.

CFP: But you were stressed trying to meet the mortgage payment?
DLM: Yes. We were put into a mortgage that we couldn't afford. That was our fault, and I blame ourselves. But I also blame the system a little bit.

CFP: So basically you had this mortgage that you were under water on. You had a good job, but it probably wasn't paying quite enough to cover everything.
DLM: That's just it. I think people assume that being an assistant vice president or branch manager of a bank means that you're making good money. When I left there, after ten years of being in this bank, I was only making $41,000 a year. So I was not, by any means, getting rich off of salary from this bank. I think that's why people never

really caught on to it. They never wondered: how can she buy this or that, or how does she always have new clothes. They just assumed I was making a ton of money.

CFP: Did you find it hard hiding it from your co-workers? You were looking these guys in the eye and knowing that you were stealing. Was that hard?
DLM: Very.

CFP: Did they ever ask questions?
DLM: Never. They never asked a single question.

CFP: Now that this is public, have you talked with your co-workers?
DLM: I have not talked with any of them. They were actually told that they were to have no contact with me.

CFP: That must be hard. They were your close friends.
DLM: At this point, I basically feel like I have no friends. Even my very best friend in the whole world works for that bank.

CFP: So you haven't even talked to your best friend?
DLM: Nope. My husband has talked to her husband. But we've had no contact with her for fear . . . I would just die if anything was to happen to her job.

CFP: And it was just you? There was nobody else involved?
DLM: Nobody else.

CFP: Stealing sounds lonely. Nobody knew about it except you?
DLM: Nobody but me.

CFP: Did your husband know?
DLM: No.

CFP: So you kept this secret from your family and from your co-workers who were like your family. Meanwhile, your mother dies.

And your mortgage is due. That's an incredible amount of pressure. Was there a certain day when it became too much and you decided to start stealing at work?

DLM: No. I don't remember that particular day. I don't remember waking up in the morning and going: *Okay. Today's the day that I'm going to steal.* People would ask me how I could stand being around all that money. And I'd say it didn't even bother me. Because money to me is just a tool. Like a carpenter using a hammer. That's how I always thought of it. I never, ever would have thought that I would be in this situation.

CFP: Maybe because you thought of money as a tool and an abstract thing, it made it easier to start stealing. It's not taking a big stack of tens.

DLM: Right. It just sort of happened. I remember doing it that day and I was *sick* all day. And all night. Wanted to take it back the next morning. Wish that I hadn't done it. Didn't do it again for a good few months. Because I was overwhelmed with guilt. It was *horrible*. And then it got to the point where it was like – to have a place to live for my kids, I have to steal some money.

CFP: So it seems like once you got started it was hard to stop, the proverbial slippery slope. Is that right?

DLM: Yes. But I always intended to repay it. I know people look at me and go *right, she can say that now*. But I always thought that I would repay the money.

CFP: How did you get caught?

DLM: I took a day off. It was by one of the customers that I personally dealt with on a daily or weekly basis – he always came in to see me. I wasn't there and he ended up going to see somebody else and had a question about one of his CDs that I had taken some money from. And that's how I got caught.

CFP: Have you talked with your kids about what you did? Did you explain it to them?

DLM: I have one daughter who is 11. So they're 11, 17, and 20. Our two older kids know more about the situation. Our youngest daughter knows that I did something wrong, knows that I have to pay the consequences. But she doesn't know a lot of the details.

CFP: What's been their reaction?
DLM: Shock. But very supportive. My oldest daughter, she's my best friend in the whole world.

CFP: That must have been an incredibly hard discussion.
DLM: It was very hard because the day that I got caught, I also attempted suicide [*breaking up, crying*]. I took a lot of pills. My last phone call was to her. She knew that something was wrong, so she had gotten in touch with somebody to come to the house to check on me and she saved my life.

CFP: So you were so distraught that you tried to kill yourself?
DLM: This sounds horrible, but I ended up in a hospital for a week because I was under suicide watch because I told the psychiatrist that I will not live, that I would not do this to my family, I will die before I go to prison. They wouldn't let me out of the hospital. So I ended up being in the hospital for just over a week. I have a great psychologist now. And strong medications. I didn't want to put them through the embarrassment of what mom had done, with them being in school. But I think that now, I have just lost my mom and I can't deal with that and I'm nearly forty years old, how would they deal with losing their mom and being kids?

CFP: And your family will be there when you get out. You were facing thirty years in prison, right?
DLM: Yes, but I got sentenced to three years. It's a camp. It's not like a prison with the bars and the doors. It's a camp. They describe it as a dorm room-type atmosphere.

CFP: Even though that sounds better than prison, being away from your family is hard.
DLM: It's going to kill me.

CFP: Well, no. You're going to get through it like you got through everything else.
DLM: Yes.

CFP: If you knew then what you know now, you wouldn't have taken the money?
DLM: No. No way. I live in a constant nightmare. I'm almost to the point where I'm agoraphobic. I don't leave my house. I'm afraid to run into people. I know so many people from my job. We live in a small community. We don't live in New York City where there's hundreds and thousands of people. We live in a small community where everybody knows everybody and goes to school with everybody and works with everybody. Thank goodness I have a son who drives and will go to the grocery store and do those things for me because I don't even leave the house. My family and people in the community have also had to bear the embarrassment of me. They would tell you differently but I know it has to bother them in some way. Even though I have a great family.

CFP: You mentioned that customer, the one who figured out his money was missing. You would never walk up to a guy like that on the street and take his money, would you?
DLM: Never. And I would never have taken a dollar bill from the bank ever in my life. It just doesn't make any sense to me now to look back and think about what I did.

Market

KATIE FORD

Because what resurrects us,
I have to admit, is our many deaths, lanterns
waiting on kerosene to seep into clothy light,
but she was slung over the bench
near market selling fast its October root vegetables,
green heirlooms, its honey-on-the-comb,
her hair matted with blood on the right side,
straw flowers in burning arrangements, the last
of the basil in the first of high winds,
bells at noon in the bare error of the cathedral,
and we were ten feet from her dire,
nine from her from her nearly-out –
it was because her eyes were open
that we kept buying goods.

Living On Someone Else's Money

TOM HEALY

What it means is flowers
always on the table,

flowers faking it gracefully
a few more days

in collectible glass and
silver ways of holding

colors no longer living,
flowers you didn't

choose yourself, names
you didn't learn,

extravagances you don't
admit you take for granted

or sometimes even tire of –
flowers and this panic.

Local Money

DOUGLAS RUSHKOFF

In my town, the tiny organic café called Comfort decided to expand to a second, larger location. John, the chef and owner, had been renovating the new space for a year, but – thanks to the credit crisis – was unable to raise the cash required to finish and finally open. With currency unavailable from traditional, centralized money-lending banks, he turned instead to his community, to us, for support. Granted, this is a small town. Pretty much everybody goes to Comfort – the only restaurant of its kind on the small strip – and we all have a stake in its success. Any extension of Comfort would bring more activity, vitality, and commerce to a tiny downtown (commercially devastated in the 1970s by the chain stores and malls on the auto-friendly main strip).

So John's idea was to sell VIP cards, which I helped him rename Comfort Dollars. For every dollar spent on a card, the customer receives the equivalent of $1.20 worth of credit at either restaurant. If I buy a thousand-dollar card, I get twelve hundred dollars' worth of food: a 20 percent rate of return on the investment of dollars. John gets the money he needs a lot cheaper than if he were borrowing it from the bank – he's paying for it in food and labor that he has in ample supply. Meanwhile, customers get more food for less money.

But wait, there's more: the entire scheme reinvests a community's energy and cash locally. Because our money goes further at our own restaurant than at a restaurant somewhere else, we are biased toward eating locally. Since we have a stake in the success of the restaurant in whose food we have invested, we'll also be more likely to promote it to our friends. By using its own currency, a local business can even undercut the corporate competition. It's not complex or even communist. It's just local business.

Local currencies are now used by several hundred communities across the United States and Europe, giving people the chance to buy and sell goods and services from one another no matter what the greater economy might be doing. Instead of favoring large, centralized corporations, local currencies favor businesses and the community members who own them.

There are two main types of local currency employed today. The simplest, like Comfort Dollars or the BerkShares created for the entire Berkshire Hills region in Massachusetts, have exchange rates for regular dollars. The BerkShares themselves can be spent only at local businesses that accept them, which keeps the currency circulating close to home. Local currencies such as these encourage local buying, put large corporations with no real community involvement at a big disadvantage, and circulate much more widely and rapidly through a community than conventional dollars. Further, the nonprofit bank issuing BerkShares is not an extractive force; no one needs to get rich or pay anyone back. Businesses that refuse to accept the local currency do worse than just brand themselves as apathetic to local development; they cut themselves off from a potential source of revenue.

Townspeople with their own money systems still need conventional currency. The three automobile repair shops in Great Barrington that accept BerkShares must still buy auto parts from Mopar or BMW with U.S. dollars. But they are willing to break down their bills into two separate categories, selling parts at cost in U.S. dollars, and markups and labor in the local currency. The object is not to replace centralized currency altogether, but to break the monopoly of centralized currency and the corporations it supports over transactions that keep money circulating locally. This is why many advocates now call local currency "complementary" currency – because it complements rather than replaces centralized money.

It's not as anarchist as it might sound. Larger businesses have begun to embrace alternative currency systems as well. In October 2008, as the credit crisis paralyzed business lending, companies started signing onto barter networks in droves. One system, called ITEX, which allows businesses to trade merchandise, reported a 37 percent increase in registrations for the month of October alone. Utilizing more than two hundred fifty exchange services now available through the Internet, companies can barter directly with one another, or earn U.S.-dollar-equivalent credits for the merchandise they supply to others. According to Barter News.com, business-to-business bartering already accounts for $3 billion of exchanges annually in the United States. As the credit crisis continues, this figure is growing exponentially.

An even more promising variety of complementary currency, like the grain receipts of ancient times, is quite literally earned into existence. "Life Dollars," such as those used by the Fourth Corner Exchange in the Pacific Northwest, are not purchased with traditional currency. Instead, members of the Fourth Corner Exchange earn credits by performing services or providing goods to one another. There's always enough money, because money is a result of work exchanged, not an existing store of coin. There can't be too much money, either, since every service provided is a service someone else was willing to be debited for.

The currency system isn't there for people to accumulate lots of money. In fact, most people's accounts are at or close to "zero" most of the time. You start with a zero balance, which goes down below zero if you get something, or above it when you do something – at rates usually determined in negotiation with the person on the other side of the deal.

It works. Economic activity doesn't have to start with a loan from a bank. All it takes is a person with a need, and another person with a skill. If the banks, in concert with the Treasury, have decided to extract so much debt-based currency from the economy that we can no longer use it for peer-to-peer exchange, then we owe it to ourselves to account for our transactions in another way.

Local or complementary currencies are as easy to begin as visiting the websites for local economic transfer systems (LETS) or Time Dollars. A local currency system can be as informal as a babysitting club, where parents earn credits for babysitting one another's children, or robust enough to serve as the primary currency for an entire region or sector.

In 1995, for example, as recession rocked Japan, unemployment rose and currency became scarce. This made it particularly difficult for people to continue to take care of their elderly relatives, who often lived in distant areas. Everyone had time, but no one had money. The Sawayaka Welfare Foundation developed a complementary currency by which a young person could earn credits for taking care of an elderly person. Different tasks earned different established credit awards – bathing someone earned more than shopping, and so on. Accumulated credits – Fureai Kippu, or "elderly care units" – could then be applied to the care of one's own relative in a distant town, saved for later, or traded to someone else. Independently of the centralized economy – which thanks to bad speculation and mismanaged banking was no longer supporting them – people were able to create value for themselves and one another.

Although that particular financial crisis has passed, the Fureai Kippu system has only grown in popularity. At last count, the alternative currency was accepted at 372 centers throughout Japan, and patients surveyed said they like the care they get through the Fureai Kippu system better than what they get from professional service agencies. Thanks to the success of the Fureai Kippu and other pioneering models, close to a thousand alternative currencies are now in use in Japan.

Complementary currencies make it easier to record and administrate value exchange in an increasingly decentralized marketplace. They initiate the process through which local regions or specific sectors learn to create value for themselves instead of having it drained unnecessarily by an artificially chartered monopoly or bank. They remind us that some of the things we have in abundance are still valuable, even though markets have not yet been created for them.

And they give us a way to transact business during a *fin de siecle*, when central banks and treasuries are more consumed with their own solvency and that of the speculative economy than they are with our ability to conduct the basic transactions through which we take care of one another.

See, the stuff in your pocket is not money. It's a *kind* of money – one loaned into existence by banks, and biased toward the interest of the already rich. It wasn't invented to help us transact, but to help the wealthy stay wealthy simply by being wealthy. There used to be other moneys – ones that weren't loaned into existence by central banks, but earned into existence by real people doing stuff for one another. These local currencies weren't invented as a means of hoarding value, but exchanging it. Instead of promoting exploitation, they promoted transactions.

It's not too late to save the economy; but we have to do it by trashing the obsolete operating system on which it's based. Our money doesn't work for people anymore. That's why we people owe it to ourselves and one another to start printing our own.

An Inheritance

DAN POPE

One afternoon I found a call on the answering machine from my Aunt Helen, asking for bread. "I want Vermont Bread," she said, "raisin cinnamon, please." There was a second message adding orange juice to the list, no pulp. A third asked me to leave the groceries on her doorstep, she was feeling ill and she wouldn't want me to catch her cold," – just ring the doorbell and she would slip the twenty dollars under –"

The machine cut her off.

I got dressed and drove to the store to get what she wanted. It took me a while to find the bread among the gourmet foods at nearly four dollars a loaf. When I rang her doorbell, nothing happened. I banged on the door with my fist. "I brought the food," I announced. She was eighty-nine and all but deaf. I banged away for a couple of minutes. I was out ten bucks and didn't want to go away empty-handed.

So I turned the handle and the door opened.

"Aunt Helen," I called. "It's Ronnie. I've got your bread here."

She lived alone in a two-story Colonial, the smallest house on the street. I went up the creaky wooden stairs and looked into the two bedrooms. The place was filthy, the walls piled high with all sorts of bag-lady crap – newspapers, grocery bags, a depressing assortment of tin cans and plastic trays. I went down to the living room and den, checked the bathroom.

I found her on the floor in the kitchen.

Two weeks earlier I had returned to my father's house in Wintonbury, Connecticut, where I had grown up. He had flown south for the winter and I was taking care of the place until spring. He usually just drained the pipes, locked the doors and had a neighbor look in from time to time, but that winter I needed a place to stay.

I'd had a job in New Jersey for the past sixteen months, working maintenance at a community college. I lived in the basement of a defunct fraternity house on the edge of campus and took my meals in the student cafeteria. It was a sweet deal. The college took a few hundred bucks from my pay every month for taxes, insurance and housing, and the rest went directly into my bank account. When I say maintenance, I don't mean pushing a broom. It was electrical work, roofing, carpentry – whatever came up. I could do all that stuff, I was board-certified. My father was a general contractor, and he'd had me working jobs since I was fourteen. "You know a trade," he always said, "and you'll never go hungry." His advice was dead-on. I'd had six years of undergraduate education and a B.A. in Philosophy but I'd never managed to procure a paying position based on those qualifications.

I liked New Jersey because you could go into a bar and light up and blow smoke all over the room. You didn't have to stand outside and shiver like a vagrant. No one likes to rush a cigarette. The point is to wind down: beer, barstool, cigarette. The three went together. The coeds were a distraction, the way they marched around campus, smelling like heaven. When did girls start to look like that? Dress like that? It must be something in the milk, the wheat, the water, the cell phone signals, the high-def heat, the wi-fi frequencies. The end of the world was near, but the girls did not know it and they had never been comelier, all costumed, as they were in North Jersey, like strippers on holiday.

One night a pack of them barged into my preferred drinking establishment, a dive called Sully's, situated at the entrance to an industrial park. I was coming up on my fortieth birthday. Maybe that partly explains my actions. Two of the girls came back with me to my basement room for some beer pong and I got a little out of hand with the paddle. I'd thought them a wee bit older. I did not learn their ages – eighteen and eighteen, respectively – until the campus police arrived and informed me of this fact. Alas, there was a non-fraternization clause in my contract.

In short, I got terminated without severance pay.

The emergency room doctor told me that Aunt Helen had pneumonia. It was good that I brought her in when I did, he said, because she was severely dehydrated and malnourished. They admitted her and I went home, out ten bucks for the groceries.

That winter, I mostly just hung around the house with the furnace roaring away, watching the snow fall. I stayed up until four or five in the morning. Name a movie that played cable that year and I can tell you the plot. In the afternoons I went into town and sat in the coffee shop, reading the print off the newspaper and observing the daily routines of the harried housewives. (Is there any creature in nature as nervous as the suburban housewife? Chihuahua? French poodle?) That was my occupation, watching housewives and high-school girls and making pithy observations to myself (see above) and snarling whenever some jackass in a business suit came too close to me with his cellphone in operation. With approximately six hundred and fifty dollars left over from the New Jersey job and a rent-free abode, I had no need or desire for employment.

A week later the hospital called and said they were ready to discharge Aunt Helen.

"Okay," I said.

The woman asked me about my care plan.

I said, "Yeah, well, she gets along pretty well by herself. I bring her groceries once in a while. She's a feisty old broad."

"With whom am I speaking, please?"

"Huh?"

"What is your relationship to the patient?"

"The nephew, you can write down."

"You are aware, sir, that your aunt is demented?"

"Demented?"

"That's correct."

I was watching TV and wasn't paying much attention to the conversation. "As in raging lunatic? That sort of demented?"

"Excuse me?"

"You should just send her home in a taxi," I suggested. "That would be the easiest thing to do."

"Hold, please."

A few minutes later a doctor came on the line. He explained that my aunt needed twenty-four hour supervision at a residential facility. Since she lacked capacity, I would have to sign for her as conservator or guardian. Under state law, they couldn't release her without a plan in place.

"Actually, I'm not her primary care-giver," I explained. I thought the phrase sounded correct in the circumstances. "My father is. I can have him call you, if that's convenient."

"You understand that she cannot remain here. This is a hospital, not a nursing home. Technically she's already been discharged. We no longer have a bed for her."

"Where is she?"

"At present, in a wheelchair in the emergency room waiting area."

"Okay, then. I'll get back to you with that information."

I hung up.

I called Florida to inform my father of these developments. His answering machine – a relic from the late eighties – had no greeting, it just gave one long beep and then the line went dead. Was the cassette filled? Broken? I called for two days without getting an answer. In New Smyrna, where he lived in a condo on the sixteenth floor of a concrete tower built on sand, you could drive up and down the main drag all afternoon and not see a single snowbird. They were there, thousands of them, holed up in their apartments and condominiums, but they only came out for dinner, like pelicans diving into the sea the hour before sundown. There was a shuffleboard court in town, but my father didn't engage in that sort of silliness. Mainly, he liked watching TV, like me.

Meanwhile, the hospital called ten times a day, speaking to the answering machine. "Mr. Milton, would you please come to the hospital to make arrangements –." I didn't answer those calls. I would look at the caller i.d. and let the nurses talk themselves blue. I didn't need that sort of aggravation. Aunt Helen herself called once too, from a payphone in the lobby, I presume, leaving the following message:

"Salvy? Salvy? Come get me, Salvy. I'm in the hallway with terrible people."

Salvatore was my father's name.

Finally, one afternoon, my father's Florida number appeared on the caller i.d.

"Dad, where the hell have you been?"

"Nowhere. Why?"

"You got your hearing aid turned on? I've been trying to get a hold of you since Monday."

"Maybe the ringer doesn't work."

I filled him in on the medical developments, just as the doctor had explained them to me – the diagnosis, the requirements of state law, etc.

When I finished, he said, "Go get her. Take her home."

"Didn't I just explain it to you? They won't let her out –"

"Sign whatever they want. Just get her out of there."

"You better call them."

"What the hell can I do from down here?"

"Besides, she's a lot better off if they keep her, you know? I mean, she's demented. That house, have you seen that place lately? She's got shit piled to the ceiling. It's a fucking catastrophe –."

"She doesn't need any goddamned nursing home. She's no more demented than you or I."

"I'm not so sure about that last part."

"Listen," he said. "Listen to me now. There's some stuff you don't know."

"What do you mean?"

"I don't want to go into it over the phone."

"What, you think it's bugged?"

"Don't be a wise guy. Just do what I tell you."

"If you must know, it's a royal pain in the ass. She doesn't even remember my name any more. And I'm out ten bucks –."

"Son, listen carefully. Are you listening?"

"Yeah."

"She can't go into a nursing home or those bastards will take every cent she's got. Her house, her savings, everything."

"What savings?"

"That's the part I haven't told you."

Once upon a time, Dad had had four older sisters, all of them spinsters. About ten years ago they retired and moved into that matchbox Colonial. Their house was a half-mile away from his, on the other side of the town's public golf course – to the right of the seventh green, to be precise. My father often found soggy Titlelists in their backyard. He would collect them and bring them home and put them in a five-gallon glass jug on his hallway table, all these grass-stained and bruised golfballs jumbled in the glass, like a modern sculpture.

For the past decade, he'd checked on the sisters every day, sometime two or three times a day, performing the same sort of maintenance I'd been doing in New Jersey, and tasks of a more menial nature as well – filling their car with gas, taking out the damned garbage, bringing them groceries every Sunday afternoon. It had practically been his full-time job since he'd retired from the contracting business, and he'd grumbled about it plenty. The only break from duty was when he flew down to Florida for a couple of months every winter, and the aunts would get along with assistance from church volunteers and Dial-a-Ride. I knew all about that. I'd helped out too, when I was a kid, cutting their lawn, but mostly I avoided them. I had no desire to get sucked into that septuagenarian chasm. They had always been old, it seemed to me, these four unpleasant women with moles blossoming on their faces and necks, wearing the same moth-eaten, wine-stained sweaters, dining on white bread and canned sardines. The four left the house only for Sunday Mass, as far as I could tell. And none of them believed in doctors, they just rotted away when they got ill. One by one the aunties had dropped into the netherland, leaving Aunt Helen the last standing spinster, the hardiest of the lot.

What I didn't know, and what he now disclosed, was this:

Aunt Helen was loaded.

The four spinsters had worked compulsively throughout their miserly, barren lives (occupations: schoolmarm, librarian, secretary, town clerk), stuffing their paychecks into the bank every Friday afternoon, and once retired, they did the same with their pension and Social Security stipends. All of this currency had been bequeathed to Aunt Helen and burgeoned under my father's wily stewardship.

In ten years, he'd more than doubled the holdings with some timely buying and selling of his favorite stock, the war-mongering United Technologies.

"How much?" I asked.

"Including the house? A half-mil."

"Seriously?"

"More or less."

"You son of a bitch. A fucking half-million. Why didn't you tell me?"

In truth, I couldn't blame him. I'd gone through a healthy share of Dad's assets in my forty years, a good deal more than the typical son or daughter was entitled – the possessions I'd whisked away in the night, the costs of rehab and attorney fees, not to mention the aggravation I'd caused. I wouldn't tell me about a family fortune either. But my wild years were behind me now, I figured, despite my recent mishap in New Jersey.

"It's not something I intended to keep from you –."

"It's okay, Dad. I understand."

"Son, that money's meant for you and your brother. I don't need it. It was going to go to you all along. You hear me?"

"Yes."

"So you're in charge now. It's up to you. Don't let those vultures get a dime."

"I'm on it, Dad."

"Good boy. Oh, one more thing."

"Yeah."

"What year did Columbus sail the ocean blue?"

"Is that a joke?"

"It's her ATM code. Find the card. Get the money out while you can."

He hung up.

A half-million dollars, I thought. I felt my chest expanding with an emotion suspiciously like the onset of love.

I had an assignment. There would be no more HBO marathons. My brother wouldn't be any help. He was off in the Far East – in a Buddhist monastery in Thailand, the last we'd heard. I didn't tell a soul. None of my friends in town could be trusted with a half-ounce stash, let alone a half-million bucks. I shaved for the first time in a long while, got into a suit, and headed downtown.

At the hospital, the social worker took me into her office. Patients suffering from dementia tend to wander, she told me. "We don't know why, but they feel compelled to walk. That's why she needs a secure facility." I listened intently, scratching my chin. She laid out pamphlets and price lists. The least expensive place wanted twenty grand up front.
"What about home release?" I asked.
"We don't recommend at-home care for this type of patient."
"Hypothetically."
"Well, it would have to be round-the-clock supervision by certified professionals. And, by state law, we would have to inform the D-E-S."
"D-E-S?"
"The Department of Elderly Services. There would be unannounced visits by a state agent to ensure an appropriate environment and proper patient supervision."
"We want the best for Aunt Helen."
"Of course you do."
It took some time, but I convinced her to release Aunt Helen into my care. I signed at least six forms, assuming full and total responsibility for her welfare. I didn't read the papers, I just kept scribbling my name.
The social worker gave me a list of businesses that provided home healthcare services. "I recommend a battery of certified nursing professionals, working in eight- or twelve-hour shifts," she said.
"That's exactly what I had in mind," I said.
She led me into the emergency room, where Aunt Helen was sitting in the hallway in a wheelchair, a blanket over her legs. In her lap she held her handbag. I said hello, but she appeared wholly catatonic. It wasn't a good day for Auntie. She peered at me with intense concentration, a look that I recognized from old photographs, when she was a plain and unhappy young schoolteacher. Perhaps she'd been

near-sighted and had never been diagnosed. Or perhaps that baleful squint was simply her natural expression, the one she'd used at Robert F. O'Brien Elementary School since 1946, terrifying generations of third-graders so severely that her visage would appear in their dreams for decades after they'd finished all manner of schooling.

The social worker and a security guard helped me wheel the patient out to the parking lot and load her into my piece-of-crap Honda. She was wearing the same clothes she'd had on when I found her on the kitchen floor, beige slacks and a blood-stained gray sweater. Her right eyeball was bruised, where she'd landed.

I strapped her in and gunned out of the parking lot. I lowered the window on her side, to suction away the aroma. She clearly hadn't bathed that day, or maybe not at all during her hospital stay.

About halfway to her house, as we crossed into Wintonbury, she perked up: "Where are you taking me?"

"We're going home, Aunt Helen. Isn't that exciting?"

"Put the window up."

"Fresh air is good for you. It'll clear all the bad hospital germs out of your lungs."

"I'm cold."

I have to admit I was overjoyed with myself. I wheeled into her driveway and shuffled her into the house, holding my breath. I found the groceries – the Vermont bread and orange juice – on the floor in the plastic bag where I'd dropped them ten days ago. I'd forgotten to lock the door, but no one had bothered to break in.

"Here we are," I said. "Safe and sound."

She sniffed and looked around. Her expression clarified. "Will they come for me?"

"Of course not. You're all better now." I handed over the plastic bag. "There's the bread you wanted. That should tide you over."

"Oh, my raisin cinnamon." She had a fearsome grip on her handbag, clutching it like a fullback on a one-yard plunge.

"Let me hang up your handbag for you, Aunt Helen."

"You've done enough already. I know how busy you are."

"It's no problem at all. I'll put it right here for you." I opened the closet door and pointed at the hook on the back of the door.

She sniffed. "Could you turn up the temperature?"

"Certainly."

I checked the thermostat in the living room. It was at 81 degrees. The radiators were clanking and humming. Aunt Helen liked a warm house. Even in summertime, my father told me, she would crank the dial into the nineties, all that oil burning night and day. I turned it down ten degrees.

"All set," I said.

"You're a good boy, Ronnie."

She seemed her coherent self, ensconced in those happy surroundings, so I decided to get on my way. There was no rush.

"If you need anything, call me."

"What?"

You practically had to scream to get her to hear you, she was so deaf. Although, oddly, at times, she could detect a whisper from across the room. I yelled my goodbyes and closed the front door behind me.

Next morning at 9:15, the phone woke me. Anyone who knew me knew not to call at that hour. I picked up the receiver and mumbled, "What the hell?" The caller identified herself as Mrs. So-and-So from the Department of Elderly Services. Unaccustomed as I was to using my faculties at these hours, it took me a few moments to understand that this was not a wrong number and that I shouldn't tell her to go fuck herself.

"What can I do for you?" I said.

"You can open the door," she answered curtly. "I've been ringing the bell for five minutes."

"Oh," I said. "You're at my aunt's house?"

"I am."

"Wait right there."

I jumped out of bed, dressed, slicked down my unruly hair, loaded a few tomato cans into a shopping bag and raced to Aunt Helen's house, nearly skidding out of control at the turn around the 14th green.

A small white car was parked in her driveway. As soon as I got out of my piece-of-crap Honda, a lady emerged from the car, holding a clipboard. She was a middle-aged gal wearing a pinched expression, with tiny shoulders and enormous, rolling hips, like a lady in a fun-house mirror.

"I stepped out to do the shopping," I said, waving my plastic bag.

"I see," she answered in a troll's voice.

I opened the door, calling, "Aunt Helen, I'm back with the groceries."

The television was blaring in the den, a human voice as loud as a fighter jet. From the doorway the D-E-S lady and I peered into the room. Aunt Helen was sitting on the couch, nibbling a piece of raisin cinnamon toast. On the TV, a nun in a brown habit sat behind a desk, pontificating at ungodly volume. The Catholic Channel, her favorite. My father said she watched Mother Angelica night and day.

I stepped into the room and turned down the volume.

"Aunt Helen, there's a nice lady here to see you."

The D-E-S woman lowered herself into a chair across from Aunt Helen and leaned forward to address her, ballpoint and clipboard at the ready. The room smelled vaguely of urine.

"How nice of you to come," said Aunt Helen. She finished her piece of toast and folded her hands in her lap. She seemed to think the lady was from the church. "Have you seen Father Alphonso? He has a wonderful singing voice, but sometimes I think he's awfully young."

The D-E-S lady proffered a litany of questions: How old are you? What year is it, could you please tell me? Where did you sleep last night?

In response, Aunt Helen sniffed four or five times, and her right eyeball seemed to bulge.

"Well?" the D-E-S lady prompted. "Can you at least tell me your name?"

Aunt Helen said, "Get out of my house. Get out before I call the police."

Then she turned back toward the TV, picked up the remote and cranked Mother Angelica to ear-damaging decibels.

After this interview, the DES lady patrolled from room to room, jotting. A pigsty, that house, with all that bag-lady crap piled everywhere. There were old newspapers and magazines and hymnals, glass bottles and tin cans filled with pens and pencils, needles and tweezers, brown shopping bags by the thousands, a plastic tub filled with buttons. Behind all this whatnot, the walls and ceilings were dust-bunnied and spider-webbed, the rugs unvacuumed apparently since placement, the refrigerator infested with fungi, the shelves empty but for a moldy head of lettuce and frozen chicken bones. The linoleum was streaked with a brown substance which may have been mud but probably was not, that had been stepped on and dragged about.

Each time Mrs. So-and-So made a notation on her clipboard, I winced.

Outside, standing by her car, she peeled off a pink sheet, the bottom copy, and passed it to me – the list of violations. She'd checked nearly every box. Underneath she'd scrawled: *No evidence of supervision whatsoever.*

"You have forty-eight hours to rectify the situation," she said. "I strongly suggest that you retain full-time assistance. I'll be back to see that you do."

Back at my father's house, I went immediately to sleep. I had always been a big believer in the restorative powers of the nap. And, as usual, I woke refreshed and clear-headed, a plan of action already formed in my mind.

I went into town and read the newspaper at the coffee shop. For dinner I had a slice of pizza at the parlor next door. Then I came back home to watch TV for many hours. When the grandfather clock chimed midnight, I went into the kitchen and lifted the key off the hook next to the wall phone. My father had hung it there before leaving for Florida, despite my protestations that I didn't want any part of it. *Just in case,* he'd said.

The golf course was silent at that hour, a snow beginning to fall. I parked at the end of the driveway. The place was as dark as a grave, not a single light visible inside or outside the house. I turned the key in the lock.

Inside, the heat was blasting. I turned on the hall light and checked the thermostat. She'd cranked it to 95 degrees. I opened the door to the hall closet and looked inside. I crept into the living room and checked the couches and chairs, looked beneath the cushions, peered inside the cabinets and bookshelves. Next I searched the kitchen. I even looked inside the refrigerator-freezer, because old ladies will keep their valuables in the craziest places.

When I returned to the hallway, a voice called out, giving me a fright:

"Salvy? Is that you?"

"Yes."

"Would you like a glass of warm milk?"

"No, thank you."

"I hear noises."

"That's me."

"Should I call the police?"

"Nope."

"Where are you?"

"I'm checking the furnace. Go back to sleep."

I opened the basement door and went down to the cellar – finding another fearsome trove of bag-lady treasure piled against the walls. The oil burner thundered away, the fire hissing inside the steel chamber, and through the casement windows I could see a sliver of the night sky and the snow falling onto her backyard.

Finally, I went back to the first floor and looked into the den.

She was sitting on the couch, clutching her purse, the TV hissing with white noise.

"You're not Salvy," she said.

"It's me, Ronnie," I said. I stepped into the light coming from the television set. "See? It's your nephew."

She picked up the phone. For a moment, I considered pulling the plug out of the wall, but I didn't need to go that far. She knew exactly one telephone number, my father's, the only seven digits that remained in her gnarled and short-circuited cerebral cortex. This was the magic number, the number that made things appear and disappear. *Salvy, there's some papers here from the bank. Salvy, something's wrong with the oven. Salvy, we need milk.* For years my father had been fielding those calls, fulfilling her requests. Now she said into the receiver:

"Salvy, there's people in the house."

While she was preoccupied, I bent and gently tugged on her handbag. She didn't resist. It slid out of her hands and into mine, an old black-vinyl thing, torn around the edges. I fished around in her purse until I found it – her ATM card. Then I passed the handbag back to her and she accepted it and clutched it again.

I said, "Do you want me to help you upstairs? I could fix the bed for you, if you like."

"No."

"Wouldn't you be more comfortable in your own bedroom?"

"I met Lucky Luciano once," she said.

"Is that so?" In truth, I'd heard the story scores of times. She'd tell it at every family gathering, practically verbatim from one recitation to the next.

"It was in Naples," she said, "in 1953. He called to me from across the square. I don't usually speak to a gentleman without a proper introduction, but in his case I made an exception. The man had black eyes, the blackest eyes you've ever seen."

"I'm leaving now, Aunt Helen."

She didn't take her gaze off the hissing television screen. "He asked me to marry him, just like that. We hadn't spoken more than ten words. I declined, of course, but I often wonder if this was the right decision. One only gets so many offers in a lifetime. What do you think?"

I said, "I'll lock the door behind me."

I emerged into that snow-covered night and raced to the bank.

What year did Columbus sail the ocean blue?

I punched in the code and there was a momentary lull – and then the dumb machine came to life. Five hundred was the daily limit, but there were many days to come. Is there a better sound than the shuffling of those twenty-dollar bills before they emerge from the slot? It was like the opening of a door onto a spring morning. The sound of freedom. I didn't know then, of course, that this was only the start of my real problems.

Barter

CATIE ROSEMURGY

Our skins, which for so long felt like being inside an arc of cream,
are shrinking. At least we seem to have discovered the first death rule:
    liquid.

Yesterday the currency was eyes, the day before, magnified fly wings.
Or more exactly the hidden leaded-glass effect. It didn't matter much

because no one had enough of either. We took to heart the lessons
about big and small and about unexpected connections, but today

we're all starving. You've got to admire the meaningfulness
of the design: an organism that crushes itself if it isn't allowed

to drink from the host planet. It's a little obvious, though.
We aren't babies anymore. Jenna ripped her long fluid arm open

trying to sneak out the window. It was the similar but different lesson
and the not always lesson and the may I lesson, reiterations

of the first new death rule: liquid. It was Jenna like mother's milk
on the floor. I know, I know, there's a system of colors and
    measurements

to what can go in and out, we'll need to buy tools.
It's hard to force ourselves outside, though, to find out the going rate.

For the time being I'm rich with the bones of my hands
digging into the doorframe.

Change

DORA MALECH

What was left
after the price
of gas
not much
in the ARCO
station outside
Desert Springs
discount fountain pop
a toilet tank
with a brick but no
handle cholla spines
whose barbs held
fast to the cracks
in the linoleum
a mirror in which
someone had scraped
Please Wash Hands
to Please   ash
gold dust
on the floor
rather regular
dust the sun
slanted golden
silver scratch-off
ticket dust sloughed
on the counter
a pen on a chain
and a Planter's can
with a slit stabbed

through its plastic
lid a nickel
for the slit above
the hand-written
request Please
Help Us Bury
Our Baby.

Immorally Bankrupt

AUGUSTEN BURROUGHS

I was wearing an Armani suit that I didn't technically own. Nor did I technically own the gold and stainless Rolex on my wrist. For that matter, I didn't even own the hair gel I was sporting. All had been purchased with credit cards and I was unable to pay a single one of them. Which is why I was sitting in the office of an Upper West Side attorney, beginning bankruptcy proceedings.

I was twenty-four years old.

"This is bad," she said, looking over my receipts. The week before, when I phoned her as an imperfect stranger and explained my financial situation, she'd told me to gather my records and bring them to her.

My "records" were already "gathered." I'd been dropping the hundreds of unopened credit card bills and envelopes from my bank into a box on my living room floor. But my "records" were also "incomplete" because several months before, I'd begun simply throwing them away. From mailbox to trash can in one easy toss.

As she went through the box opening envelopes, she made neat piles and I was filled with longing. I wanted to be the kind of person who could organize his finances. Instead, I was the kind of person who stored socks and tax returns in his oven.

"Oh, this is just terrible," she said.

"Yeah, well. I know," I stammered. I wanted to ask, "Don't you see this all the time? I mean, you're a bankruptcy specialist who advertises in the Yellow Pages." Surely she entertained a daily parade of hopeless souls in financial ruin. I had a high-paying advertising job. Could I possibly be in worse shape than her other pathetic clients? Did I need to start lining up friends to visit me in prison?

She was looking at my American Express Platinum card records now. Pages and pages, columns of charges, all delinquent.

American Express was my client. I created their ad campaign. Therefore, shouldn't I be exempted as a tradeoff for suffering through meetings where I was told, "Can you make the card a little bigger?" when it was already too big?

Finally, she set the papers aside and looked at me. It was the level, even gaze of a logical woman with an advanced degree. "You have a real problem."

Here, I laughed. Of course I had a problem. I was unable to pay my bills. And the reason I was unable to pay my bills is because I was born without the gene that enables a person to write a simple check, even when they have enough money in the bank. "Tomorrow," was my mantra. But somehow tomorrow was always several weeks away, when my electricity and phone service were cut off. Long before I was in debt, I was in inertia.

She looked at me with a bit of disbelief. "No, you misunderstand me. Your financial situation, yes. It's not good. But that's not what's so terrible."

I felt strangely hopeful now. "Oh?" I said.

She slid the American Express papers across the glossy table. They nearly floated across the surface at me, the polish was so high.

I glanced at them, forcing myself to take in a few of the details. Most of the charges were from one place, which seemed pretty efficient to me. So what was the big deal? "What am I looking for here?" I asked.

"You have over forty thousand dollars," she said, "in bar charges."

Did I? "Let me see that again," I said.

Her expression softened to pity.

I glanced again at the documents. Sure enough. This chick had a good eye.

"You need help," she said.

"I know," I said. "That's why I'm here."

"I don't mean that," she said. "I mean, you need help with your drinking."

"Oh, that!" I said, finally understanding. "No, I'm okay in that department. I mean, I drink a lot. But I'm in advertising, you know? And it's not like I blackout – it's more like a brownout. And besides,

I never get hungover."

She became tender, which shocked me because I was unaccustomed to tenderness when it wasn't attached to a penis with motives. "Sweetie, you *are* hungover. Can't you see that?"

And truthfully, I just couldn't.

I left her office feeling conflicted. On the one hand, I was horrified that in a month I'd be in court having my financial freedom stripped away. On the other, all I would have to do is stand before a judge for ten minutes and I'd be absolved of all my debt. I'd get to keep my suits and my watch and everything else I'd acquired, without having to pay a dime for them.

And that's when I made my decision. I needed to stop drinking. My lawyer was right, I did *have a problem*. And just acknowledging this gave me a huge sense of relief.

So to sort of mark the occasion, I figured I'd go pick up a pair of excellent shoes at Barneys, using the one card that still had some available credit.

The Back of the House

J. C. HALLMAN

Paul Anka was playing the hotel. Some nights, after his show, he swung by the casino. I had never seen him, but people I knew had stories about Anka: about dealing *to* him if they thought he was nice, or dealing *with* him if they thought he was an asshole. All over the casino there were commemorative cheques – chips – that had been made up in his honor. The photo on the cheque was of a vibrant forty-year-old, though Anka was in his sixties.

I was on a $100 craps game. My end of the table was empty, dead. People like to stand and watch the $100 craps game because it's high action, but we make them stand back from the table a pace or two: sorry, chief, special rules for the $100 game. Sometime around 1 a.m., a woman walked up to the table and just stood there. She was thirty-two or three, Italian, attractive but not gorgeous. She watched the action at the other end of the game. I had not looked over there because – important rule – dealers are not allowed to look away from their layouts.

I asked my floorperson, Jimmy, if it was okay for the woman to stand there, and Jimmy, a bored forty year-old divorcee, looked from the woman's face to her chest and said sure it was okay for her to stand there.

Four or five rolls went by: two crap, point of eight, out, nine centerfield, hard four. Then the woman asked for one of the commemorative chips. She produced five dollars cash, and I dug one of the cheques from the bankroll: we completed the trade, a Lincoln for an Anka.

I said, because it was my job to be nice, "You know, he comes to the casino sometimes, maybe you could get him to sign it."

She looked at me strangely. She looked at me as though I was an animal that had just performed a behavior she found particularly repulsive. "Oh, izzat so," she said, her voice thick with Jersey

149

influence. She turned to the other end of the game. "Hey, Pawlly. This dealer heah says you might sign my chip. Izzat true? Would you do that fo' me?"

Anka was at the other end of the table. I looked over there – breaking the rule – and saw a short, nondescript man, sixtyish, with glasses and a seven-inch cigar stabbed into his mouth. He was nothing like the face on the cheque. The woman was part of his entourage. Daughter, mistress, niece, wife: she might have been any of these, and all casino employees have been warned against making assumptions regarding couples whose ages appear disparate. It's one of many guidelines meant to lower the risk of giving offense, and it occurred to me even as I was embarrassed that I had broken the opposite of the rule: I'd assumed no relationship where there was one. In any event, the vision of the real Anka, disguised by age and ugliness, made the rule seem like a bylaw of an even more fundamental fact of casino life: people are rarely as they seem, and they are never as they are billed.

Anka ignored the woman, but there was laughter from everyone else. Paul Anka was at my table and I didn't know it. Jimmy laughed the loudest, long and strained, the way people laugh only in the presence of celebrities. He squeezed my shoulder like an overbearing father.

"He's right there! See him! He's right there!"

The woman looked at me again, glanced at my nametag for some reason, and wagged her head sadly.

"I was just trying to be friendly," I said to Jimmy.

"I know you were!"

Anka threw the dice. He was wild with them. The dice are sharp when they're new, and if they hit you, you can bleed. Later that night, I saw Anka get so mad he threw a die at another player, and nearly caught the man's cheek. Anka's cigar smoke bothered all of us, the brown drift of it like the stink of his aura, his worth. In a casino, dealers work primarily for "tokes," or tips. By 3 a.m., Anka had won something like four thousand dollars. He walked off with his entourage laughing and happy with the world, and we smiled and waved after him. He left us nothing for our trouble but the kindly face on our money.

When I tell non-casino people that I work as a dealer, there's always a moment of pause as they weigh the possibility that I have just brazenly announced a drug association.

"Oh," they say, "you mean like in a casino."

The interrogation usually continues with the standard inquiry into why I would ever accept such a position. Casinos are a seamy, ugly world for bright, educated people to avoid. My response to this – it's a good job to have while you write, decent pay, time off, etc. – never satisfies the inquirer or me. The truth is I don't know why I am a dealer, except to say that it feels like fate. Gambling has always been a prominent feature of my personal topography. And as I draw a line through the significant turns of my life, the various games and questionable wagers, I see a direction indicated, a course predetermined.

My first specific memory of gambling comes from 1976, when I was nine years old, playing odds and evens with a kid named Ed Totty in the back of our grade school classroom. There was one run of tosses when Ed called "odds" sixteen times in a row and sixteen times in a row both our coins came up heads. I made eighty cents. Ed quit playing with me after that, and the expression on his face as we turned back to our lesson was the same one I saw him wearing fifteen years later when he pumped gas for me at a service station in our home town. He didn't recognize me.

Casinos are sometimes called "houses." As in: "So, what house do you work for now?"

The "back of the house" describes the area of the hotel property designated "employees only." Usually, it is a display of noxious abundance: fluorescent-lit hallways lined with dozens of room service trays, rows of maid carts stuffed with the dirtied linen of the horny droves, massive rubbish containers brimming with rotted food. I once saw a pornographic sight: a fifty-gallon trash drum piled high with disposable chef's hats.

The single step from the back of the house to the "front of the house" – where patrons are permitted – recalls Dorothy's emergence into Oz: she moves from the stale black and white interior of her tornado-flung home to the Technicolor wonderland of costumed dwarfs and brilliant matte paintings. Before work, the dealer/munchkins stand just outside the casino dragging on cigarettes until the moment when lateness will result in disciplinary action, then push through the swinging doors. It's like walking through a façade onto a soundstage: there's lights and action, but no cameras, strict house rule.

Liza Minelli was playing the hotel. She was good, the local paper said, but she had sung the same songs for 20 years. She had just had hip replacement surgery, and between shows she was carted through the back of the house in a wheelchair. A security team cleared the hallways for the transport, either because Liza did not wish to be seen in her convalescence, or because she didn't like the back of the house and wanted to get through it as quickly as possible.

One night, I was standing outside the uniform shop as they prepared to push her through. An acne-faced security guard in a maroon blazer told me I had to leave the area, Liza was coming.

"I'm sorry," he said. "She's usually pretty tanked before she goes on." He thought about it a moment, then added, "Like mother, like daughter."

I stood in a cubby outside the bathroom to wait. The guard's radio crackled with hoarse commands as she approached. "Whee," I heard Liza say as they rounded the corner. She rolled by me in a sequined flash, and the guard – a different kind of munchkin – jogged after her.

In a few seconds more, the hallway was filled with Filipino maids.

In the late 80's, my parents bought a condominium near Atlantic City. We celebrated my twenty-first birthday with a casino trip. I played twenty-one for nine hours and won $800. My mother – who has long since explored the possibilities of video poker addiction – had taught me the game on our kitchen table with the same tattered deck we had used to play gin rummy when I was eight. My mother had never spoken to me of sex, had never taught me how to cook or do laundry. But when I became a man she taught me basic strategy blackjack.

I have never played to excess, or lost a great deal of money, but these are relative terms. I once took a diagnostic test distributed by an organization for gambling addicts. The test had questions: answer so many "yes" and you may be a "problem gambler":

Do you feel a need to 'chase' after money already lost? *Yes.*

Have you ever lost money set aside for rent or bills? *No.*

Do thoughts of gambling occupy you while you are not playing? *Sometimes.*

Do you frequently lose all the money you bring with you? *Yes.*

Have you ever hidden money from a spouse/loved one to gamble it later? *No.*

My final score, out of twenty, was two points below the cut-off for people who should seek help.

In 1994, I borrowed the money to go to dealer's school. In deciding on this course, I thought of all the reasons I still give – relatively good pay, flexible hours – but I knew even then that the reasons were bullshit and that I had an affinity for this world I couldn't describe. I knew there was something bad about it, I knew it exposed everything awful of human behavior, but even so I liked it. It gave me a base and selfish thrill.

One day, I returned from break to find a dealer on my table in my time slot, a heavy black woman. "You goin' to Pit 10, honey," she said. "Watch out! You dealin' bee-jay to The Doctuh!"

The Doctor, I knew, was a regular. Had been a regular since the casino opened twenty years before. He was called The Doctor not because he was a medical professional, though he may have been, but because he bet a lot of money.

I checked in with the pit boss in Pit 10, a man named Joe. Joe was a tall prematurely gray man whose innate friendliness hibernated while he worked. "Listen," he said, "you ever deal to The Doctor before?"

"No," I admitted. "But I've heard the stories."

He nodded. "It's best just to stay quiet. Dummy up and deal. Got it?"

The dealer I tapped out was a young, pregnant Asian girl. A few strands of hair had come loose from her bun, and it made her look haggard but sexy. She cleared her hands for the cameras and glanced back at me with gratitude.

I stepped up to the game. The Doctor's appearance fit the basic doctor stereotype: tall, balding, well-groomed. He sat back in his chair and stared off into the casino, pretending not to notice the change of dealers. Dealer changes are considered bad luck by almost everyone.

The Doctor was infamous mainly for his intensity while he played: intensity the euphemism for becoming angry when he lost. The Doctor chewed his thumbnail like a pacifier. He pounded the padded rail in front of him that was padded because people pounded it all the time. He ran his hands roughly through his balding hair and cursed frequently, but turned his head to one side as he did it, the way smokers look away to expel a hit.

I burned a card and arranged a few cheques in the rack. My supervisor stood a few paces back, as far away as he could while maintaining something of an authoritative presence. Though The Doctor's anger was rarely directed at anyone overtly, he was unpleasant to be around, that bad vibe like a pocket of polluted air, a sphere of discontent that followed him everywhere.

Our game began. The Doctor's play by play was continual, and I was silent as instructed.

"There, look, you see? Thirteen. Why you always gimme thirteen? Okay, fine then, gimme a seven . . . queen. Of course." He looked away, said "Fuck" to the wall, and turned back again. "Okay, do it again . . . oh, now the twenty. Sure. Wait 'til I got the one chip up, then give me a hand. Of course."

The Doctor pressed his bets slowly as he won. His initial unit of wager was $100. If he won, he pressed to $200, then $300, then $400, then $500. If he lost at any point, he returned to $100. This is a reasonable system, if not actually a winner. (There is no such thing as a winner.) Losing five hands in a row would lose $500, but winning five in a row would win $1,500. Thus, a run of five losses followed by five wins – even, in terms of the cards – would nevertheless net $1,000.

"Okay," The Doctor said, "three in a row, good. Finally. Here's $400, take it. Ace-three. Gimme soft fourteen 'gainst a nine, sure. Hit it. Six! Ha! Good boy! Attaboy, kid! Pay me! Okay, now the five spot. The fin. The hump. Get me over the hump, kid, I'll take care of you, I swear ta God. Two, okay, gimme a nine . . . eight! Double!" He put up another $500, and now had $1,000 bet on the hand. "Gimme a ten! Gimme a monkey! Picture! Color TV! Nine. Okay, now the little one. Turn it easy, kid. Oh, no! No, not the . . . *fucking* twenty-one!" He slammed the edge of the table and ran his hands into his hair. His grammar failed him completely. "I . . . fuck the . . . that's just fucking . . ."

He lapsed into despondency as I gathered his cheques and racked them. I felt him looking at me. Everyone has a different policy regarding these moments, and my own was to avoid eye contact. Don't look at them.

"You're a piece of work, kid. Now I know why they fucking brought you over here. Twenty-one every time. Every goddamn hand you've got twenty-one." He picked another cheque off his stack and presented it, holding it between us like a pill he would prescribe for me as medicine. "Hey, look at me. Look at me, kid."

I hesitated a moment, for myself. Then I raised my eyes. The Doctor's eyes were stressed and wet.

"I'll make you a bet, kid. You're so goddamn good. How much you wanna bet I lose this next hand?"

What you learn of dealing in dealing school is a little like what you learn of war in Boot Camp. There's a lot of basic training that has very little to do with what it's like to work in a live casino, an unlikely cousin of combat.

Essentially a vo-tech setup, there's no real classroom work. Instead, there's a large mock casino where the silence is conspicuous: a soundstage of a soundstage. Four days a week, five hours a day, students put in time toward the completion of "degrees" in various games. What you learn are the fundamentals: how to riffle cards, how to drop-cut cheques, the proper way to "clean" your hands for the overhead cameras, how to protect yourself from chip thieves. Eventually, they cut to the quick, the thing everyone cares about: tokes. This means taking care of the customer.

In the casino industry, the verb "to take care" has two meanings:

the first is to provide exemplary service. Polite hosts. Complimentary meals or suites. The dealer's management of a player's money during play. Of course, the more you bet, the more you get: "care" is more careful for the higher roller.

The second meaning of "to take care" is simply a player's generosity in response to having been taken care of in the first place. A player who tokes frequently is said "to take good care" of the dealers. Such a player might also be called "the best," even if there are others who toke more.

As in: "Mr. Smith? Oh, yeah. If he wins, he takes *good* care of you. He's the *best!*"

This odd parlance is as important a lesson as any, and dealing school is ultimately an incomplete introduction to a perverted Wonderland. The curious transaction of "taking care" has nothing to do with taking care, but the irony goes undiscussed. My craps instructor once gave a lesson on servicing the customer. "Hand off the last come bets," he said. "Remind them when they forget to place their numbers. *Service* them. If you take care of *them*, they'll take care of *you*."

One night, a massive fat man pushed his way through the crowd to get to the spot on my craps game just next to me. He pushed and pushed, and when he arrived his whole bulk seemed to settle into place, finding the unlikely balance of a boulder in the desert mounted on the thinnest of perches.

"Good evening," I said.

"Hey, how ya doin', kid?" The man's voice was nasally and squirrelly, like an impersonation of someone friendly to the point of annoyance. His eyes went up to my forehead and down to my lips in a way that struck me as odd. "I'm from downtown Jersey City," he said, "but it's a good thing I don't live up in Alaska there or they'd think I was one of them whales, uh?"

He smiled. Stand-up comics may make a living ridiculing themselves for weight problems on stage, but such effacement one-to-one is embarrassing and sad. I smiled back and nodded.

The man continued to stare at my lips, which are not spectacular in any way. "Oh, you like that, uh? You like a little *you-mer*. Good kid."

He played for a few moments, ten pass line, double odds, eighteen each six and eight. A nine rolled, then a five, then a winner. I paid everyone, and stood up again.

"Way to go, kid," the man said. Then he did an odd thing. He reached down and touched the back of my hand, stroked it twice with his finger. It didn't seem possible to move away.

My floorperson walked over. He was a man I didn't know. He shook the fat man's hand in familiar greeting, and called him Harry. He nudged me and said, "Take care of Harry, here. He's the best."

"You got it," I said.

"Oh!" Harry said. "This is a good one, this kid. Good dealer. Handsome, too."

"We pick 'em careful," the floorman said.

"Good-lookin' kid," Harry said. "Look at 'im. You Irish, kid? Good, solid Irish boy."

The dice rolled. "Winner," the stickman said.

"Winner!" Harry said. He grabbed my hand and brought it up to his mouth to kiss my fingers. I felt the warmth of his breath and the soft flesh of his lips.

I paid the line, and stood up again.

The floorman slapped Harry on the arm, congratulating him. I glanced back once, to see if I could catch the floorman's attention: part of his job was to protect me, to take care of *me*. But he wouldn't return my glance. Another roll came, another winner.

"That's a *good* kid," Harry said.

The floorman was gone.

The house is more Big Brother than corrupt gangster.

There are cameras everywhere. There are teams of people whose sole job it is to investigate others doing their jobs. The house exists to take care of you, like it or not. A computer system tracks the complete lives of guests: where they eat, how much they win or lose, how frequently they leave the property. The house is an information ministry and a fully functional bank. In the back of the house there are framed posters on the walls, service propaganda disguised as friendly reminders: Smile! 'Cause The Next Person You See Will Be A Customer! The house operates with a dumb omniscience, a spooky sterility.

The house is based on decentralized human power, standard democratic checks and balances. No one floor manager is aware of how the property conducts itself as a whole, and executives are oblivious to the details of the lower bureaucracies. Surveillance personnel do not mingle with casino personnel, and there are only rumors of those associated with the "count," the actual cash the games take in. Thus, the idea of the house, as in "the house edge," refers to no specific individual. It's as slippery a term as "culture," or "the system."

I had a dealer girlfriend . . . well, not a girlfriend, really, but someone I was very close to, a beautiful Vietnamese woman. She got a lot of attention from players. It might have bothered me once. But after I became a dealer I never got jealous. It meant tokes. I watched her one day from across the casino, chatting with a player, an Asian man, Vietnamese himself. They joked and laughed, and spoke softly in that unruly tongue. He made a comment, and she blushed and her dimples appeared, one of them a recent surgical implant. She reached to touch his hand, a congratulatory flirt when he won some money. I felt nothing. I thought: *You've almost got him.* He tossed her a $25 cheque, and out came the dimples again. "Dealuh money!" I heard her say, and down it went into our toke box.

In Atlantic City, dealer tokes are pooled: $1/500^{th}$ of that for her, $1/500^{th}$ for me.

Even dealers disagree over how to best describe casino life: tending bar, factory work, amusement parks. Nothing fits. Consider the following: as a dealer, there are only certain places inside the house you are allowed to go. You smoke when you can, and the food they give you is ridden through with viral concerns. Employees sometimes form a unified front, and sometimes go at one another like animals. We all wear the same clothes, and everyone has a number on their shirt. You're never sure who's sleeping with whom, and clandestine drug use is rampant. Everyone likes to talk about what they will do once they "get out" of the industry.

Casino life has these things and more in common with prison life.

Stories about being a dealer tend to glamorize it, though, and what gets lost in the process is the tedium. Dealing is subject to the pilot's formula: 95% boredom, 5% terror.

Because it's dull, dealers will talk about anything on dead games, and scams are a common preoccupation. A scam is a plot on the part of players or dealers to rip off the casino. It's tempting. We all admit that. There's a lot of money right there in front of you, and you can't help noticing the procedural holes through which you might, over the course of a month or two, slip a couple hundred thousand.

The house, of course, does *not* like to talk about scams. So much so that when dealers are caught stealing, they're rarely prosecuted. It's bad publicity. The scammers are arrested, sure: there are stories of dealers being cuffed right in the pit and paraded through the casino like Christ bearing his cross through the streets. But this is for the rest of us: it's what's available short of a stoning.

There are a million scams. And for every dealer who is caught, it is said, there are ten who get away with it. It's true that casino employees are supposed to watch each other, but people don't *like* to do it: it's a sign of respect and friendship to turn your back on someone.

The cameras are everywhere, yes. But eventually you learn that there are blind spots, and that there are only so many monitor screens in the surveillance room. It's said that there's about a one in six chance that your table is being watched at any given moment. One in six is like rolling a die.

I was on a dead game once. The tedium was incredible. I picked at a cuticle for a dozen minutes, then did leg stretches to battle cramps. For several long seconds, I leered at a woman who agreed to leer right back at me. Then I looked down at my rack. Ninety thousand and change. Not a floorperson in sight. Curious, I glanced up at the nearest security globe, a half-sphere imbedded in the ceiling covered with the gold reflective material NASA uses on space helmets. It was nearly opaque, but through the glass I could just see the LED light of the camera inside blinking at me like a laser sight.

Gambling's critics sail deep for the big fish: the "problem gamblers" who end up in debt, bankruptcy, suicide. Surprise, surprise: they find them. Stories of suicides circulate through the city every month or so – sometimes, they come in bunches – and I myself once took $40,000 from a man, the entire value of his auto-shop: well beyond anger or shame, he just sat quietly, amazed that the game would then go on without him.

While bankruptcies and suicides make for effective blurbs, the statistics – money and death – are reductive and misleading. They are the same statistics through which wars and natural disasters are reduced to forgettable figures, equations that fail to move.

The casino industry's argument – jobs – is a big one. They may stretch the numbers to their advantage, but they don't have to stretch them far. The casino business is filled with people – the under-educated, immigrants with little English – who, were it not for gambling, would make less money in uglier businesses. The casino industry is pretty ugly itself, but the thing that makes it such a target is the discrepancy between how it is advertised and the subsequent reality. The fact is that most players who come to your table are not problem gamblers. In generous estimates, problem gamblers make up only 5% of the gambling population, and the real number is more like 2%. Still, it's an ugly thing to watch.

I once dealt blackjack to a young white guy for whom the abbreviated diagnosis certainly applied: he had it bad. He needed to gamble, and he needed to hate me for beating him. To take a hit, this guy shaped his hand into the shadow puppet of a phallus – middle finger extended, ring and index alongside like stubby testicles – and tapped the table with that sign language "Fuck you." If he broke, he continued tapping. "Fuck you, fuck you, fuck you." Also, he called me a nigger.

"You fucking nigger bastard," he said.

He seemed to realize it didn't make much sense. As he bought in for another $1,500, he paused to apologize. It was just the way he was when he played, he said. I told him I understood, and as a gambler myself, I did. The odds beat you, the anger accumulates, and you have to figure out what to do with it. The first choice is to give it to someone else: not a surprise, really, this game of tag we've all been playing since we were four years old.

This is the industry price that gambling's critics have forgotten to measure, the "problem" that the definition of "problem gambler" doesn't contain. Even decent people behave badly when they play, and they hand that angst off to the dealer, to their spouse, to their chauffeur, to their children. It's an effect that lacks the drama of a death or bankruptcy. But that bad vibe, that sudden inexplicable hate, takes its little toll when you are its unwitting victim, and the transaction is so much more common that its accumulated price outweighs those higher-profile costs – the costs that wash with the vast benefits of casino revenue anyway.

I, myself, was a better gambler before I became a dealer. I used to make smaller bets and raise them incrementally, and I counted cards a little, though counting cards is not the advantage that people think. And I did okay. I won some, lost some, rode the rollercoaster. I paid bills and dues, alternately. It worked like it was supposed to.

Now it's different. On becoming a dealer, my sense of casinos changed. It's not contempt, it's apathy. Oddly, I still get the impulse to play.

It creeps up on me. I'll find myself daydreaming about a game: craps, blackjack, poker. I can see the cards coming the way they are supposed to, see the dice falling obediently. A French mathematician, Joseph Bertrand, said, "A [flipped] coin has neither conscience nor memory." Gamblers have little of the former and a selective version of the latter: just as my clearest gambling memory from childhood is a 16-flip winning streak, gamblers tend, when the hankerin' hits, to focus on memories flush with luck. Now, I always recall the 24-hand bank run I once saw while dealing baccarat, the 90-minute crap roll that cost the house $200,000.

So I take a shot. I go for the big score. I make bad bets and power press them. I play badly now: I leave everything on the layout, hoping for the long roll. That long roll, or run of hands, is so many standard deviations away from the mean as to be effectively irrelevant. But as a dealer, you see it, and if it comes at the right time . . . .

I always lose. I sate the impulse with $100 or $200, like a shot of methadone, and it goes away as mysteriously as it came.

Dealers count out currency on the table. Different houses have different procedures for how the money should sit: rows of four, rows of five. Large cash sums have an inexplicable fascination: this holds even when you see it every day. I once counted out $3,000 in ten dollar bills for a Chinese woman. My supervisor stood behind me as I spread them out, and when it was all there on the table he whispered to me that the woman owned a Chinese restaurant in a neighboring town, and that upstairs from the restaurant she ran another business.

"300 blowjobs," he said, motioning with his pen to the swarm of bills.

Players sometimes ask dealers if they don't feel guilty for having taken the player's money, their $100. It's a silly question when you think about it: these are not the ovens at Auschwitz. Still, when cash from drug sales or prostitution passes through your hands, it's tempting to feel like a conspirator in the crimes. Sometimes, you're even closer to it.

One day, a young dark-haired kid walked into Baccarat and requested a marker. $8,000. Daddy's money, we guessed. He bet $100 at a time. If he lost, he doubled it. If he lost the $200, he went to $400. If he lost the $400, then $800. Etc. This is called the Martingale System. It's a couple hundred years old, but people dream it up on their own now and again and think they're onto something *big*. You will, in fact, probably win a little with the Martingale System, but if you lose, you lose it all. I did the math in my head for the parameters the kid was playing: $100 bet, $8,000 buy-in.

"What is it?" I said. "Seven losers before you get burned?"

The kid smirked, enjoying his moment at the center of attention. "Something like that."

I saw him get his bet up to $3,200 once, but he won the hand, scrambled back to an even keel.

Several days later, I saw a notice in the paper. A kid from Long Island had killed himself over gambling losses in Atlantic City. He had a strange method: he bought a toy gun, then drove around like a madman until a cop pulled him over. He climbed out of the car brandishing the toy, and the cop had no choice but to gun him down. The kid left a message on the car seat, an apology to the officer who killed him.

The printed picture of the kid was a little bit like the kid I dealt to, but really I didn't remember him too well. The paper listed his losses as something near $8,000.

Was it the same kid? Was I culpable? I never actually took his money, but I was part of the system that beat him. The assignment of blame is always tricky work, and the ultimate question is whether every casino employee is responsible for the desperate acts of every crazed gambler. The kid seemed to think not: his letter of apology was addressed to the cop.

Sometimes when I wake up, I've forgotten that I'm a dealer. For a brief moment, my life seems to have turned in a more progressive direction, and the world is more pleasant to be in. Then I spot the disgusting shirt of my uniform hanging near the ironing board, and it all comes back. In the end, there's a debate in my mind: a part of me approves of dealing because it is honest work, a somewhat-skilled labor, but a larger part feels a widespread variety of shame.

When I go to work, I tend to notice hands. I look at peoples' fingers, how they use them. I rarely look at faces. I might notice a deformed lip or an abnormally large nose, but mostly I don't bother. Hands and bets. People are what they bet.

I didn't notice much about the man when he walked up to the table and asked for $17 on the inside numbers: he could have been any elderly Caucasian. He was tall and wore glasses, and his hands were wrinkled like an old grocery bag. That was all I could say about him before he teetered and fell backward onto the wild carpet, collapsed from the action even before the dice rolled.

It's not a new story, people dying on the casino floor. It's the paradigmatic casino moment – the senseless poignancy of someone's life ending in a place where all that is good about being alive seems to have been set aside, the fallacy of a man's last words being a wager made with a stranger.

The guy went down. He broke his fall with his hands, but that doesn't mean he wasn't already unconscious. I was the first to see this, I realized, the first besides the players just next to him, who did nothing. I immediately called for security, and the pit boss scrambled for a phone.

I looked back to where the guy had fallen. I could have helped, but I stayed where I was. A dealer may never leave a live game. Never. This rule is brainwashed into dealers to the point of its being an ethical consideration. Do Not Leave The Game. I could have helped the old guy in only a token way, but perhaps looking back I feel less heroic than had I gone around to elevate his feet or just hold his hand until the paramedics arrived.

In a minute several security guards appeared and surrounded the man. Nobody so much as checked his pulse. The guards stood about in impotent vigil, holding their walkie-talkies aloft and glancing into the near distance as though for enemies in the underbrush. A moment later, my boxman decided to continue play on the game. This is one of the most disturbing details of casino life: the audacity and faux romance of the game continuing at all costs, like a newspaper press. But we couldn't continue quite yet. The guy had money on the table. The procedure went like this: the first thing we did for him, the first thing before wiping his brow and whispering into his ear that he was going to make it, you better believe it, was put all his cheques into a plastic bag, seal it with a tie, and place it securely into the possession of a security guard who made $8 an hour for all this shit and hassle, $10 tops. Business was the first order of business.

Now, the game could continue. There was a nice little roll going, actually. I was surprised that I could do all the calculations despite the distraction: the scene had given me a heady push of epinephrine, and I was able to divide up my attention neatly. As the roll went on the players pressed their bets more aggressively, I thought, as though it would continue as long as everything stayed as it was, as though the scene had augured luck, as though the dice themselves were distracted by the man's seizure and would refuse to come up seven until he was wheeled away or out and out died.

Perhaps eight minutes had passed. Finally, a security official in a vinyl windbreaker climbed on top of the old guy and began pumping his arms into the man's naked chest. I was surprised how distended the man's belly became on the thrusts, how rounded and smooth, the navel nearly flattened like a pregnant woman's. The security official's hands almost disappeared into the man's flesh, the sharp bend of his rib cage. The treatment was awful in its violence, but perhaps more horrible in just how routine it seemed. The security official didn't seem to care much about the man he was attempting to resuscitate, and his thrusts were half-hearted even in their brutality. It was just another old fucker who was going to die doing something he shouldn't have been doing anyway, and the security official was paying about as much attention to him as I had when I looked at his crinkled hands, set up his bet, and went to the next guy.

The security official tired after a while and settled back on his haunches to rest. I got a good look at the old guy's face, finally. His eyes were open, lids peeled horrifically back over globes fixed at the ceiling, and his mouth was gaping, lips sucked in over bare gums. He was unconscious, but looked terrified.

The E.M.S. crew arrived a few minutes later, and the security team turned over what little information they had. The lack of action during the transition was like dead air on the radio. The paramedics took their time breaking out the defibrillator kit. Someone put a ventilator bag on the man, and pumped the bladder so that his chest rose and fell. For passers-by, this motion constituted evidence that the man's condition was nominal and under control.

My attention kept veering between the scene and the game, and eventually, as they began to shock the man ("Clear!"), it occurred to me that the split in my life between gambling and writing was somewhat like this division: I bounced back and forth, doing dice math while trying to sustain a generalized compassion. Then I looked around the casino at the faces of the players, locked on the scene. They watched with the interest of a grave revelation.

In craps, people have a tendency to watch the dice at all times. In blackjack, the shuffle commands a ridiculous fascination. In roulette, it's the ball. As though fate rests in the nature of that hard matter, it is difficult to take your eyes away from the tools of the games. The faces around the casino studied the scene in that same way. The crowd's eyes were as hard-fixed as the dead man's, and the collection of ages and races made it a universal moment. I was pleased that I had found something less desecrating than the man's death to consider. Then I stopped. I paused at the face of a homely Asian woman maybe forty, with long silky hair, heavy jowls, and sculpted red lips. She was not looking at the man. She was looking at *me*.

At last, the gurney arrived. The paramedics shocked the man once more and hefted him onto the bed. They pushed him away, and we would never know for sure whether he died or survived. The roll on the table continued a moment. Then petered out. Then seven'd out. And the game died at once as though the man's spirit had in fact been the thing that sustained it.

Old Money

MICHAEL HEFFERNAN

I bought a Roman silver denarius
at Hudson's Department Store in Detroit,
with a week's collection from my paper route
when I was 12. Marcus Aurelius
still looks surprisingly like one of us,
approaching 60, and a little tired
from things that kept him always on his guard.
He seems to be there just the way he was
after the middle of the 2nd Century,
and in the 17th year of his reign:
one of the nicest tyrants in history
having to glance away from everyone,
who never got to know him personally,
passing from palm to palm on a gray coin.

Limited Time Offer

RONALD WALLACE

I guess God knew what He was doing
when He set up his earthly economy –
what choice did we have but to buy into it? –
though it seems we're getting short shrift,
always losing the shirt off our back,
going bankrupt, being brought low.
Even Adam was reduced to barter –
What do I hear for this rib? –
& kicked out of bliss for shoplifting
into a world well-stocked with woe.
It seems life is finally a closeout,
a clearance, a liquidation,
with God up there hawking His wares.
The bottom line: Everything Must Go!

$5 American Poem

L. B. THOMPSON

        — what came into my hands
        as change, I didn't discover
        until later. We were home
        when I showed Paula

the marvelous ordinary 5
dollar bill with those few
handwritten lines on its
pillared building side, in the top
right under the circled numeral
5, plain

        and quickly scribbled with the kind
        of pen you might find chained
        to the counter at the bank —

blue letters, two of them
almost hidden in the green bushes
at the base of the Lincoln Memorial:

        Small
        Jerk Chicken
        Sweet
        White rice

Just like that.
We couldn't stop staring at it —
Little food order on a 5 dollar bill.

Maybe it's the journey from earning to eating –
we even
talked about keeping
the money; not spending it;

                maybe framing it double-
                sided for the living-
                room mantle, but we'll probably
                end up tipping with it –

Nannies, Maids, and Money

KATE CLANCHY

The Maids is the name of our local cleaning service. I often see their vans parked in nearby streets, jauntily emblazoned with a saucy round-bottomed lady with a lace apron. Ironic, of course – no one says *maid*. The pallid, heavy-footed gangs of women I occasionally see dragging mops from the van or smoking in the front seats wear badges which say *cleaning operative*. "Their pay is shit," says Antigona. They are low-grade women, stupid. Polish. "Imagine," says Antigona, "if you had your EU papers and you still needed to work in a job like that. Ha." She tosses her black ponytail.

I think of the salary list of an Edwardian grand house: handwritten in cursive, arranged by hierarchies: scullery maid, under kitchen maid, kitchen-maid, under-cook, cook; bootboy, under-footman, footman, butler; skivvy, housemaid, housekeeper; the upper servants and the lower, the body servants – ladies maid, valet – the between stairs people – governess, companion. We visit to be horrified by these now, the ranked bells, the attic bedrooms, the back stairs – but at least they acknowledge the scale of the task of housekeeping, and differentiation of skills. In terms of raw number, if not of proportion, we probably have more servants now in Britain than we did at the turn of the century, but their jobs are not differentiated – cleaner, cleaning operative, housekeeper – and their proper names are very often not recorded. When people have no rank, even a lowly rank, we tend, I think, to treat them worse.

"My mother says *maid*," says my friend Monique. She is from Trinidad. The maid, Diana, has served her mother for twenty-five years. She is twenty years younger than her employer, but now they are both old, just a pair of old ladies gossiping in Creole on the terrace. For twenty-five years, Monique's mother has paid every doctor's visit for Diana and her family, written all letters, made all official phone calls, and built Diana's house. In return, Diana has cared for the house, nursed Monique's grandmother, and now Monique's mother. Actually, says Monique, Diana no longer cleans, but how can you fire someone who laid out your grandmother's body, pulled her twisted ribs into alignment, someone who will, you may be perfectly certain, hold your mother's hand when she dies?

The woman up the road is not allowed to employ Antigona. Her husband forbids it. They get *The Maids* in instead, once a week for four hours during which time she is always in the playground so that the children don't witness any of the process. "It's the personal element," she says, helplessly. "I mean, don't you find that difficult? Talking to them? And my husband's worse, he's terrible! He just doesn't want to know, you know, who is cleaning his personal things. Gives him the creeps." She shrugs, smiles. Men. "Silly, but then, at the end of the day, it's his money."

The personal element. The individual. Yes, I should say to my neighbour, it is difficult, it is embarrassing. It makes explicit a relationship which I would rather ignore: the relationship of my freedom to another's labour, my wealth to another's poverty. Maybe it would be easier to pretend it is not happening, easier to employ a firm called *The Maids* and call *cleaning operatives* – machines – not women, in the same way, it suddenly occurs to me, as I found it easier to send Sam to a nursery rather than a child-minder. A child-minder is an individual, and individuals demand interaction. They make you feel worse.

But Sam was never happy at nursery. He wanted an individual. In 2004, he was due to start state nursery school and I was due to have a new baby. My friend Jeannie, meanwhile, had a seven-month-old baby, two older children, and a new job. Neither of us was able to pretend we could have it all, anymore. Neither of us wanted to hand another baby into group care. But neither of us wanted to give up our jobs, either. We both knew and employed Antigona, and we knew that *Nanny* was a title she fancied more than *cleaning operative,* and so we had our obvious but brilliant idea.

Together, we reckoned, by paying her most of my earnings and about half of what Jeannie takes home, we could employ Antigona five days a week and pay her £16,000 a year, which, from our reading of Working Tax Credit regulations (we have both received it) should still entitle Antigona to some support and, more crucially, to Housing Benefit. In return, Antigona would solve The Problem for us. Antigona could work in my house in the morning, taking care of the babies and picking up the little ones from nursery school, and at three o'clock could move to Jeannie, collecting Ylli from school on the way alongside Jeannie's son. It would help Ylli. Antigona could do an NVQ child care! We were excited by our benign, liberal plan. We couldn't wait to tell Antigona.

Except she will have none of it. It's not the child-care – she wants to do that. It's the taxes. She refuses, point-blank, to go legal. She will end up paying tax, she will not have enough money. I realise, with a crunch, that going legal was what the owner of the sweet factory wanted her to do. Rather than take her passport; he was trying to rid her of the man taking her wages and filling her with fear about the tax system. Now, Antigona says, she knows no one who pays tax. But she already pays tax, we point out, for the restaurant. Maximum tax, actually, in the name of Anna Grimaldi, an imaginary Italian. If she was legal, she could get that back. Antigona says she could not possibly declare that much income, because then she would lose her Housing Benefit which is more than a thousand pounds a month. We say that if she starts paying National Insurance she will be entitled to a pension. She looks at us as if we were cretins.

Also, we say, it is one thing for us each to employ her four hours a week and pay cash. That's not even illegal. But employing her full-time without tax is different. We are committing a crime. Antigona says no one is ever caught for this crime. We say they are. Who do we know? asks Antigona. We say no one – but we've read about them. Antigona thinks nothing of such evidence. Antigona says we know nothing of the real world by which she means the black economy. We say we've read about it. Ten percent of GDP, isn't it? There, says Antigona. You see. One in ten, and how many get caught? Maybe one in 10,000. Impasse.

Jeannie and I start to ask ourselves: *How Much is Antigona Earning?*

And we add it up: *A Large Sum.*

Income Support and Child Benefit: £135
Cleaning 30-40 hours a week, variable rates: £250
Restaurant approx. 30 hours a week £4:50 an hour: £100
Restaurant tips, approx £20 a night: £100
Average weekly income: £580

But Antigona also receives more than £300 each week in Housing Benefit. She needs this because, though her house was built by the Council, it was bought by its tenant some years ago. A few changes of hands later, it has become a rental property whose high commercial rate has to be met by the Council because they have a shortage of properties because tenants keep buying them. If Antigona had a council house with a £70 rent, she could afford, she tells us, to pay tax.

Including the Housing Benefit, her weekly income becomes nearly £900, or given that she has no paid breaks, about £50,000 per annum net income. For a tax-paying person to bring home such an income, she would have to earn at least £70,000 gross. So, though my hourly rate can sometimes be a great deal higher than Antigona's, and though I have a house which through no virtue or talent of mine accumulates yearly more than Antigona can earn, I am a long way from being able to employ her. My gross income varies between £10,000 and £16,000 a year, Jeannie's new job pays £29,000.

I am depressed by my sum. I have never been one for the *Daily Mail*, never believed in a plague of black – market immigrants living it up off benefits. Clearly, Antigona is not living it up. She is glassy-eyed and stick-thin and never sleeps. But, even allowing for the fact that she never actually sees the Housing Benefit, she must still be saving money. Where, then, is she putting it? I ask her. She is, she says:

1) Still paying back her own and her husband's passage money (the £13,000 has grown to nearer £20,000) to her brothers so that they will not fall foul of the nefarious figures they bribed in the first place.

2) Saving up to go to Albania to look for her family.

3) Saving up so that she will not be penniless if she is deported.

I find it hard to argue with any of this. I also know that it is true that she is one of very many. Migrant labour, very much of it illegal, sustains our catering and cleaning industries and, if you figure in private cleaning too, much else. All the working women I know employ a cleaner: Jeannie and I are the only ones wrestling with the extremely complex tax credit system. Even the Home Office, it emerges a couple of years later, is cleaned by illegal migrant labour.

And I know that Antigona is right to say that very few get caught. How can I ever persuade her to come and work for me when she earns so much more than I do? How can I make working for less money an attractive, even possible idea? Jeannie says we can't. We dig deeper and work out how to pay her more. We get in a third family for some afternoons. We get the exact Housing Benefit figures from the Council. They're on a sliding scale actually: not so bad. We put this new proposition to her. We wait.

Nothing. I try again.

"Antigona," I say. "I think you should pay tax because it's part of belonging to this society. Taxes pay for schools and hospitals and the police, and you like all those things. And it wouldn't be very much tax, and I'll pay it. Really, we can work it out."

Antigona shoves another load in the washing machine. She won't meet my eye. "I'm going to Albania," she says. "Next week."

"What? What about the children?"

"Ylli will come with me. The girls will be okay."

"No they won't."

"Flora is seventeen."

"Still . . . Are you going to look for your family?"

"Yes."

"How? I mean, where?"

"Tirana – capital city. Then Vlores, in south. There is nice beach there. Then . . . around."

"But, Antigona. We went through this, remember? The Red Cross? We checked all the lists?" I'm saying her family are dead. Understandably, she is not listening.

"You don't understand. In Albania, they don't have lists."

This seems plausible.

"So, my job – you will make up your mind when you come

back?"

"When I come back."

The trip is of course a much bigger deal than that. I have to buy the air tickets, which she says are too expensive. I have to lend suitcases, find the bus times. Antigona is calmly adamant about all this, and I start to believe she will make her way coolly through Heathrow, perhaps even track down her family by simply badgering an official until they take down some forgotten ledger and trace their names with an inky thumb.

Of the wisdom of leaving the girls I am less convinced. They have a school term to finish, true, and exams, and Antigona simply believes they will go there every day, and come back and cook in the empty house. She leaves them money. I call them a few times while she is away, and they giggle but I am heavily pregnant and have my eye off the ball.

Antigona is gone three weeks. When she comes back, she is tanned from her sojourn in Vlores, but strangely dead round the eyes. She found nothing, though she asked at many agencies, and trekked through three major cities.

She says she will take my job, and we go to the job centre and sign many hundreds of forms. She lends me a tenner on the way out, to buy fruit in the market, and we both laugh our heads off. She is doing it for me, she says. She does not accept anything I have to say about the future, or pensions, or GNVQs, or strengthening her case to remain here. But I am like her sister here, and this is what I want. And her real sisters are dead, we have to assume now: Vera, Blerta, Jehona, and their children. Her own mother, Fatmire, who was such a tower of strength to Antigona, is dead, we have to assume.

When my baby is born, Antigona cries with joy.

The Price of Waterfalls

MICHAEL GUISTA

I grew up on a farm of grapes and plums. I loved to watch the yellow berries of Thompsons swell over summer, green leaves rustling in the wind, the pink blossoms of Santa Rosas budding. But it wasn't the plants or the scurry of lizards and squirrels that got to me. It was watching the water course down the furrows.

And I don't know why. It's not something a kid decides to do. I didn't wake up one morning as an eight-year-old and say to myself, "I'm gonna watch water my whole life!"

But I have. I first studied water by sending little sticks down the furrows, canoes traveling down the heavy currents caused by bumps in the irrigation beds, crooked plowing, stones. Then I noticed tiny falls where water would build up behind some clods until finally making its way over a ledge. Or I'd make waterfalls by building dams and then cutting a trough at the tops. My brother would sometimes put ants on the sticks, just to see what a creature would do on a canoe. Not me. I was a water purist.

When I go to the mountains now, I'm drawn to rivers and waterfalls. You can see waterfalls just about everywhere: where melting snow splashes over mounded boulders, where a drain pipe juts out the side of a mountain, where water after a rain pours off the road into a gutter obstructed by rocks and limbs, where a depression in a log pools up with water and overflows onto the leaves below, one leaf filling and spilling into the next. I enjoy fishing not so much to catch fish but to walk up and down the banks of rivers, through them, across them, even beneath waterfalls in the space between the falls and the granite sheering.

Even at my jobs water has been a focus. I worked as a farm laborer during summers for about five years and I remember when I got promoted to "irrigator." What a job. Watering oranges all day long.

Later, I became a "ditch man," riding up and down a company-owned ditch, selling water to farmers, controlling the flow of water into their fields.

It now seems my thoughts were hackneyed and innocent for more than half of my life. I thought work was something that should be enjoyed, and if possible, involve water. My disdain of business was absolute. It was exploitative of laborers. I hadn't read Marx, but it was obvious: you were having someone work for you, and if he cost you ten dollars an hour, you were going to have to make more than ten dollars an hour off of his labor. I reached late adolescence during the Seventies when corporations were under attack. What was Vietnam about after all? Corporations. What was smog about? Droughts? Corporations. And a small business was just as culpable if on a smaller scale. Exploit and gather your riches.

But I just wouldn't.

I carried this sentiment into my own first business, which, I believed, was not actually a business but – and I would use this phrase – a labor of love. And so it was.

No businessman would ever claim I had more than the business sense of a clam.

Although I had two master's degrees, I barely used them. For a while I taught English part time at local universities and community colleges, but I gave it up. Instead, I brought in water fountains from Mexico and sold them. I loved them, much more than my customers did. My business was in a terribly sweet location in a quaint little town I adored. But few customers came. I was losing my rent money and not getting a cent for my labor. I was an idiot. But I loved hearing the fountains. My business was indoors and water splashed onto the hardwood floors. I'd talk to someone on the phone and exclaim, "Hey, you hear all that water? That's my fountains! That's my water!"

I moved to a better location and got more customers than before. But my rent doubled. I still wasn't selling enough. I turned down jobs teaching at a university where I used to work. I turned down a job working for the government. I got calls on the phone and said, "No. I have a business to run."

I was losing money every month to run it, becoming one of those sad statistics: four out of five small businesses fail within 18 months. The owners of these dying businesses not only earn a poor wage but in many cases – like mine – actually have to pay to work. Yeah, a real labor of love, paying to work. But to many businessmen, I've come to believe, the job is a hobby, and hobbies cost money.

That's what farming was for my dad. He lost money many years, broke even others, made a little half the time. He worked twenty or thirty hours a week after his regular job to do the farming. He could have sold the acreage for a huge profit. But he wouldn't. He had offers up until his death but he wouldn't sell. I was that foolish about fountains. The only time I made any money at all was when I plastered "Going Out of Business" signs all over the building. "Good Bye and Good Riddance." "Lost and Forgotten." "Thanks for ruining my life, Santa Maria!"

But the signs lured customers. Suddenly my business was popular. My employee and I carved waterfalls out of lava rock and sold them at four times our cost. We were selling ten to twenty waterfalls a day. This went on for a week. Then two more weeks. My little shop was finally making money, but the mini-craze for waterfalls didn't last. I shut the doors and counted my money. After a year of hard work and no wages, I had lost $20,000. All I had left was a dozen pumps and some tubing.

Then seven or eight years later, tabletop fountains were everywhere. I knew they would be. I'd predicted it back when I was in business but had no idea how to do anything about it. I wanted to be back in the water business, even though I was teaching English at a junior college.

"I have some pumps," I told a friend of mine. "We'll make our own fountains and sell them on eBay."

We did. It was surprising, but we did. And we made money off the hobby.

We'd drive to the beach for driftwood. I'd go to the mountains and get rock. I learned how to pick bowls at Home Depot that would hold water well with the right kind of plugging at the bottom. We'd spend twenty dollars on a fountain and sell it for forty-five. We made a profit of maybe twenty-five dollars a week.

It was a blast. We started making trips to Los Angeles to buy better bowls at cheaper prices. We started buying pumps in large enough quantities to get discounts. We bought air plants from a huge Tillasandia greenhouse. We added miniature ceramic Asian fisherman costing twenty cents each. Sometimes we cleared a hundred dollars per week profit.

But bowls cracked in shipping. Claims had to be filed. Packing a box took as long as making a fountain. I said, "You know, Jim, we ought to sell pumps."

He thought about it. I'd been getting cranky by then. Not really a nice guy to be around. I wanted to make money. Enjoyment was leaking out of the equation. I'd started to calculate how long it would take to make each fountain if we created a crafts assembly line, first plugging up all the bowls, then drilling a dozen holes in slate, then inserting the pumps and tubing. And so on.

At the time, Jim was chair of our department at the junior college. "I'm an English teacher," he said. So he gave up his share of our inventory, which was worth about a hundred dollars.

And I got out of the fountain-making business. I built waterfalls on the side, huge ones for people's backyards. I didn't know what I was doing. I didn't understand anything about plumbing. I just knew what a good waterfall looked like. But mostly I started selling pumps. At first I had students make a website for me. Then I gradually got around to adding online sales. I bought some more pumps. I was ecstatic the day I owned 300 pumps, all paid for by me!

A fellow businessman said, "Hey, Mike, why don't you buy the pumps directly from China? Why pay a middleman?"

So I bought from China. I was such an amateur. But that's what I did. And now I buy and sell hundreds of thousands of dollars worth of pumps each year.

But still, I sell pumps! They're made of plastic and copper. They're ugly.

We don't have a single fountain at our home. My wife is sick of them. She doesn't want to have to worry about water. Can't I just be happy that water makes us so much money?

So I learned to get my feelings out of business. It's not a labor of love, not if it's going to be successful. I have no love for pumps. I don't despise them. It's indifference. I've substituted my love for water with a business plan and lots of spreadsheets. Instead of watching water, I concentrate on how to divert money so taxes don't get too high, on making sure part-time employees do the physical work and higher-paid full-timers do the clerical work to keep Worker's Comp premiums down. My time is invested in locating the best foreign factories for pumps and the best foreign software engineers for web design. It's about precisely calculating the impact of product return and shipping costs and predicting inventory needs. It's about selling lights and tubing and diverter valves to get more hits on the Internet so that Google keeps giving the company a high page rank.

People call our 800 number for advice on how to build waterfalls. I start to get enthusiastic. Then I think to myself, how big of a pump is this guy actually going to buy? It's just one pump. How long can I afford to talk to him on the phone? My voice gets icy. "I don't design waterfalls. I sell pumps. It takes a hundred gallons per hour for every inch of water. How wide you want the waterfall to be, that's up to you." I just don't think that way anymore.

I go outside when I'm done with work. The small drainage pond at the end of the building ripples with tadpoles. The water sinks into the ground and the pond nearly empties every day but fills up again at night when the sprinklers come on. In that precarious space the tadpoles survive, breathing in the water before it almost disappears for good.

Loaded

DENISE DUHAMEL

This morning on CNN I see a white hamster
lounge between two black piano keys.
The hamster's gnawing away
on popcorn, its paws holding a kernel
that it twists like corn-on-the-cob.
Everything seems out of proportion,
the giant kernel, the tiny rodent.
I think about my failed marriage,
how my ex hopped off the wheel
while I kept running. How he loaded up
a suitcase and left me with all our debt
and creditors looking for him to pay his bills.
The hamster lazes on its back, lifting
its hinds leg in what seems like pure bliss.
I imagine my ex, who has been gone
for a while now, living like this
on the money I gave him in our settlement.
When he first went missing,
I kept seeing a mouse run across the wall,
so I set out traps, globbed
with peanut butter my ex had left behind.
Every morning I checked, sure I'd find
some awful dead thing, but the traps
were empty. It took me a few days to realize
the mouse I thought I'd seen was the shadow
of a bird who flew above the balcony outside.
Once again I was wrong. Once again I saw
something that wasn't there and missed
the obvious. Look how cute!

The CNN announcer coos about the hamster,
today's YouTube sensation.
As I leave for work, I say *By the way, I hate you,*
to the pampered hamster, who is playing
on a loop, on every channel,
serenaded by big well-meaning hands.

Fair Is Fair: A Dialogue Between Husband and Wife

KELLY CHERRY

I was incensed. "Even if it's true
that the best things in life are free, there are not
enough of them. Or else some damn idiot
got a good deal more than any fool is due.
Meanwhile, the poor cannot afford to sue
Congress for a chicken in every pot.
Justice? I guess it's just that hell is hot.
In death the rich can live on Supply Side Stew."

My gentle husband said, "Suppose justice
isn't a balancing of scales, an equation
       between terms, but rather a singular gorgeous thing
       to be weighed against sheerest emptiness?"

"Plato's metaphysics are out of fashion."

"So what?" he said. "Has the North Star stopped shining?"

Money as Water

KURT BROWN

"Cash Flow" "liquid assets" "pooling our resources" –
it's clear that money falls from heaven,
drops in pennies, nickels, dimes, to gather
in the small depressions of our hands.
It's clear how profit swells and streams of money
merge, how waves of money move
through nations, cause a "rippling effect"
and soon recede. How some people
drown, while others stay afloat and keep their heads
above the flood. How banks are "bailed out"
like wounded ships and panic follows,
bubbles burst, small investors find it hard
to breathe. It's clear how money
passes through our hands like water,
and our sources, once dried up, leave us
thirsting after more. How funds
diverted, often vanish, and those without a "safety net"
go "belly up." How all we have
goes down the drain, and we get soaked.

Sixty per Bird

SAMANTHA PEALE

Martha Zelenko made paintings of barns and farmhouses in Spain based on photographs she'd taken her junior year abroad. Each lonely little building made me shudder, as if she'd shown me her soul. I wasn't the only one who hated her for being so far ahead. When Martha turned her easel around, the whole class gasped.

"Mah mother used to wear a brown turtleneck sweater quite like this here color." Martha pointed to her canvas, the first one she showed us. You could hardly understand a word. Martha was from Virgilina, Virginia and her high squeaky voice was knotted and twisted by her rural accent.

"Mah parents died in a car accident last summer and I just can't stop thinking about that sweater," she said.

While our work was critiqued, Martha ate rusty looking stews out of a plastic thermos. She pushed her glasses up her nose with a dirty finger.

"In Virgilina, mah home, the townspeople leave their old glasses in a wooden box at the library, over by the book drop. Anyone can help herself." Martha picked up a pair each autumn. She chose the lenses closest to her prescription and wore them until her eyes adjusted.

"These belonged to the children's librarian." She touched the greasy frames. "The headaches only last a week or two."

We all stayed far away from her. We were eighteen, ruthless and self-conscious, afraid to be associated with anyone peculiar. Martha established that she was the best painter among us before the first week of freshman year was out. But she was an orphan, poor, ugly and awkward, with slimy hair and pilled acrylic sweaters. I doubt she made a single friend during the four years she studied in New York. After graduation she disappeared.

I was thirty-one when I moved to Los Angeles from Brooklyn. I'd been out of graduate school for two years and hadn't made much headway with my paintings or getting people to see my work. I'd become lazy and spent more time chasing boys and watching movies on my laptop than painting. I was bored and ready for things to be different.

A few artists I knew had come to California already and I'd heard the art world here was more open to outsiders, but it was still hard to get a foot in the door if you hadn't studied at CalArts or Art Center or UCLA.

I spent a week with a girl named Cassie who'd been a classmate but wasn't really a friend. She taught art at a private school in Pasadena and rented a big Craftsman house there.

"Remember Martha Zelenko?" Cassie said.

"I'll never forget her."

"She's in L.A. She applied for a tenure track job at UCLA and they wanted to hire her but she's just too fucking weird."

"Have you seen her?"

"Hell no. Martha's a creep."

Martha remembered me. She'd rented an apartment below an exterminator's office in a depressing little neighborhood overlooking an on ramp to the 101. She had four rooms – her studio, a big square kitchen, and a bathroom. The largest room was empty.

"Why'd you decide to live here, Martha?" The walls of the bathroom were stained with mold and the gray linoleum floors were chipped at the seams.

"It's cheap. In February I sold two paintings and a drawing at a gallery in Echo Park and I haven't worked since. I was waiting tables out at the airport. It was a nightmare for me. You can't imagine."

Martha wore new glasses but she still looked like a strange underground animal, with chalky skin and wet feverish eyes. A dozen years out of Virginia hadn't made her any easier to understand. Her paintings were more staggering than ever. She painted people now, bumpy sweaty animal people, with dark beady eyes that stared out at you in fear.

"What's happening in here?" I pointed to the big empty room.

"It's for rent. I can't find anyone to take it. No one wants to live with me." She took a bottle of Hawaiian Punch out of the fridge and poured two glasses.

I didn't have a place to live so for four hundred and forty dollars a month I rented Martha's best room. The neighborhood turned out to be a hub of gang activity. There was gunfire every other night. Martha didn't flinch. The exterminator and his wife were pleasant to us and moved the trash bins out of our yard to the side of the garage and took some rodent precautions on our behalf.

Martha had a picture in a group show in August, when any person with two nickels to rub together would be on vacation.

"It's better than nothing. I've got to keep going if I'm going to get any serious action. I'm not going to be one of the people who complains for ten years. I'll quit before then. Or shoot mahself," she said.

"That's what we all say," I said.

"We'll see what you say, Anne-Marie. You better get cracking. You haven't made a thing since you moved in."

I'd only been there two days.

Sunday afternoons Martha emerged from her studio to create the disgusting concoction she called Brunswick Stew. She stuffed chicken, tomatoes, corn, and beans in her crockpot and cranked it up until it turned into sludge a few hours later.

"Here's a big bowl for you," Martha said.

"Maybe this will help my painting," I said.

"In Virgilina we make it with squirrel."

I stifled a gag.

"We should have been roommates in college, Anne-Marie. College was a nightmare for me."

I sat on the porch or in our weird backyard – a puny cement slab, a few rose bushes and a half dead bamboo grove – and watched birds zoom back and forth between the mature trees in yards on either side of mine. Black Phoebes, mostly.

"Why aren't you working, Anne-Marie?" Martha waddled over and dropped to the ground in a heap.

"How do I start? I can't remember." I was still under the impression that I was the one who was being nice by living with Martha beneath the exterminator, making myself available for breezy conversation in the yard.

"Why don't you paint one of those stupid birds you watch all afternoon? Mah goodness, you can pass the time watching those little things fly."

Martha had no shortage of ideas, but unlike everyone else I'd ever met in my life, she didn't volunteer them. She waited to be solicited.

"Get up off your derriere and do some work. What are you waiting for?"

This wasn't rhetorical. Martha didn't have the gene for entropy.

"I'm waiting to be inspired by life in California." I thought this was a legitimate answer but a fiery look passed Martha's face and she practically hollered at me.

"Inspiration is bullshit, Anne-Marie." Martha couldn't be light and breezy either.

"You were born inspired, Martha. It's different for you."

"I was born poor and I saw mah parents get killed. That is different than being a debutante from the Main Line."

"I was not a debutante!"

She waddled back toward her studio. When she got to the hallway she made a sound, maybe an angry sound, a laugh, or a self-satisfied snort. I didn't recognize it at the time because I wasn't accustomed to be being openly disdained.

First, I drew Black Phoebes in a notebook, learning the shape of their little bodies.

"How's it going?" Martha ducked her head in my room.

I didn't look up. "You were right. Thanks, Martha."

Then I made a painting of the Black Phoebe that sat on a bough above our laundry line and caught flies. I sent the first bird painting to my mother for her birthday and she was delighted. She left two consecutive messages on my phone telling me how talented and generous I was and how she always believed in me and was so proud.

"Thanks for your nice messages, Mom." If she didn't hear from me within forty-eight hours after she called she started to worry and then her worry turned to anger. I had to be careful with her.

"I can't stop looking at it. I don't even like birds."

Three days later I got a thank you card from her with a snapshot of the Phoebe hung over her desk at home and a check for five hundred dollars.

"Would you make one for your Aunt Gillian?" she wrote.

I painted another Black Phoebe, this one perched on the neighbors' fence. I sent the picture to Aunt Gillian in Bryn Mawr and got a two-page handwritten letter and another check.

I started painting Black Phoebes on square canvases, small ones so the birds were life sized, or larger than life sized. Phoebes were only about five inches long. I could do two in a day if I started by eleven.

Within a month my room was lined with Phoebes. I began branching out into other birds as well. I sent photos of the paintings to galleries and I applied for every grant, residency, and fellowship Martha told me about but no one in a position of authority wanted anything to do with my birds.

"They're too pretty," Martha said. She'd had three promising studio visits since she made her mole-people and their dirt mounds darker and more barren.

"No, they're not." But I got a sick feeling in my gut and my throat went tight.

"They're songbirds. Songbirds are pretty. I don't know what you can do with them. How many have you done?" Martha said.

"Hundred twenty-five."

She shook her fat little head. I followed her advice and now she was telling me I'd made a mistake. There was no point protesting. Martha had a feeling for painting that our teachers had recognized, everyone felt it, and a keen awareness of how prettiness – physicality and materiality – factored into any situation. Unlike her paintings, Martha herself was a mess to look at. Living with her had afforded me an intimate view of the sad cycle of dandruff, nervous rashes, and plaid dresses that pulled across her soft stomach.

"What kind of bird is that?" Martha pointed to the canvases I'd done over the last week.

"Those are crows and ravens. Ravens are bigger, their caws are deeper, and their feathers creep down their beaks a bit. That one's an African Grey Parrot."

"Too pretty, Anne-Marie. If it matches the bedspread it's too damn pretty."

Martha picked up a picture of a Black Phoebe flapping over the laundry line, sallying forth to fly on a field of flat lavender grey.

"You can have one if you want it," I said.

She took the painting to her room and hung it over her bed. It looked great on the cold white wall.

We went out to the yard with bottles of beer and watched the sun go down.

"What's your plan?" Martha said.

"When I reach two hundred I'm going to find a way to present them. I don't know where though. Something will happen. My aunt loves hers. My mother calls her a bellwether."

"No disrespect to your family, but you have to change your game," Martha said. Then she played a stupid tune blowing across the lip of her beer bottle.

I couldn't stop painting the birds and I was too proud to ask Martha for a new idea. Also I needed to earn a living if I didn't want to end up back in Philadelphia or word processing in a law office with a bunch of men who played fantasy football and talked about the sporting events they TiVo'd.

The only place in Los Angeles that ever got crowded was the Hollywood Farmers Market on Sundays. I submitted an application for a vendor's permit. I would pay the market five percent of the gross and a twenty-dollar stall fee.

I couldn't wait to have a small success with my art, too. I wanted Martha to be happy for me. It's embarrassing to think of that now.

I set up my wares on Selma, by the children's clothes, scented candles, Mexican jewelry and bags, kettle corn, hand woven rugs, and cheap summer dresses. I'd invested in wooden shelves and painted them a pale silvery gray and arranged a clever display of the Phoebes with a shade structure covering the whole thing so I wouldn't cook my brain for five hours. I sold twenty-three paintings that first Sunday.

"Anne Marie, you can't sell your paintings in an outdoor market and then get a gallery," Martha said. "You'll ruin your chances at a real career."

"I charge sixty per bird."

"Stop it. Anne-Marie. You didn't go to art school and graduate school to sell your paintings to farmers."

"What's wrong with farmers?" I expected Martha to appreciate my ingenuity, not strive to perpetuate an elitist gallery system.

"Where do I start? The tobacco farmers I grew up around were ignorant, malicious, and violent. Mah father and his two mean brothers and his mean brothers-in-law. They all hated me and tried to tamp me down. I would not let them shut me down, Anne-Marie." She exhaled dramatically.

I didn't know what to say but Martha changed the subject.

She said wanted to live near the water one day.

"There's no water in Halifax County," she said.

I've always loved looking at pictures of artists' rooms. Most photographs and paintings of studios show the space without the artist and you get the sense, in her absence, that it's possible to discover the details, the secrets that set her apart from everyone else.

Once I went into Martha's room when she was at the supermarket. As usual, the door was open. I had a burning curiosity to find something concrete that was unique to her, a detail that would reveal the source of her artistic excellence and single-mindedness. I didn't think it was wrong, or that she'd especially mind if she found me there, though in truth, we only spent time together in the kitchen or the yard.

Martha's twin bed was covered with a pine-green chenille spread. Beside the bed was a pink and orange striped rug with fringe at both ends. The rest of the gray linoleum floor was bare; a few books were stacked in the corner haphazardly. The dresser was missing most of its knobs. A metal office desk and chair she'd found on the street occupied the corner, beneath the window. She had two easels, one she'd brought from Virgilina and one she built herself. Both were empty. She'd painted the long wall white and that's where she hung the canvases she was working on.

Martha's aesthetic interest didn't extend to her room. Her studio didn't have any charm or beautiful curiosities or arrangements. Perhaps the pine spread or the way she lined up her slippers and clogs against the wall beside the door might one day appear special in a photograph. I got my camera from my room and took a few random pictures of the unfinished paintings, the desk, the bed, her shoes. Nothing in the room spoke to me. Martha's genius went straight from her brain to the canvas via her hands and it hurt to know that her psyche was simply worth more than mine.

My mother sent me a card with a snapshot of Aunt Gillian and her Black Phoebe hanging over the chair where she reads and knits. "Would you paint one for Uncle Martin? You know he fancies himself quite the ornithologist!"

Martha got a solo show at a gallery in Culver City. She painted around the clock. The door to her room was always open, the light blazing, Martha stood with her right hand on her hip, her dark eyes boring into those canvases.

Everyone from our graduating class who'd moved to Los Angeles and hadn't quit painting yet came to the opening. All three of them. The Ossendorf twins brought their bored boyfriends. They all taught adjunct drawing classes or worked in film production. They stood apart from the crowd and didn't say much to Martha, just a quick congratulations after they'd looked at her paintings. Her work had gotten bigger and more detailed, more abstract, and darker. I wondered if anyone remembered Martha's mother's turtleneck sweater.

I was the only one who went to the dinner afterwards. Martha introduced me to the gallery owner, a scrawny little guy named Malinowski.

"This is Anne-Marie, mah roommate." She didn't say we went to college together or that I was an artist too. It was an indictment.

I sat between Malinowski's wife and a journalist and we talked about the food. I couldn't believe how much I had to say about artichokes, it mortifies me to remember. We all toasted Martha.

The show hung for a quiet month. Then there was a review in the newspaper and another in a British art magazine with reproductions. Then everything sold – nine paintings and six drawings on paper.

I'd seen her prices. At 40% – the gallery took 60% – she made at least $35,000.

I'd have to sell six hundred birds. This year I sold 387, averaging almost seven per week.

"I deserve every penny," Martha said. "Getting this far has been a nightmare. You have no idea." She closed the door to her room. There was no Brunswick Stew that week. Or the week after. Martha was out looking for a new place to live.

"I need my own space," she said.

In another two weeks she was gone. To keep the lease, I had to start selling Phoebes at the South Pasadena farmers market on Thursday nights.

I don't know where Martha lives now, or if she's even in Los Angeles any more. I assume she's by water. She shows her paintings in San Francisco and New York and London.

I'm still painting birds in the apartment by the 101. They still sell at a regular clip. I've added hawks and quail to my repertoire, raised my prices fifteen dollars, and there are different sizes, too. Martha's room is available but I haven't found anyone suitable. It should be a painter but I don't really know anyone who paints. Cassie still teaches the brats in Pasadena how to make brown from red, blue, and yellow. The others have been swallowed up in prop houses and design firms. My family is proud of me and they tell everyone how I accomplish the impossible, and actually make a living as an artist.

Compared to Martha Zelenko, of course, I put square pegs in square holes – for a pittance. Whereas she's turned her nightmares into fame and wealth. How strange to think of Martha as rich. She was lucky to have had a miserable background because it gave her drive and material. But I don't want people to be repulsed by me while I clutch an old brown sweater. It wouldn't be worth it. I don't have nightmares, nor do I want any. I do regret giving her a Black Phoebe painting for free. I should have held out for a trade.

The Economist's Daughter

dawn lonsinger

Wherever she goes, trees follow, flash their blank
greenback hands in deaf applause, nervous

excitement, as if to flag her down or surrender,
as if to imply a state of emergency, carve up the wealth

of light, but she walks through the forest
that clumps around her like it's the biggest nothing

to note. Despite this ticker-tape parading,
she skips to the slow messy churning

of her own heart. She shies away from addition
but gathers lilacs in her skirt, arcs her back into

a bridge to broaden her own custody. She seems
confident that her interest will not falter.

She tells her father that in her dream there was enough
water for everyone to go swimming, but

he only hears a faint fraction. He's too busy
listening to registers humming, money heaping

like bees to the hive. Her dreams may be instrumental
since he's always on the lookout for an apt metaphor –

"The economy is a small girl in the blight of morning;
it's an ocean, the tossing about of slippery schools

of glittery fish; it's butter-smeared, whipped, melting.
The economy is bubble, crater, rocket, a green shoot."

She has gone outside again, into the glut of spindly things,
amid the dim cloying microbes poised over the dumb yard.

He's trying to coin just the right phrase, to say succinctly
what we are about to lose. He's pacing, thinking things

can't get more fraught, but when he looks out the window
he sees all the leaves suddenly drop down around her

softly like play money. It is the most beautiful schism,
a plunder he can not name. He can see in her eyes –

all spark and slalom – that she is not easily enumerated.
She is a bright light in a landscape of numbers;

when she smiles the zeroes flower into lust.

A Consistent Property

REGINA DERIEVA
TRANSLATED FROM RUSSIAN BY J. KATES

Rising prices do not increase the value
of conscious existence, no.
Paying debts and lamenting
expenses, we can not buy even
a single smidgen of consciousness
to augment what we already have, no.
We are awarded only what
there is, and don't you expect anything more . . .
Really now?
The consciousness we have been issued
so quickly passes, melts away,
evaporates, until nothing
at all remains, no.
Consciousness is the constant
denial of the denial of life,
its final page.

Old Soup

DREW DEGENNARO

On Sunday
Christians
tried to
recruit me
outside
Hopewell
Mall

they were
collecting
pennies
for the
poor by
banging
on old
soup cans
blocking
the doors

I gave
the girl
a dollar
asking
for change

claiming
it was
my last

she gave
me seven
dimes,
one quarter
and four
pennies
back

and I made
my way
into the
99c store.

Old Money

TERESE SVOBODA

The sisters are old money, so old the eagles and Indians have worn off the currency, threadbare money where mother and father left only the dregs at an early age, money embroidered with worthless graces learned from retainers unrelated, as only old money can provide, but retainers that, unlike legal fees, vanish if unpaid. But the sisters are now of an age that doesn't need retaining, they are of an age that requires new money, or, as it is known in old money circles, marriage.

Together the sisters sit beside the window on an old wrought iron chaise – old money moved inside – looking at their feet. Maybe the sun will melt the sky's gel and great gobs of blue will slide to earth in big valuable quantities says Alice, and that's what it appears they are waiting for, looking at those feet and not around, not at the sky or at anything actually money-making.

Old money is always unearned, the earning having been tossed out with the ugly trash things No Money buys to keep, the earning of it left forgotten in a drawer somewhere. This is how Louise replies. With old money so used to being unearned, Alice is not really asking for any, she is just making her need known in this blue-before-sunset reverie of gel and wrought iron, the iron rusting its red flakes if she moves, but she doesn't. Louise, the purse-pinching eldest with an unfashionable wild-haired chignon, moves to press the door closed where the plumbing is dropping parts with every odd flush or hint of stopped sink, she moves the door carefully, it lacks a hinge. Then she searches a cupboard empty even of sweet Chinese sauce in plastic packets they have both become so fond of to find the discarded Sunday paper Alice has brought to twist into logs. She makes no reply to what Alice has asked for under that blue gel sky but the way Alice has begun to tie those papers into logs suggests she is tying up money to burn.

Louise's reflection.

Alice ties up the newspaper logs section by section. When Louise tries to help, she gets stuck on the football scores, holds onto them with her fingertips spread, as if those armored men were about to run up her arm and not just blacken them. Last week they acquiesced that a football hero would help, that that's who could really help them, having no luck at all with the financial page, and less with the arts section, and none in the least with the social. But Louise tosses it down anyway. He has a bicep? she says, showing her own.

Just light the logs, says Alice.

Louise is actually about to light the logs, the whole kit and caboodle, her match set on the cover, the cover closed, when a squirrel runs down the flue.

Louise claps her cold newsprinted hands to her face.

Rabid, mostly likely, says Alice.

They both jump to the couch when the squirrel takes such quick steps toward them.

You have to clean the chimney now and then, says Alice.

That's expensive, says Louise. Look at the size of its tail.

The squirrel brandishes it as if it could push them off the couch. Then two more squirrels fall down, tiny ones, enough infant that one does not get up.

You have been feeding them, says Alice, recoiling.

They're just squirrels, says Louise, leaning over the couch to poke at the downed squirrel infant with a roll of newspaper. Two other squirrels, a mother and daughter says Alice – not two sisters – climb the wrought iron chaise making noises with their mouths as if they have eaten through the bricks of the chimney.

The two women flee the couch for the kitchen but not for long. Wallpaper shredding, a long bad sound, draws them back in. Oh, my god, shrieks Alice. The squirrels are climbing the walls, planting their claws into the wallpaper and racing for the corners. Louise darts past them and wrenches the front door open with a screwdriver they keep on a nearby chair. The squirrels run through the door, holding their tails in that held-comma way that squirrels have, they run into a street of dark parked car crevvies and up some poles.

Louise points at the left-behind infant corpse. Look at that.

Alice covers it with her log. We'll make a pyre and scare them off with the stench of it.

You always were a savage, says Louise, and Alice smiles demurely. We won't eat it, she says as if she would if Louise left the room.

Louise maneuvers the squirrel into the garbage.

Soon the newspaper fire blazes up in its short life, and Alice turns her hands in front of it. Women throw themselves on pyres, she says in the trance of heat.

I wouldn't give twenty cents for a man. I mean it, says Louise.

Twenty cents and interest, I wish, says Alice. No men are ever going to marry us. You might as well make a wish.

Louise purses her lips as if a wish could be whistled. If I wish, won't I get something like having a sausage grow on my nose instead?

A remark like that is the reason nobody will ever marry us. Alice pushes past her, closer to the fire.

If we had money they would. Even with our interesting minds. Louise touches her hopeless hair.

The fire complicates itself and in its flare all the squirrel prints show, soot scribbles on the floor in front of the fireplace.

At least you have the house, says Alice. All I have is a miserable studio.

We need to get the black off the floor, says Louise, and she pulls off her ring and leaves it on the mantel. Sweeping is easy, she says when she returns with the broom, you just keep pushing it toward the dustpan – and she leaves again to empty it in disgust when Alice won't even try.

While she is out the second time, Alice pockets the ring.

They burn the rest of the newspaper while they talk about the desperation of the squirrels and the condition of the chimney, while they singe single slices of pale bread skewered onto forks to nibble butterless, better for their figures, and who has butter? Alice promises to call if she needs anything – it is something they say, while she lets the out-of-plumb door bang behind her. Oh, excuse me, she whispers to Louise at the window, making a face.

Alice wears the ring to bed that night and when her sister calls the next morning, she tells her the squirrels must have taken it, that's what squirrels like that do, if they are muddled enough to come down a chimney. But she can't bring herself to sell the ring or even to pawn it. She wears it turned around on her finger so the glitter doesn't show on her next visit, and she boasts to her sister she's engaged.

Congratulations, says Louise, tucking up her loose chignon-neck hairs. She asks nothing about the suitor, nothing, nothing, nothing she is so jealous.

Alice volunteers nothing. They toast their unbuttered toast several successive weekends in a silence seemingly related to their last bad bet on tech until a soccer ball crashes through the window, followed closely by a Realtor who is tall and bald but very admiring of the lines of the living room.

The house is sold soon after Louise marries him. The Realtor gets his commission then of course half the proceeds and they buy something smaller. It is only at Louise's daughter's christening, the lace on the long old money gown against Alice's arm catching on the diamond side of the ring that Louise notices. Louise has been complaining about all the junk mail she gets now that she owns a new house, about the toxic new cupboard smell, its big pretend fireplace that Alice just has to come see whenever her beau isn't too busy.

Louise says Oh, at the ring caught in the lace, and then in the same rushed voice that she's had since the Realtor arrived, That's okay, it wasn't really mine anyway. I took it out of a box of cufflinks I found in the attic.

Alice holds the ring up to the watery light of the baptistery. You never told me about it, she says.

You never saw our mother wear it, did you?

Oh, Louise, Alice says. She hands the baby to the Realtor who is talking at some blond woman with a saltbox to sell instead of at the baby, and takes both Louise's hands in hers as if she is older and wiser. Oh, Louise, she says again. It wasn't so bad before, was it?

Louise touches the tip of the jewel lightly, as if it will burst into flame.

The Price of a View

CASTLE FREEMAN, JR.

Years ago, when our young family was searching for a place to settle in southern Vermont, we heard of a house for sale on Newfane Hill, in the West River Valley. We were shopping on a pretty tight budget, and had been in the market for some months. We'd looked over a lot of properties. One summer morning, I visited this latest place with Dottie, a Realtor from Brattleboro.

It was a likely spot, I found. In fact, *likely* didn't say it. The house itself needed work, but the setting needed nothing: on the eastern slope of the high hill, with little meadows all around enclosed by stone walls and shady woods. It looked like a place that would do for us; more than that, it looked, in the mysterious way of these things, like the right place, the destined place, the only place. (Every inexperienced buyer of rural real estate will know what I mean.)

Casually, I inquired about the asking price. Equally casually, my new friend Dottie quoted me a figure that puzzled me. The number of dollars she named seemed to me to be calculated to buy four or five houses. I only wanted one. Had Dottie not understood? I put it to her.

"Price seem a little high?" Dottie replied.

"More than a little," I said.

"Well," she said. "But, look at what you've got . . . "

She pointed to the east. I followed her extended arm and saw, far away on the horizon, a vast blue pyramid rising above the intervening hills.

"You've got the view," said Dottie.

I'm afraid I looked blank. I was a newcomer to Vermont, to New England generally.

"That's Mount Monadnock," Dottie explained. Together we silently contemplated the far-off eminence, I reflecting on its power to add value, Dottie (no doubt) figuring her commission. The next day, we bought the place, lock, stock, barrel – and Mount Monadnock.

It is one of the oddities of Vermont that, for those in its lower right-hand corner, the best-loved piece of the landscape isn't Vermont's at all. Mount Monadnock dwells in New Hampshire, about 50 miles east of my dooryard. Over there, they're proud of their mountain. Of course, they are. For its New Hampshire owners, Mount Monadnock is the emblem of their region, the geographical focal point of the whole southern quarter of the state. It's also a tourist destination and a recreational resource. Monadnock, its promoters tell us, is, after Mount Fuji, the most visited, most hiked-over mountain in the world.

For Vermont, the mountain's value is comparable, but harder to define. Its value is purely emotional. Mount Monadnock is in our neighbor's domain, but it's in our heart.

Monadnock is a hard-rock cone with wooded flanks and a bald summit. At 3165 feet, it's by no means the tallest mountain in these parts; at least three nearby Vermont peaks – Stratton and Glastenbury mountains and Mount Snow – are considerably higher. Monadnock, however, is a solitary mountain, sitting quite by itself on the surrounding plain. In its isolation, it draws and holds the eye from a distance as the higher mountains do not. They are grand. Monadnock is something better than grand: it's singular.

It's also, somehow, benign. Over here, that lonely mountain floating on the visible world's farthest edge becomes a calm, reassuring presence. It rests and restores the eye. As constant, as permanent, as it is, however, it's also full of pleasing variation. On a clear fall morning, the mountain is a deep royal blue in color; in a summer haze, it's pale gray, and on a white day in February, it's almost no color at all, a distant glittering palace of ice. In any season, it's a welcome part of the landscape, inspiring not awe, not transcendence, but affection.

From our hillside, we saw the upper two-thirds of Mount Monadnock. Indifferent to that view as I had been, I soon learned to appreciate it. Mount Monadnock was nearly the only thing about our new home that didn't require large infusions of either labor or cash. The house, a Cape Cod-style farmhouse approaching its 200th birthday, was in a condition, not critical but, say, akin to walking wounded. For a couple of years before our arrival, we were told, it had stood empty. We discovered that that was not at all the case. The house had indeed been lived in – by mice, snakes, wasps, bats, squirrels, and also by a larger furbearer that might have been a porcupine, might have been a raccoon.

We swept and scrubbed and painted, and, later and for years to come, we repaired, re-sided, re-silled, reglazed, replastered. We confronted the dilemmas, the painful enigmas of home improvement. Do you do it yourself, or do you do it right? How come the biggest, most expensive jobs are invariably the ones whose results are the least visible, the least to be enjoyed? How in the world did the builders of the early Federal period manage to produce houses with no right angles in them at all? We shimmed up, shored up, fixed up. We lived and we learned – and always with Mount Monadnock presiding from afar over our education.

Time has passed, and after unremitting effort and appalling expense, we have brought matters on this place to a curious pass. We have about stood our little world on its head. The house, which was a ruin, is today quite habitable. The view of Monadnock, however, which was so splendid, is, finally, no more.

It couldn't have been otherwise. The great Robert Frost, who, in his lifetime, made a fair bid to be the Mount Monadnock of American letters, wrote a famous poem that begins "Something there is that doesn't love a wall." He might have written, "Something there is that doesn't love a view." Frost is referring to the way the Vermont soil shifts in its seasonal freezes and thaws, dismantling the region's familiar stone fences. The force opposed to the integrity of our view to the east was equally inexorable: the upgrowth of forest trees.

For some years I labored to protect our glimpse of Mount Monadnock. As long as doing that was a business of pruning, chopping, and clearing roadside trees and brush, the job was easy enough. In late years, however, it has grown difficult and at last impossible as more distant woods have put on mature growth that blocks the view, not near at hand, but from increasingly far away.

Today, to get a look at Mount Monadnock from our place, you have to climb the hill behind the house to the edge of the woods, or you have to get up on the roof of the woodshed. Fortunately for me, I regularly find reasons to do both. The mountain is still there, in its distant azure realm, and though it's no longer available around a corner of the house or through a window, it still affords unfailing refreshment and repose to the onlooker. Whatever that view had cost was worth every dollar. Or, at least it was to me.

What *had* it cost?

Once I asked Dottie, the realtor, that question. What did a view of Monadnock really add to the price of one of her properties? She smiled.

"It depends," she said.

"Depends on what?"

"The buyer," said Dottie. "Is he a grownup? Is he practical? Add one percent, two percent. Is he . . . the opposite? Add five percent."

"How much did you add for me?" I asked.

"Seven percent," said Dottie.

Plunder

JANE DELURY

During the day, Clémence takes a walk along the beach, empties her husband's bedpan, holds his feather of a hand. At night, lying next to him, in what was once his study and is now a sickroom, she dreams about the manor. She has spoken of it before, first to Herman when they met long ago near the base where he was stationed. Later, to their friends in America when she moved with him here. It was part of her story, mixed in with the good things that she missed about France – fresh baguettes, walkable distances, the attention to detail she found lacking in this culture of speed and disposability. Now, in her sixties, what she misses has become an impression, but the contours of the manor stay sharp.

She barely knew the Jews, as the couple was called. Just before the start of the war, they had bought the manor deep in the forest and only came into the village to do their shopping. Unlike the cartoon Jew on the poster by the town hall, who had rat teeth and a truffle of a nose, their faces were thin and careful. The woman wore white gloves and real stockings when most women just drew on the seams. Her husband carried a leather satchel and used a cane, though he didn't look older than anyone's father. The children whispered about them as they passed by the school courtyard on their way to the bakery or butcher's. One boy had heard from his mother that the woman had a diamond as big as a chestnut. Another said that the man owned all the banks in Tours. Every night, they ate goose liver for dinner. She bathed in champagne. "Theirs is the finest house in France," Clémence said. "My father says so, and he's been to Paris."

She saw the woman up close once, while playing ball in front of her father's garage. The couple had come to pick up their car, which was long and sleek as an eel, speckled with rust on the doors. The ball rolled away, under a truck parked on the road, and the woman, waiting outside for her husband, fetched it for Clémence, who couldn't reach far enough. Clémence pushed herself out from under the truck and saw a soft chin and two gloved hands. "Let me help you," the woman said. She draped her gloves over the side view mirror of the truck, then crawled under the carriage. Later, when she and her husband disappeared – this was how Clémence's father put it when she asked – Clémence was unable to conjure up the woman's expression as she reemerged with the ball, but she could still see the ladder running down her leg from a hole in the knee of her stocking.

    The children trade off calling each morning at eight. Today, it is their daughter. "How are the little ones?" Clémence asks in French before her daughter can say, "How is Papa?" When she first explained the experimental treatment she had found for Herman, the children too felt hopeful. But then they consulted their own sources. "Papa wants to do this," she argued when they brought up their doubts. "It's our job to help him." He might make it to the birth of a grandson expected in June. He might be sitting at their daughter's graduation. "It isn't your decision to make," she said finally.

    The receiver tucked against her chin, she draws back the curtains of the study. The baby, her daughter tells her, has finally cut his first tooth. She cracks open the window, then mouths her daughter's name to Herman, who has woken up. "He's ready for you," she says into the phone, but what she means is that her daughter is ready for Herman. Clémence is the opening act that warms the hitch out of the children's voices, moves them away from cell counts and scans.

    Herman picks up the conversation where Clémence left it hanging: their son-in-law is trying to build a shed and their daughter thinks it looks like a shanty. Clémence can hear him laughing as she goes down the hall to fix his breakfast. She stands at the stove and waits for the kettle to boil. Outside, the sky and the ocean are two tones of gray. An egret stalks the shore, shooting its beak into the thin water, coming up with nothing. This landscape is still unfamiliar, though she and Herman retired to the island three years before. She has thought during her more irrational moments that if they had never left Boston, he would be all right.

She stops the kettle before it whistles, then spoons loose tea into a pot. Herman can't stomach much more than tea and toast. The egret, she sees, has snagged something dark and flapping, not a fish, perhaps a piece of rubber, a strip of tire or carpet. She learned quickly that the pristine surface of the ocean is a delusion. Herman would walk the shore each morning, gathering the stray wrappers and plastic bags delivered by the tide. She has kept up this ritual for him, as if preserving the beach for the day that he will leave for the sand at dawn, returning with his bag of trash, the name of a new migrating bird, the intact shell of a horseshoe crab to save for the grandchildren. This morning, though, she barely found anything, only seaweed and driftwood, innocent waste. She does not understand why some mornings the beach looks as it should.

"Did she tell you about the tooth coming in?" she asks when she brings Herman his tray.

"What a relief." He tries to raise his arms dramatically but manages only to get them just over the sheets.

She helps him sit up. In these moments, he reminds her of the Raggedy Andy that they gave their son one Christmas, a long, unmanageable doll whose limbs were forever flopping over the back of the couch.

"We have to get you ready," she says. "Your treatment's at noon."

She watches his face as she moves his legs to the edge of the bed. "OK?" she asks.

He nods, but his teeth are set so tight that his jaw bulges. When they first made love, forty years earlier, he kept asking her if she was all right until she put her hand over his mouth. He was so worried about hurting her, and now she hurts him over and over again.

She brought Herman home a few weeks after their first date. Already, she knew that she was falling in love with him, or perhaps only the idea of him, this quiet American with the easy humor and nice teeth. They had met near her university in Châteauroux, at a café where the girls went to find soldiers, though she told herself that she was going there to practice her English. For months, she sat at a corner table in her best dress, reading *Moby-Dick*, but none of the soldiers seemed to notice. She was not beautiful like her mother, who had been courted by every boy in the village. She took after her father, whose people had come from Toulouse; her skin was thick and quick to darken and her eyes, her father said, were sailor brown, tough enough to stand up to the salt and sun.

She had an idea of the soldier who would approach her: he would be tall and lanky, as all the Americans seemed to be. He would offer her a cigarette, which she would decline, and then, looking down at her book, he would say something interesting about Melville. She did not fully understand the book in her hands, but a man who had read it, who was drawn to her because of it, would be someone with whom she could talk of other things that she did not yet know. Instead, she met Herman, who stood only a head above her and was, though only twenty-five, balding on his crown. He did not even notice her book. After apologizing in surprisingly good French for bumping into her table, he said, "It's better with ice" and pointed to her Coke.

The one nagging doubt that Clémence had about Herman was that he was too kind and therefore too simple. He let her talk longer than she thought he should. He didn't pressure her to make love as she had heard the other soldiers did. When he could get off the base, he took her to the patisserie in the village and ordered enough cakes for four people. His grandmother had been from Marseilles – she had taught him her language – and he seemed to ascribe to the French a goodness that made Clémence nervous. She had told him about her father's death when she was twelve, about how happy she was to have escaped her village and life with her mother. She tried not to make herself sound perfect. But over the plates smeared with chocolate and cream, Herman listened to her with an alarming interest and sympathy. At any moment, he might wake from this spell she had unwittingly cast and see her for who she was.

That day at lunch, her mother became tipsy with the aperitif, and by the fish course was giggling and asking Herman whether in the United States people really drank champagne out of shoes. As she chattered on, Herman answered her questions with good humor, pretending not to notice that she was flirting with him and looking over at Clémence for translations when he was lost. Her mother had used the good silver and covered the table with the cloth she'd trimmed out of her wedding dress, a fact that she reported to Herman when she brought out the meat. "Of course, it looked better on me than it does on the table," she said, and then she told him her parents had ordered the silk all the way from Italy. "They didn't have much," she said. "But they wanted me at my best on the altar." She reached over and tucked a tendril of hair behind Clémence's ear, a gesture she had never used. Clémence had known when her mother opened the door, wobbling in heels, what this lunch would be like. She wanted Herman to see where she was from – it seemed the honest thing to do, but now panic rose into her throat.

"Isn't my Clémence pretty?" her mother said, smiling at Herman as if giving him a challenge.

"No," he said. "I think she's beautiful."

It was the defiance on Herman's face when he smiled back at her mother that convinced Clémence to show him the manor.

"I warned you," she said as, after the coffee, they headed into the forest. "She can't hold her wine."

"She seems lonely," Herman said. "She must miss your father."

"She was lonely when he was alive."

Her mother, she explained as simply as she could, felt that she had married below her. She never said so exactly, but she made it known by small acts, like making the tablecloth, by never inviting anyone to dinner or coffee because, she said, their plates didn't match and their furniture was shabby. "When he had the garage, Papa would scrub his hands before dinner with a potato brush to get the grease off. She kept slipcovers on the arms of his chair. I wouldn't be surprised if she never let him touch her."

They had left the thin trees at the edge of the forest. The path now skirted the stone walls of the manor. A few minutes later, they came to the iron gate with the rusty lock that her father had broken open with his pocket knife.

"I want to show you something," she said as she turned the handle.

"I thought so," Herman said. "This didn't feel like a stroll."

Beyond the gate, the grass was so tall that it would have come to her waist when she was a child, though now it only came to her knees. They walked the path to the back of the manor, passing a fountain clogged with moss and beds of nettles studded with roses. The facade rose above them, and they quit the grass for the flagstones of the courtyard.

"Everyone called it the manor," Clémence said, "but it's more like a castle." She pointed at a balcony. "Those are gargoyles. You can't really tell for the vines." Ivy had swallowed all three stories, tentacles fluttering off the gutters and downspouts. The shutters, which still hung strong on her last visit, tipped from their hinges, and the chimney had collapsed. "When my father and I first came here, it had been vacant for years. We would go to the woods to check the rabbit traps and end up in this courtyard." She pointed to a stone bench. "We sat there and ate our lunch. My feet didn't reach the ground."

She told him that they never went to the front of the manor. She didn't know why, perhaps because her father was afraid of being seen. The manor was for sale and there must have been people who came by, since it was sold eventually. "And we could never look inside because it had been shuttered."

She took him around to the side, where the windows were not boarded. She wiped the grime from a pane with her sleeve.

"What happened?" Herman asked, after putting his face to the glass.

"The people who bought it. They were Jewish. They must have thought they'd be safe here, in the middle of nowhere. But they were taken away."

"The Germans did this?"

"No," she said. "Some men from the village. They thought there was money hidden inside."

Herman looked again through the window. "They massacred it," he said.

"My father was one of them. My mother won't admit it, but I know he was."

She felt her eyes fill. It made her feel silly. Herman had turned from the window and was watching her the way he did sometimes – head cocked to the side, the suggestion of a smile on his face but serious eyes. "My father," he said in English, "kept a mistress I met at my mother's funeral. Not quite a draw but close."

He leaned in and kissed her, on the cheeks as they had done that morning, then slower on the mouth. "You're a serious girl, aren't you?" he said. And something about not quite understanding what he had said and the way he had tilted her chin back as the American men did in the movies made her laugh despite this being a place that she considered as hallowed and haunted as a cemetery.

Sometimes, she cannot bear the sight of Herman's face and now, helping him sit up, is one of those times. The night before, as she dipped the tines of a fork into a jar of mustard while making herself a salad, she thought, this is the color of Herman's skin.

He has regained his breath, and she hands him the cup of tea that has been cooling on the desk he never could keep clean. Now it is blank and glossy as a sheet of ice. He takes a small sip. He smiles and she recognizes him again.

"Do you remember worrying about them not getting teeth?" he asks. She shakes her head. She has become good at conversations that move around shoals.

"Only about them not speaking French, though that's all they do now." When they moved to Massachusetts, Clémence spoke English with Herman, because she wanted to become fluent. But with the birth of their first child, Herman suggested they speak French at home. He was right. English nursery rhymes felt false in her mouth. Herman encouraged all of it: the Cake of the Kings in the oven during January, the trips they took when they could afford it to Paris and Brittany. She never went back to her own village, though. She had, as her mother accused her only once and softly, turned her back on that place.

Herman smiles. "They're being nice to you. You have me to thank."

He lifts the cup to his mouth. She always loved the veins of his hands, thick blue snakes darting up the backs of his arms. Now they are ruined, powerless things. In a few hours, she will again watch a nurse go fishing, continuing the regime that the doctor says is working better, meaning not as poorly as the last. They had a few blissful weeks after the initial round of treatment, before his first scan. Then there it was: Herman's liver, glowing on the wall, and the oncologist's pointer circling the bright constellations.

"We got most of it," he said. "But it only takes one rogue cell."

"Cut it out then," she said.

"Clémence," Herman said. "He can't take out everything." She saw on his face something she had never seen before. He did not seem despondent or discouraged. He was looking at the X-ray as one might gaze out a window at a view.

On the way home, in the car, she turned to him. "Do you remember," she said. "What you used to call liver when I served it?" He didn't, so she told him. He could never get the gender of the article right. The masculine form of the word meant liver. The feminine form meant faith. "Do it for me if you have to," she said.

Not long after the Liberation, the furniture started to appear in the village. A grandfather clock in the neighbor's kitchen. An embroidered divan at the hairdresser's. A green silk chair that stayed a few weeks in the sitting room of Clémence's house, a delight of a chair to sneak into when her mother was upstairs having her nap. The garage had long shut down with the petrol shortages and vehicle confiscations, and Clémence's father spent most of his time at the café with the other unemployed men or doing odd jobs. When she heard her mother's door close, Clémence would hike up her school jumper, the better to feel the cool silk on her legs. She knew that the chair would not be in the room long – her father had explained that he bought it for a price and planned to sell it – but sitting there, even for a few minutes, made her feel hopeful. Her father would find work again and start coming home for dinner, rather than arriving late and covered in dust from the construction job he had found. He would lose that rough cough. When she asked if they could go to the forest, he would say that he was too tired and that anyway, all of the rabbits were gone.

It was years later that Clémence connected what happened to the manor with the chair and the other fine objects scattered around the village. "It was done innocently," her mother said when she asked. She had brought her mother to Boston so she could meet her grandchildren. Her mother moved around the house as if she were afraid of marking the floors with the soles of her slippers. She was kind to the children, but Clémence knew that she wanted nothing more than to get back on the boat and return home.

"What's innocent about plunder?" Clémence burst out. They were at breakfast, Herman doing his tie, Clémence spooning food into the mouth of the baby. Her mother was drinking coffee out of a cereal bowl, rather than a mug, and perhaps it was this further proof of her inadaptability, or the set to her wrinkled cheeks, that made Clémence bring up the furniture in the first place. She scraped cereal from the baby's chin and said, more calmly, that nothing was innocent about what happened to the couple. "I don't blame you, in particular," she added.

She felt she had been conciliatory by saying that she did not blame her mother, though they both knew she did. She wanted what she had wanted since she first saw the inside of the manor: for her mother to admit what her father had done. But her mother shook her head. She turned to Herman. Her voice steady and measured, she told him what it was like during the war, how they fueled the fire with horse patties, how breakfast was an egg to split in three and dinner boiled potatoes. Her husband lost the garage that he had sweated for all his life.

"We did what we could," she said. "We weren't young, and there was Clémence to look out for."

"I don't deny that it was hard," Clémence said.

She put the spoon to the baby's mouth. She thought that the conversation would end there, but her mother spoke up again. "The manor," she said. "She won't let it go. She acts as if a murder was committed." She wiped a drop of coffee from the side of the bowl with her napkin. "There were rumored to be thousands of francs hidden in the walls of that house. Why wouldn't people go looking? And she's wrong about my husband. He had nothing to do with it."

Clémence's heart lurched. For a moment, remembering the war, she had felt a thawing, but now she clinked down the spoon. "Of course there was a murder," she said. "It just happened off stage."

"She's an old woman," Herman said that night as they lay in bed. "Can't you let this rest?"

"I'm only asking her to tell me."

"What does it matter? Your father is gone."

She knew he did not mean to be cruel, but it felt as if he had slapped her. She turned to the wall. "You don't understand," she said. "How can I forgive him if I don't know?"

"Forgive him for what?"

"We used to call it our palace. I wanted them gone."

On the way home from the hospital, Herman asks her to stop at the diner in town. "Let's have breakfast," he says, though it's five o'clock. Clémence holds his elbow and pushes open the door. The woman at the counter comes around and takes Herman's other elbow. He jokes with her. The pancakes, he says, are worth getting out of a sick bed. She is thick and high-haired, one of the locals that Herman has won over during their time on the island. She says that he's looking good, though Clémence noticed the strain on her face when they walked through the door. More and more, when she is out with Herman, it seems that everyone is wearing a happiness mask.

"What can I get you, sweetie?" Herman asks once the waitress has left. The menu flutters in his hands. It is a joke between them, the sweeties and hons of their new home.

"Everything," she says. She wants to come around the booth and put her head on his shoulder as she used to do. But now it is her shoulder and his head.

When the woman returns, Herman orders pancakes with a side of bacon. Clémence almost says something, but holds back. Later, on the road home, she pulls over when he asks. She stands next to him as he throws up the barely anything he ate. In front of them, the embankment drops into rocks, then into the water. The ocean is swallowing the sun.

"Do you think it'll be bad for the fish?" Herman asks. He doesn't make those sour jokes much anymore. He wipes his mouth with the napkin she found in the glove compartment, a cocktail napkin from their old life in Boston. She tells him they should go – it's getting dark

– but he doesn't move.

"I'm tired," he says. He folds the napkin into his pocket.

She takes his arm. "Let's get you home."

"No," he says. "I mean I'm tired."

* * *

When she first started to hear about what had happened to the manor, not long after her father's death, she decided to go see for herself. The back door was padlocked, and there was a trespassing notice signed by the mayor. She found a set of glass doors with a broken pane, and she squeezed through the jagged opening into a room with ceramic floors. This, she realized, blinking in the sparse light, must have been the kitchen. Shards of white tile glittered under her feet. A ventilation pipe gaped where a stove had once stood. The walls and ceiling had been knocked clean away, leaving only beams and furring.

She continued on through the other rooms, around heaps of baseboards, an island of bricks. She thought about going upstairs, but all that remained was a backbone of a banister, sweeping to the next floor over absent treads. A marble mantel – too heavy to move? – lay a few feet from a fireplace taller than she was. A chandelier, half stripped of its crystals, hung crooked from a beam. Her throat was dry with dust, and she thought of her father's cough in those last months before he died. The construction job that brought him home long after she'd gone to bed. The sour smell of his neck when he kissed her goodbye in the mornings, the smell, she now realized, of plaster.

By the time she walked back outside, she had stopped trembling. She sat down on the bench and brushed off her clothes. She remembered looking at the manor from the top of the stone wall, after the couple had moved in.

"They aren't outside," she told her father.

"Maybe they're waiting for you to go."

"Like fairies?"

"Sure," he said with a laugh, then lifted her down. "Don't worry," he added on their way home, "We'll be back there one day. Maybe even living in it. You can have the whole top floor to yourself." She knew he was teasing her, but she believed him anyway.

She did not leave by the back garden. She walked down the front drive. Had a set of these grooves in the gravel been made by the car that drove the couple away during the night? No one knew where they were taken, probably to one of the internment camps. Someone must have informed, people said, because the Jews were not registered. They had never worn the star. The mayor was thinking of putting together a commission to examine what had happened to the manor. The property now belonged to the commune. "If a house isn't claimed," he had said in a speech. "Everyone owns it."

She kept walking down the river of gravel, feeling herself quitting more than the manor, feeling as if she could walk on to the main road and out of the village, to a place she did not know. She saw again the ball in the woman's hands. And father walking out of the garage with the man. Hadn't he looked friendly; hadn't he smiled? But then, too, the dust in his hair those nights. And herself on the wall, watching the manor. The desire she'd felt.

Herman calls his doctor the next morning to say that he wants to stop the treatments. After giving him the phone, Clémence goes to the bathroom and stands under the shower, not washing her hair or her body, staying there until the water turns cold. "Hold on a little bit longer," she told Herman the day before as they stood by the road. "Look at me," he said, and she knew he was pleading.

She dries off and puts on a robe, then brings Herman a basin of warm water so that he can shave. His cheeks make the same noise that they did when they were full. When he's done, she takes off her robe and lies down next to him. They can't make love. They haven't in months, but they kiss and she curls next to him and he touches her breasts. She tries to think of the trembling in his hands as passion.

"I've been dreaming about that house by my village," she says. "The one that was owned by a Jewish couple."

"The one you fought about with your mother."

"You're the only one who can understand. The only other person in my life who saw it."

"Did I?"

"Of course. The first time I brought you home. Remember?"

He circles the mole on her shoulder with his finger. "I remember your mother made clafoutis and I didn't know what to do with the cherry pits. And that she kept talking about your father."

"We walked there through the forest. You kissed me for the first time."

He shakes his head. "I kissed you for the first time in my Jeep. In front of the base."

"It's impossible that you can't remember."

He runs his hand down her waist. "Let me tell you something sweetheart," he says in English, affecting the Bogart accent that used to make her laugh. "When you're dying, you hone your memories."

It is the first time either of them has used that word. She makes herself think it in French.

"You're going to be fine," he says when she buries her face in his neck. "I knew that when I met you. You're one of those people."

"Right before I took you to the house," she says, through her tears.

He laughs. "Right before I kissed you in the Jeep."

Once he falls asleep, she unbuttons the top of his pajamas. She traces with her eyes the humps of his ribs, the path of the scars over his belly. She looks until her eyes start to close, then she lies down next to him. Soon, she is back at the manor. As in the other dreams, she is pulling bricks from the fireplace, but each time she gets one off, another appears. One more and she will see something. Just one more. This time, though, she is not alone. Her parents are next to her, throwing bricks over their shoulders. "You'll stain your dress," her mother says. Clémence looks down and sees that her hands are bleeding. "You need a tool," her father says. He reaches into his pocket and he gives her his knife.

Back of the Envelope

GREG MCBRIDE

You're still drowsing upstairs, crumpled
    under the comforter. I'm in the kitchen,
wrapped in my robe at breakfast, peering
    through swoops of frost at sun-bathed snow outside:
the veiled lawn and stubble, lamp post, roll and roll
    beyond the pond, the sheen a mile to the pines.

I'm doodling on a security envelope,
    a #10 – so handy for shopping lists,
for reckoning mortgage amortizations,
    for juggling our shrunken life expectancy
with income, savings, expenditures,
    for indulging arithmetic fantasy:
that our last dollar might be spent on our last day.

This time, though, I'm thinking about last night:
    how in our heat we smoldered into sleep
before we could re-sense or re-dress ourselves,
    how we melded to embrace our warmth,
the way a cabin stoked for night turns in
    upon itself, snow-draped in winter woods,
how we woke in the quiet of first-light,
    eyes on eyes, lips pouting with last night's love.

Hmm. 31.5 times 365,
    plus eight leap days, and days magnified
by Saratoga, San Francisco, Princeton,
    Portland, all of it compounded over years.
I hope you'll come downstairs soon. I've made
    coffee and a fire. I've found some old photos
that show us in our strength.
    I'll put on the mackinaw and tuque,
shovel to the shed to get the sled, and soap
    its runners well. But first, let's watch the logs
rearrange themselves in their diminishment,
    how the embers crackle stars until the very end.

Money

TOM SLEIGH

Two drinks down, and there's money
begging to be fucked by me, to fuck me silly,
money's hand clutching at my sleeve –
foolishly aware of how money must rave

all over the city, demanding, begging,
telling lies I need to hear and money
needs to tell. It's ridiculous and sad,
this wanting sharpening money's naked need

as if money were a cock, a cunt that can't stop
coming, and the more it comes the more
it has to come, money money money
making me feel what I can't shut down enough

not to feel in this wanting of not
having I have to have even as I have it.

Money

C. J. SAGE

Of course it matters
if you are rich
or poor. The silver dollar song

holds even the ears
of infants. o how I admire
women who covet

it and nothing more.
Neo-nurture equals closed eyes
plus open hands.

Demonophobia: false start
of the newly bolded brain.
It isn't the money god that takes

your girls' innocence. It isn't
the money god that takes
your cattle away;

your brooms tied to their tails
mask the footprints
all the way to the bank.

After every set,
Ray Charles took his wages
in only one dollar bills.

The money god will teach
your children cunning.
Such a burden, deselecting for need.

Nature equals faith plus sleep.
Chrematophobia: end-game
of the pre-pragmatic brain.

The big question:
What would it mean to trade
in only laughs and glances?

The final answer: Don't be ridiculous.
Look – there are people carrying
their own hearts. Drip, drip.

So you want to be a lover,
not a saver? Come on. Just think
how long free love's been on its knees.

Solve for this: where x is hope
and y is your future, what is surely finite?
(A bed of roses makes a barrier to reason.)

Where the Money Went

KEVIN CANTY

When the thing was over, Braxton sat down at the kitchen table of his apartment and tried to figure out what they had done with the money.

Some of it went for schools, of course, good private schools – the hippy school for Lucinda and the Spanish Academy for Steve. The hippy school was a parent co-op. Braxton remembered sweating through a parent meeting, drunk: the affluent and lawyerly, trying out their voices on one another. On and on. It was like being in the eighth grade again, stupid with boredom, ready to flee. Plus the parent co-op was more expensive than the academy, ten thousand a year versus six. Plus the afterschool care. Plus Brenda, the sitter. The weekend art lessons, the tennis clinics, swimming.

Not that the public schools were terrible. They were fine.

Some of it went for cars, landscaping, clothes, vacations. The four of them flew to Honolulu for Christmas, Vail for Presidents' Day. He sat with pencil and envelope-back (he was pre-approved for fifty thousand dollars more) and tried to figure how a simple skiing weekend could cost so much: lift tickets, lunches, the fat, hourglass-shaped skis he bought himself and then, out of something like guilt, bought his wife. It wasn't the skis he bought himself that were wasted, he thought. He was a decent skier, he enjoyed it. No, it was the skis he bought his wife, hoping to encourage her. She used them that weekend and never again. Five hundred for the skis, one-and-a-quarter for the bindings. Then of course new boots.

That was a waste, he thought.

The snorkeling equipment, the Windsurfer, the mountain bike. A Klein, he remembered. He had spent some months researching what the absolute best kind to get was. The little crazy expensive bike he bought Steve so they could tool slowly around the playground on their thousand-dollar rides, father and son.

They threw a party when the pool was done. Everybody they knew, under the lights. Braxton spent a thousand dollars at the liquor store alone, not to mention the catering, the lights, the pool itself. And then she had gotten drunk, early in the evening, some accident where she had forgotten to eat. It didn't happen constantly or even often but she loved to be drunk. She raced around the pool in the shadowy light, chatting, flirting. She was standing with her back to the pool, talking with the Andersons, when she took that one slow inadvertent step backward and could not right herself. He watched her topple slowly backward into the water, watched her dress bloom around her in the underwater light like some bright colorful flower and in that moment he had not disliked her. In fact he loved her, just in that moment.

Then heard the whispered word: "drunk." It passed around him, hand to hand.

Then she got out and she didn't even care, she went around the rest of the night in her wet dress, her nipples poking through the wet cotton.

The parkas, stereos.

The afternoon he figured out how bad it was, how bad it was going to get, he was in their bedroom, which faced the pool. Looking up from his bills and figuring, he saw Steve bobbing in the deep end on a silver plastic raft, eyes closed, hours on end. He had turned fat with his tenth birthday – "husky," she called it. Every time Braxton looked up, his son was there, immobile, drifting. He gets it from her, he thought angrily. That indolence. He looked on his son with disgust.

The rest of the money, what there was of it, went for the lawyers.

Contributors

Jonathan Ames is the author of eight books, including *The Extra Man* (now a film, starring Kevin Kline) and *Wake Up, Sir!* He is the creator of the HBO show "Bored to Death" and has received a Guggenheim Fellowship. In addition to writing, he has had two amateur boxing matches, fighting as "The Herring Wonder."

Geoffrey Becker's most recent books are *Hot Springs* (Tin House Books) and *Black Elvis* (University of Georgia Press). His *Dangerous Men*, a collection of short stories (Univ. of Pittsburgh Press), won the Drue Heinz Literature Prize. His story, "Black Elvis," was included in *Best American Short Stories*, 2000. He lives in Baltimore.

Don Bogen has published four books of poems, most recently *[an (A)lgebra]* (Univ. of Chicago Press). He teaches at the University of Cincinnati and is poetry editor of *The Cincinnati Review*.

Jenny Boully is the author of *not merely because of the unknown that was stalking towards them* (Tarpaulin Sky Press). She is a Ph.D. candidate at the Graduate Center of the CUNY and teaches at Columbia College, Chicago.

Kurt Brown is the founder of the Aspen Writers' Conference. He has published five poetry collections, including *No Other Paradise* (Red Hen Press), and teaches poetry workshops at Sarah Lawrence College.

Augusten Burroughs is the *New York Times* bestselling author of *You Better Not Cry, A Wolf at the Table, Possible Side Effects, Magical Thinking, Dry, Running With Scissors,* and *Sellvision*. He lives in New York City.

Kevin Canty has authored three novels and three collections of stories, most recently *Where the Money Went* (Nan A. Talese/Doubleday). His work has been published in *The New Yorker, Esquire,* and *GQ*. He lives in Missoula, Montana.

Kelly Cherry has published nineteen books of fiction, poetry, memoir, criticism, essay, and translations of two classical plays. Her most recent titles are *Girl in a Library: On Women Writers and the Writing Life* (BkMk) and *The Retreats of Thought: Poems* (Louisiana State University Press).

Kate Clanchy is an award-winning UK poet with three collections from Picador. *Antigona and Me* won the Writer's Guild Award for Best Book. She won the BBC National Short Story Prize in 2009.

Drew DeGennaro is an undergraduate at Augsburg College in Minneapolis. His first chapbook, *The Man in a Little Red Dress,* will be published by Pudding House.

Jane Delury is the author of a new book of non-fiction, *Writers and the Words They Love and Loathe* (Sarabande Books). Her stories have appeared in *Southern Review, Potomac Review, Prairie Schooner* and other magazines. She teaches at the University of Baltimore in the creative writing and publishing arts MFA programs.

Regina Derieva was born in 1949 in Odessa. Since 1999 she has lived in Stockholm. Her two-volume collected poems, *Sobranie Dorog (A Gathering of Roads),* were published in Russia in 2004-5. Marick Press will bring out a selection of her poems, Corinthian Copper, translated by J. Kates, this year.

Mark Doty's *Fire to Fire: New and Selected Poems* (Harper Collins), published in 2008, won the National Book Award for poetry. He teaches at Rutgers University.

Denise Duhamel's fourth collection of poems is *Ka-Ching!* (University of Pittsburgh Press). A recipient of a National Endowment for the Arts fellowship, she is an associate professor at Florida International University in Miami.

Tony Eprile grew up in South Africa where his father edited the country's first mass-circulation multi-racial newspaper. He is the author of *The Persistence of Memory*, a New York Times Notable Book of the Year and Koret Jewish Book Award winner. He teaches at Lesley University's MFA program and lives in Bennington, Vermont.

Katie Ford is the author of *Deposition and Colosseum* (Graywolf). She is the recipient of a Lannan Literary Fellowship. Her poems have appeared in *The New Yorker, Smartish Pace, Bayou, Blackbird* and *Seneca Review*. She teaches at Franklin & Marshall College and lives in Philadelphia with her husband, the novelist Josh Emmons.

Dolly Freed wrote *Possum Living: How to Live Well Without a Job and With (Almost) No Money* at the age of 18. Published in 1978, it is now a cult classic and regarded as a forerunner of the sustainable food movement. Dolly became a NASA engineer and college professor. She lives in Texas.

Castle Freeman, Jr. is the author of four novels and many short stories, essays, and historical studies. His latest novel is *All That I Have* (Steerforth Press). He lives in southeastern Vermont.

Michael Greenberg is the author of *Beg, Borrow, Steal: A Writer's Life* and a memoir, *Hurry Down Sunshine* (both from Other Press). He is a columnist for the *Times Literary Supplement*. He lives in Manhattan.

Michael Guista is a writer, community college English teacher, and president of Fountain Mountain, Inc. which has never been more than $100 in the red and in 2007 grossed $1,000,000 for the first time. His collection of stories is *Brain Work* (Houghton Mifflin).

J. C. Hallman, no longer a casino dealer, is the author of *The Chess Artist, The Devil is a Gentleman,* and *The Hospital for Bad Poets.* A work of non-fiction, *In Utopia,* is published by St. Martin's Press.

Tom Healy's first book of poems is *What The Right Hand Knows* (Four Way Books, 2009), nominated for the *LA Times Book Prize.* He teaches at Pratt Institute.

Michael Heffernan has published seven volumes of poetry, most recently *The Odor of Sanctity* (Salmon Press, 2008). He teaches creative writing at the University of Arkansas, Fayetteville.

Tony Hoagland's fourth book of poems is *Unincorporated Persons in the Late Honda Dynasty* (Graywolf). He teaches at the University of Houston. His essays, also from Graywolf, are collected in *Real Sofistikashun: Essays on Poetry and Craft.*

Michelle Huneven's novels are *Round Rock, Jamesland,* and *Blame,* nominated for both the National Book Critics Circle and *LA Times Prize* prizes for Best Novel of 2009. She is the co-author, with Bernadette Murphy, of *The Tao Gals Guide to Real Estate,* a book for women buying houses. She lives in Altadena, California, one mile from where she grew up.

Ruth Ellen Kocher has published three books of poems, most recently *One Girl Babylon.* She teaches in the MFA program at the University of Colorado-Boulder.

Hailey Leithauser's poems have appeared recently in *The Iowa Review, Poetry,* and *The Best American Poetry 2010.* She was a Discovery/*The Nation* award winner in 2004.

Sonja Livingston's new memoir *Ghostbread* (University of Georgia Press) won the AWP Award in Nonfiction. She holds an M.S. Ed. from SUNY Brockport and an MFA from the University of New Orleans.

dawn lonsinger is pursuing a doctorate at the University of Utah where she is managing editor of *Western Humanities Review*. Her second chapbook is *The Nested Object* (Dancing Girl Press, 2009).

Dora Malech's first book of poems is *Shore Ordered Ocean* (Waywiser Press). A 2005 graduate of the Iowa Writers' Workshop, she has published in *The New Yorker, Poetry, Poetry London* and *The Yale Review*.

Randall Mann's second collection of poetry is *Breakfast With Thom Gunn* (University of Chicago). A winner of the 2003 *Kenyon Review* Prize, he is co-author of the textbook *Writing Poems* (Pearson Longman). He lives in San Francisco.

Greg McBride's chapbook is *Back of the Envelope* (Copperdome Press, 2009). A Vietnam veteran, he writes after 30 years of law practice and edits *The Innisfree Poetry Journal*.

Donna Lee Munson is a former bank assistant vice president who is now serving a three-year sentence for fraud in an undisclosed U.S. Federal facility.

Samantha Peale's first novel is *The American Painter Emma Dial* (Norton). She is a graduate of The New School and The School of the Art Institute of Chicago.

Robert Pinsky, former U.S. Poet Laureate, has published seven books of poetry, most recently, *Gulf Music* (Farrar Straus & Giroux, 2007). He teaches at Boston University and is the poetry editor of *Slate*.

Dan Pope is the author of a novel, *In The Cherry Tree* (Picador). A 2002 graduate of the Iowa Writers Workshop, he is a writer in residence at the MFA program in Creative Writing at Western Connecticut State University.

Katherine Ann Power spent more than a decade on the FBI Ten Most Wanted Fugitives list after she was involved in a 1970 bank robbery that resulted in the death of a Boston police officer. She lived underground for many years, turned herself in, and served six years in Federal prison. She lives near Boston and is nearing the end of her 20-year parole.

Catie Rosemurgy is the author of two poetry collections, *My Favorite Apocalypse* and *The Stranger Manual* (Graywolf). The recipient of a Rona Jaffe Foundation award and an NEA Fellowship, she lives in Philadelphia and teaches at The College of New Jersey.

Jess Row is the author of *The Train to Lo Wu*, shortlisted for the 2006 PEN/Hemingway Award. His fiction has appeared twice in *Best American Short Stories* and has won a Whiting Writers Award, an O. Henry Award, and a Pushcart Prize. He teaches at the College of New Jersey and the Vermont College of Fine Arts.

Douglas Rushkoff is the author of a dozen books on media, technology and culture, including *Cyberia, Media Virus, Coercion* and, most recently, of *Life Inc: How the World Became a Corporation and How to Take It Back*. He also wrote the novels *Ecstasy Club* and *Exit Strategy*, and the graphic novel *Testament* and the upcoming *A.D.D.*

C. J. Sage's latest book is *The San Simeon Zebras* (Salmon Poetry, 2010). C. J. edits *The National Poetry Review* and works as a Realtor in Santa Cruz County, California.

Elaine Sexton is the author of two collections of poems, *Causeway* and *Sleuth* (New Issues). Her poems and reviews have appeared in *American Poetry Review, Poetry, Art in America* and other periodicals.

Mona Simpson's novels include *Anywhere But Here, The Lost Father* and *A Regular Guy*. She teaches at Bard College. She was named one of *Granta*'s Best Young American Novelists and has won the Whiting Writer's Award, a Guggenheim grant, the Hodder Fellowship at Princeton University, and a grant from the Lila Wallace-Reader's Digest Foundation.

Tom Sleigh has published six poetry collections, most recently *Space Walk* (Houghton Mifflin), winner of the 2008 Kingsley Tufts Award. Graywolf recently published his essays as *Interview with a Ghost*. He lives in Brooklyn and teaches at Hunter College.

Terese Svoboda's most recent book of poetry is *Weapons Grade* (University of Arkansas Press). Her third book of prose, *Trailer Girl and Other Stories,* was re-issued in paper by Bison Books.

L. B. Thompson's *Tendered Notes: Poems of Love and Money* won the Center for Book Arts annual chapbook contest in 2003. She lives on the North Fork of Long Island and works as an English teacher and freelance writer and copyeditor.

Tabitha Vevers (cover art) received her B.A. from Yale University and studied at Skowhegan School of Painting & Sculpture. She is the recipient of numerous awards and honors and is a co-founder of artSTRAND. She lives and works in Cambridge and Wellfleet, MA.

Ronald Wallace has published seven volumes of poetry via the University of Pittsburgh Press and founded the creative writing program at the University of Wisconsin in 1975. He is editor of the University of Wisconsin Press Poetry Series.

Acknowledgements

"America" by Tony Hoagland, reprinted with his permission, was first published in *What Narcissism Means to Me* (Graywolf, 2003).

"Tycoon" by Michael Greenberg is reprinted from *Beg, Borrow, Steal: A Writer's Life* (2009) with the permission of Other Press.

"Eros" by Randall Mann, reprinted with his permission, first appeared in *Complaint in the Garden* (Zoo Press, 2004).

"Income" by Dolly Freed is reprinted from *Possum Living* (2009) with the permission of Tin House. *Possum Living* was first published in 1978.

"Stage" by Don Bogen appeared first in *[an (A)lgebra]* (Univ. of Chicago Press, 2010) and is reprinted with the permission of the author.

"Inman Square Incantation" by Robert Pinsky first appeared in *Gulf Music* (Farrar, Straus and Giroux, 2007) and is reprinted with the permission of the author.

"Free Meals" by Jonathan Ames originally appeared in *What's Not to Love?* (Vintage, 2001).

The two sections from Sonja Livingston's memoir *Ghostbread* (2009) are reprinted with the permission of University of Georgia Press.

"Coins" by Mona Simpson, reprinted with her permission, first appeared in both *Harper's Magazine* (August, 2002) and *Best American Short Stories* 2003 (Houghton Mifflin).

"Class" by Elaine Sexton first appeared in *Causeway* (New Issues Press, 2008). It is reprinted with her permission.

"The Entrepreneurs" by Tony Eprile, reprinted with his permission, first appeared in *Glimmer Train*, issue #13.

Donna Lee Munson's interview appeared in a different form in *Insidious*, published by Memento Press in 2009.

"Living on Someone Else's Money" by Tom Healy first appeared in *What the Right Hand Knows* (2009) and is reprinted with the permission of Four Way Books.

"Immorally Bankrupt" by Augusten Burroughs originally appeared in *The New York Times* and is used with permission of the author.

"Back of the House" by J. C. Hallman appeared earlier in *GQ* and is reprinted with the permission of the author.

"Limited Time Offer" by Ronald Wallace is reprinted with the permission of the University of Pittsburgh Press. It first appeared in *For A Limited Time Only* (2009).

"$5 American Poem" by L. B. Thompson, reprinted with her permission, was first published in *The Women's Review of Books*.

"Money as Water" by Kurt Brown appeared first in *Return of the Prodigals* (1995). It is reprinted with the permission of Four Way Books.

"Where the Money Went" by Kevin Canty is reprinted from *Where the Money Went*, with the permission of Random House, Inc.

IOU is an experiment
in publishing and community.

And now you're part of it.

This book is free. All we ask is that you give money to a group you support or someone in need. Where and how much you give—that's completely up to you. Just chart your donation at our website, www.concordfreepress.com. Then—and we know this is the hard part—**pass your book along** to another reader so that the reading and giving can continue.

The Concord Free Press is about inspiring generosity. Thanks for yours.

Chart this book's progress and donations at:
www.concordfreepress.com.

YOUR BOOK IS # 2292

OTHER BOOKS BY CONCORD FREE PRESS

The Next Queen of Heaven
by Gregory Maguire

Push Comes to Shove
by Wesley Brown

Give and Take
by Stona Fitch

Please sign your copy of *IOU*
before you pass it on.

WHO	WHERE

1. _____

2. _____

3. _____

4. _____

5. _____

6. _____

7. _____

8. _____

9. _____

10. _____

ABOUT THE COVERS

IOU is published in four different covers, each using original artwork by Tabitha Vevers, who graciously allowed the Concord Free Press to use paintings from her Value Added and Nest Egg Series. All paintings are oil (and gold leaf) on US currency, $2^{5/8}$ x $6^{1/8}$ inches.

For more information on the artist and her work: www.tabithavevers.com. All images © 2009, Tabitha Vevers

Cover #1: Eyes
Value Added Series

Watching I
Five FA73305241A (after John Snow)
Sally Hemings
Two A00879514A (after John Snow), Private Collection
Eye of Providence
One B35581293J (after John Snow)
Watching II
One Hundred HB156988013B (after Hank Paulson)

Cover #2: Eggs
Nest Egg Series

Nest Egg
One A7525796A (after Hank Paulson), Private Collection
Nest Egg
One A94411733D (after Hank Paulson)
Nest Egg
Two A01481441A (after John Snow)
Nest Egg
Fifty AJ54367859A (after Robert Rubin)

Cover #3: Nudes
Value Added Series

Free Fall I
Five CC56288641A (after Paul O'Neill), Collection of Wayne Petty
Free Fall II
Five HF39567469A (after Hank Paulson),
Collection of Arlette and Gus Kayafas

Cover #4: Monetary Miscellany
Value Added Series

Novus Ovum Seclorum
One B24141354J (after Hank Paulson),
Collection of Arlette and Gus Kayafas
Hung Out
Ten BJ02137239A
Pay to Play
One Hundred HA15380977A (after Hank Paulson)
Aftermath
Five FB04666196B (after John Snow)